Unwanted Stress

"Is it . . . a lot of money?" A.J. asked Mr. Meagher.

"Between the Eriksson real estate, the studio, and its subsidiaries, you're roughly worth in the neighborhood of eighteen million dollars."

A.J. gulped.

"That's a lovely neighborhood," her mother, Elysia remarked. "You'll enjoy living there."

"You're a very wealthy young woman," Mr. Meagher said, maybe thinking she had missed the point.

"I guess so." She knew she was disappointing Mr. Meagher, but she couldn't help thinking that this was bound to look like she really did have a motive for murder.

"Of course, with great wealth comes great responsibility."

That's what I'm afraid of, A.J. thought.

Mr. Meagher gave another of those polite coughs that seemed to be part of his stage craft.

"One hesitates to bring up sensitive subjects, but . . . do you have a will, my dear?"

Corpse Pose

Diana Killian

BERKLEY PRIME CRIME, NEW YORK

THE BERKLEY PUBLISHING GROUP
Published by the Penguin Group
Penguin Group (USA) Inc.
375 Hudson Street, New York, New York 10014, USA

Penguin Group (Canada), 90 Eglinton Avenue East, Suite 700, Toronto, Ontario M4P 2Y3, Canada
(a division of Pearson Penguin Canada Inc.)
Penguin Books Ltd., 80 Strand, London WC2R 0RL, England
Penguin Group Ireland, 25 St. Stephen's Green, Dublin 2, Ireland (a division of Penguin Books Ltd.)
Penguin Group (Australia), 250 Camberwell Road, Camberwell, Victoria 3124, Australia
(a division of Pearson Australia Group Pty. Ltd.)
Penguin Books India Pvt. Ltd., 11 Community Centre, Panchsheel Park, New Delhi—110 017, India
Penguin Group (NZ), 67 Apollo Drive, Rosedale, North Shore 0632, New Zealand
(a division of Pearson New Zealand Ltd.)
Penguin Books (South Africa) (Pty.) Ltd., 24 Sturdee Avenue, Rosebank, Johannesburg 2196,
South Africa

Penguin Books Ltd., Registered Offices: 80 Strand, London WC2R 0RL, England

This is a work of fiction. Names, characters, places, and incidents either are the product of the author's imagination or are used fictitiously, and any resemblance to actual persons, living or dead, business establishments, events, or locales is entirely coincidental. The publisher does not have any control over and does not assume any responsibility for author or third-party websites or their content.

PUBLISHER'S NOTE: The recipes contained in this book are to be followed exactly as written. The publisher is not responsible for your specific health or allergy needs that may require medical supervision. The publisher is not responsible for any adverse reactions to the recipes contained in this book.

CORPSE POSE

A Berkley Prime Crime Book / published by arrangement with the author

PRINTING HISTORY
Berkley Prime Crime mass-market edition / April 2008

Copyright © by Diane Browne.
Cover art by Swan Park.
Cover design and logo by Lesley Worrell.
Interior text design by Laura K. Corless.

ISBN: 978-0-425-22090-0

BERKLEY® PRIME CRIME
Berkley Prime Crime Books are published by The Berkley Publishing Group,
a division of Penguin Group (USA) Inc.,
375 Hudson Street, New York, New York 10014.
The name BERKLEY PRIME CRIME and the BERKLEY PRIME CRIME design
are trademarks belonging to Penguin Group (USA) Inc.

PRINTED IN THE UNITED STATES OF AMERICA

10   9   8   7   6   5   4   3   2   1

To Jacky Sach. *Namaste*.

Prologue

∿

There was only one car in the parking lot on Saturday morning when Suze MacDougal's baby blue Beetle lurched to a stop outside Sacred Balance Studio.

Quel perfecto, Suze thought as her Volkswagen sputtered and died beside Diantha's battered Volvo. This was working out even better than she'd planned. It was nearly forty-five minutes before the Sunrise Yoga class, and Diantha was already inside. It was now or never.

Suze caught her reflection in the rearview mirror, and—remembering Jennifer Stevenson's crack about looking like Dopey—licked her fingers and tried to paste her cowlick down. She took a couple of deep calming breaths—it wouldn't do to show up breathless and flushed when she was trying to demonstrate how worthy she was to train others on achieving spiritual insight and tranquility through the ancient discipline of yoga.

Sliding out from behind the wheel, she grabbed her gym bag and locked the door. The New Jersey September morning air was crisp and invigorating despite the chill.

The ancient pine trees leaning precariously over the new building that housed Sacred Balance Studio threw the parking lot in deep shade.

Diantha Mason had waged a battle to keep those pine trees intact—even threatening to pull out of escrow if the new location for Sacred Balance Studio was going to mean the demise of the evergreen giants. She had not won friends over her tree-hugging stance. That was nothing new. She *had* won the battle to preserve the surrounding trees. That was nothing new either. Diantha won all her battles. That was one of the things Suze most admired about her.

She checked as something stirred along the edge of the lot. A fat possum with a long pink tail waddled out of the shadows and headed fearlessly for the trash Dumpster at the far end. It must be an insomniac possum, Suze thought. She had never seen one in the daylight, though she had seen plenty of other critters. Diantha was as fierce a protector of the local fauna as she was the local flora—and her woodland neighbors seemed to know it. On more than one occasion squirrels, rabbits, and even a timber rattlesnake had found their way into the new building on the outskirts of town.

Chuckling, Suze continued up the front steps. The glass doors were unlocked, which did not surprise her. As more staff and more classes were added, the studio rarely closed. Suze had overheard Diantha telling Lily, her protégé, that the ultimate goal was to turn Sacred Balance into a kind of twenty-four-hour spiritual community center. Lily had been oddly unenthusiastic, but then Lily had not been her usual self for some weeks. In fact, Suze had overheard the two instructors arguing Wednesday evening. Well, if Lily was falling from favor, it just might work to other people's advantage.

Inside the building the lights were all on, which did give Suze a moment's pause. Diantha was very conscious about not wasting natural resources—or money. The entire building had been fitted out in full-spectrum lighting, which made it about ten times more expensive to maintain, so Diantha was kind of a grouch about people leaving lights on after hours.

"Hello?"

There was no response. In fact, the building seemed eerily silent. Suze could practically hear the potted plants photosynthesizing. Her eyes flicked to the vintage black-and-white art posters of women frozen in yoga positions—they seemed to be listening, too. *It Could Happen* read the caption at the bottom of the posters. It was Diantha's motto, the slogan of the entire staff and all the students.

Suze shrugged away the flash of unease and kicked off her shoes. She stuffed her bag into one of the empty cubbies.

Even now Diantha was probably brewing her morning green tea in her office, with one of her soothing James Asher CDs playing softly in the background. Suze tried to visualize Diantha inviting her in for a chat and a cup of tea, but the picture wouldn't quite come. Still, maybe it would happen once Suze confided her ambition and somehow convinced Diantha that she was serious, that she was ready. Heck, she'd given up fast food, hadn't she? And she'd cut up her credit cards—well, most of them; that *had* to mean something.

It could happen.

She swiped at her cowlick one last time before heading for the stretching room.

As she passed Diantha's office, she called out in what she hoped was a serene voice (she didn't want Diantha to accuse her of screeching again).

"Hello?"

No answer.

The low lights bathed the stretching room in golden luminescence. The wall of mirrors reflected the tawny sheen of the polished hardwood floors. Suze's eyes took a moment to adjust.

She froze in the doorway, recognizing Diantha lying spread out in the Corpse position, the final relaxation pose of a good yoga session. Diantha seemed to barely breathe, her body as still as though she were in a trance, unaware of Suze or the outside world. But then no one had the control or focus of Diantha. Back in the 1960s she had studied in India with the most respected of the yogis.

Careful not to intrude by so much as a stare, Suze tiptoed in a wide arc around Diantha. Across the room she self-consciously seated herself on her mat, folding her legs into the Lotus position. She inhaled slowly, exhaled evenly.

Inhale. Exhale.

Inhaaaaaale.

Exhaaaaale.

She was doing a lovely job of it, too, breathing deeply in and deeply out—her exhalations were a thing of mint-scented beauty.

Several minutes of this passed with no comment from Diantha. Could she really be observing Suze, evaluating her performance? Shit. Er, shoot. She'd never had this kind of attention from Diantha before.

Suze continued to breathe in and out. She began to feel light-headed. Instead of the calm of mind and body she was laboring for, she was tense, waiting for that familiar English drawl to cut the silence. It really wasn't like Diantha to keep quiet for so long.

Oh no. What if she had walked out? She moved like a cat; Suze might not have heard her leave.

She cracked one eye open.

Diantha lay motionless on her mat.

Suze's breathing slowed, she stared. Diantha was so still, her chest didn't seem to move at all. Her face was turned away.

Cautiously, Suze got to her feet. She tiptoed a few feet

closer to where Diantha lay. Not a flicker of awareness from the older woman. Suze cleared her throat.

Nothing.

In the golden light of the stretching room, Diantha's skin looked as grey as her close cropped hair.

Reluctantly, Suze stepped forward to see her face.

What she saw had her sucking in her breath in an unapproved fashion before letting it out in a long, bloodcurdling scream. . . .

One

∞

A.J.'s cell phone was ringing. . . .

But then her cell phone was always ringing. Actually, it was more of a chirp than a ring. It sounded cute and friendly, like she had a pet bird in the pocket of her Versace pantsuit, but lately A. J. Alexander had come to hate the sound of her cell phone.

Maybe that wasn't the ideal reaction from an up-and-coming freelance marketing consultant trying to make it in the cut-throat world of big league promotion, but more and more, A.J. found herself resenting the electronic leash, resenting being on call 24–7 to people with more money than talent or good sense. Where had all her energy and enthusiasm gone?

"Wonderful party!" gushed a woman in a gigantic black hat. Did she think she was at Ascot or a funeral? "I was wondering . . . could we *talk*?"

Ah, a prospective client. Again A.J. was struck by her own lack of eagerness. This was her bread and butter, but she just wasn't hungry anymore.

She nodded, still smiling at the woman in black, and reached into her pocket.

"I just have to . . ."

"Oh, of course!" Of course. Everyone understood that people dialing in came before the physically present.

A.J. flipped open her cell with a practiced flick of the wrist, like one of the world-weary crew of the Starship *Enterprise* who had been there, done that—and killed whatever got in her way.

"A.J. here," she said crisply, offering a fleeting apologetic smile as she turned a shoulder on her perspective client. Why did women kid themselves that baggy clothes were effective camouflage for a weight problem? That dress made the poor thing look like a baby buffalo.

"Is this Anna Jolie Alexander?" The voice was male and unfamiliar. But what really registered with A.J. was the fact that he knew her full name. Not many people knew her full name—she took a lot of trouble to keep it that way.

"Speaking."

"This is Detective Jake Oberlin of the Stillbrook Police Department."

Stillbrook? Aunt Di. This was something to do with Aunt Di.

"Ma'am, I've got some bad news."

Yes, the bad news was that she had reached a point in life where men called her "ma'am." Then his title registered. A detective? A cop? This was not good. Something not good had happened to Aunt Di.

Please don't let this not good thing be a really bad thing. *Please. . . .*

"What is it?"

Detective Oberlin's deep voice seemed to drop another octave or so. A.J. pressed the phone closer to her ear, closing her eyes, trying to focus on the words.

No. That couldn't be right. It was hard to hear in the crowded room. She started walking, brushing through the ribbon tails of the balloons pressing against the low ceiling of the room like orange cloud cover.

A.J. pushed open the nearest glass door and stepped outside onto the rain-slick sidewalk. Cars passed, tires hissing on the wet streets, but the rush of Manhattan traffic was soothing compared to the din inside the restaurant.

"Sorry. I didn't hear what you said."

There was a pause and the detective said carefully, "I'm afraid I have bad news regarding a Miss Diantha Mason."

"Aunt Di?" Miss? Aunt Di would hate that. She always insisted on "Ms."

"Your name came up as her next of kin. You and a Mrs. Eliza Alexander. We've been unable to reach Mrs. Alexander. Looks like she lives overseas."

"Elysia Alexander," A.J. said. "My mother. Aunt Di's sister." She managed to stop herself from explaining that her mum chose to live most of the year in London, only occasionally staying at her New Jersey farm where they had spent most summers when A.J. was growing up. What did this unknown cop care where Elysia lived or what the relationship was? She was just stalling. She was just putting off the inevitable moment when she had to deal with whatever this bad news was. Because somehow she knew what the bad news was. She could feel it in her gut like a lump of cold snow.

A laughing couple pushed out through the glass doors, and A.J. smiled with bright insincerity in their direction. "So what's happened?" she said tersely into the phone.

"There's been an accident," Detective Oberlin said slowly and carefully. "I regret to have to tell you that your aunt is dead."

She had been bracing herself for something like this, but it still felt as though someone had knocked her down on the sidewalk.

"That's not possible," she said.

"I'm sorry."

"Are you *sure*?"

He said very patiently, which told her that everyone asked this same question, "Yes. I'm sorry, but there's no mistake."

"How did it happen? When did it happen?"

"We don't have the coroner's report yet, but she was found strangled at—" His voice fell away for a moment as though he had turned from the phone.

"Strangled!"

Silence.

"You said it was an accident? How is that an accident? You mean, she was *murdered*? Is that what you're trying to say? Is that what you're trying to tell me?"

He intoned, "Well, if I could get a word in, that's pretty much what I would have to say."

A.J. held the phone away from her as though trying to see through the lit up screensaver of She-Ra, Princess of Power. This yokel cop *dared* to be smart-assed about her beloved aunt's death?

Thank God. Thank God she could vent her rage on this jerk because that gave her time, time to avoid dealing with pain, with grief, with loss.

"Who's in charge there?" she snapped. "I want to talk to someone in charge. Listen, Detective Overload or whatever the hell your name is, maybe this is routine for you. Maybe it never occurred to you that—"

"I apologize, ma'am," Detective Oberlin said, his deep, calm voice slicing through her rising hysteria. "I realize that may have sounded insensitive."

A.J. opened her mouth, but all that came out was a little croaking sound.

Just as though she had said something quite intelligent, Detective Oberlin said, "We can talk more once you get here."

"Do you know who did this?" she managed finally. "Do you have the person who . . . killed my aunt?"

"We haven't made an arrest."

"But you have a suspect?"

"Like I said, we can talk in depth once you get here."

Yes, of course. She would have to drive up to Hicksville to make the . . . arrangements. She would have to take charge now. She would have to be the adult. She would have to phone her mother.

Of all the discoveries of the past ten minutes, that was nearly the most shattering of all.

Her phone began to chirp again as she hailed a passing taxi. Her client, Devorah Volvic, was probably wondering what had happened to her. A.J. let it go to message and climbed inside the cab. She couldn't deal with Devorah right now. She couldn't seem to think past the shock of her aunt's death.

Not just death. *Murder.*

It made the tragedy all the more terrible. Who would do such a thing? Why? It was so unbelievable. It was surreal. Murder did not happen to people like Diantha Mason. It just . . . *didn't.*

She shivered despite the curry-scented heat of the taxi. She realized she had left her raincoat at the restaurant. The launch party seemed like a lifetime ago.

Her phone rang again. Automatically she checked the number. A number that was as familiar as her own— because it used to be her own: Andy. She swallowed hard and hit Talk.

"Sweetheart, I just heard." Andy's voice was warm with sympathy and concern. "It's unbelievable. I just can't get my head around it. Are you all right?"

For a weird moment she considered pretending that she didn't know what he was talking about, letting him flail and flounder as he faced trying to break the dreadful news himself. Instead, she said huskily, "Thanks."

"What do you need? What can I do?"

That was why Andy was hard to hate. He was so god-damned nice. Even when he was destroying her life he had tried to handle it in the most considerate way possible.

"How did you hear?" she asked.

"Some cop called here looking for you, and for a minute or two I sort of let him think we were still married."

A.J. laughed without humor.

"Sweetheart—"

"*Don't* call me sweetheart," she bit out.

"Sorry. A.J., tell me what I can do."

"You can call Mother. She'll take it better coming from you."

She was not serious, of course, although the truth was that Elysia *would* take the news better from him. A.J. was pretty sure her mother had not been totally joking when she asked to be part of Andy's half of the divorce settlement.

"She already knows," Andy said. "I just got off the phone with her. Apparently your aunt's lawyer called her this morning—kind of a breach of etiquette, but your mother does have that effect on people."

That was one of the effects. Suicidal urges was another.

A.J. tried to focus as Andy ran on. "She's catching the first flight out of Heathrow. She should be arriving at Liberty International tomorrow morning. I have her flight info."

A.J. knew that the rush of resentment she felt was un-reasonable, even childish. Of course Elysia was coming home, and there was no reason why she shouldn't commu-nicate the details through Andy. She could have tried to call A.J. and been unable to reach her.

It could happen.

Yeah. Right.

She tuned back in to hear Andy asking, "Did you want me to take Lula Mae while you're away?"

Lula Mae was the four-footed feline thug that A.J. roomed with. She and Andy had found Lula Mae abandoned in an alley when she was a few weeks old, on their way home from a revival screening of *Breakfast at Tiffany's*.

"I thought what's-his-name was allergic to cats."

Andy said quietly, "His name is Nick, and he's fine with taking her for a few days—or however long it takes. Did you want to drop her off or shall I come and get her?"

"You can come and get her. I'm not going over there, that's for damn sure."

There was a sharp silence filled for A.J. by the shushing of tires on wet pavement and the rattle of a window loose in its frame.

"Why won't you at least meet him?"

"I have met him, remember? Twice. Once would have been enough. We're not going to be friends; we're not going to be one big happy family. It's not like it is on the sitcoms, so get over it."

"Have it your way," Andy said curtly. "Anything else I can do?"

She opened her mouth, but then let it go. What a bitch she was turning into. Unhappiness did that to you.

"There is something, if you're serious. I left my coat and my client at the 212 Restaurant. We were in the middle of her book launch when I got the call."

"You want me to smooth the client down?"

"I want my coat."

"You've got it," Andy said. "I'll see you in about an hour."

A.J. started to click off, but Andy was still hanging on the line, not speaking. The hair prickled at the nape of her neck.

"What is it?"

He said hesitantly, "We can talk when I get there, but maybe you should think about speaking to a lawyer."

"A lawyer? Why?"

"I just got the impression talking to that cop that . . . um . . . he . . . the police, that is . . . consider you a suspect."

TWO

꩜

"**What** do you mean the police consider me a suspect?" A.J. asked, opening the door of her apartment at Andy's knock.

But Andy was staring at her, his expression stricken. "Oh my *God*. What have you done to your hair?"

She was too upset and preoccupied to enjoy his reaction to her new pixie cut. She'd known he would be appalled; he loved her hair. Loved the length, loved the color, loved the highlights she paid a fortune for at the John Barrett Salon.

"You look like you've been having chemo. You look like Joan of Arc before they burned her at the stake—and who could blame them with *that* do."

"Oh, for crying out loud," A.J. said, taking her raincoat from him. "It's just a haircut, Sampson. It'll grow back."

"That isn't a haircut. That's assault with a deadly weapon. That's insult added to injury. That's—"

"*Alright already!*" yelled A.J. "Jeez. Give it a rest, Andy. I've got more important things on my mind than my hairdo. Why do you think I'm a suspect?"

"Hairdo?" Ignoring the question again, Andy said, "*That* is a hair *don't*." Satisfied with having the last word, he bent to scoop up Lula Mae, who had wound herself ingratiatingly around his long legs. "I smoothed down Devorah's feathers," he added.

"Thank you," she got out grudgingly. No one was better at stroking ruffled egos than Andy. "I appreciate it."

Lula Mae, who had the manners one would expect from someone named Lula Mae, meowed widely in his face. Andy kissed her pink nose.

"Someone wuvs her daddy, don't she?"

Watching them, A.J. felt a rush of emotion. It was so damn hard. They had been married for ten years, and while it had not exactly been the stuff of a Harlequin Romance, she had been happy, content, secure. All that was gone with the realization that the love she had believed in was a lie.

What were not gone, even though she wished they were, were the memories. The good memories.

Now she gazed at Andy, and it was like staring into a mirror—and only partly because she knew him so well. The new rule was never marry a guy who could pass for your brother—let alone your sister. Same tall, lanky build, same chestnut brown hair (though there was no argument Andy had the better cut). Andy's eyes were blue while hers were brown, but otherwise they could pass for blood relations.

"So what makes you think *I'm* a suspect?" she repeated.

"*I* don't think you're a suspect; I think the police might think you are."

"Why?"

His so-blue eyes met hers, but she couldn't read their expression. "There's a hell of a lot of money involved, right?"

"I'm still not following you."

"Diantha's estate. It sounds to me like you're her sole heir. Or rather, heiress."

"What?"

"Close your mouth, sweetheart—you'll catch flies." Andy let the already restless Lula Mae down, so A.J. couldn't see his face when he added, "Don't tell me you weren't aware that she was worth millions."

She. Andy had never cared much for Diantha, and the lack of feeling had been mutual. That was one reason A.J. had seen so little of her aunt over the past couple of years. That, and the fact that she had been too busy carving out a career she was no longer sure she even wanted.

"What are you talking about? You're suggesting the yoga studio is worth millions?"

"The yoga studio, the books, the product endorsements for everything from workout wear to organic peaches. And let's not forget the bundle she inherited from Gus Eriksson—including that farmhouse in Stillbrook, which sits on several hundred acres of prime real estate." He raised one eyebrow. "Have you quit reading the *Wall Street Journal*?"

He sounded like a minister asking when she had last cracked open the Bible. A.J. wasn't about to admit she hadn't even bothered to renew her *WSJ* subscription when it expired three months ago.

"I had no idea," she said at last.

Andy's mouth curved wryly. "I don't know if the police will swallow that. Your mother knows, so I doubt if it was supposed to be a secret. Where's Lou's carrier?"

Automatically she turned and headed for the hall closet. She pulled out the vacuum cleaner; tossed a pair of purple galoshes, the crutches Andy had used after his accident, and her skis out of the way; and finally hauled the carrier out of the back.

Lula Mae had long since skedaddled.

"What specifically did the police say to make you think I might be a suspect?" She handed him the carrier.

Andy shrugged. "It's more what they weren't saying.

Besides, it's common sense. You're the main beneficiary, maybe the only beneficiary. Do you . . . er . . ." He paused delicately.

"Do I, er, *what*?"

"Have an alibi?"

"What the hell is *that* supposed to mean? I don't even know when she died. All I know is that she was . . . strangled—" Her voice cracked. Unexpectedly tears were pouring down her cheeks.

Andy moved to hug her, but she waved him off.

"I'm fine, I'm fine!" She turned away to the bedroom, yelling, *"Lula Mae, get in here!"*

Like that would ever work.

But chasing the cat gave her time to compose herself, and by the time she hauled the wailing Lula Mae out from under the bed she had once shared with the stranger waiting patiently in the hall, A.J. was dry-eyed and in control again.

"I've got to meet—go," Andy said as she stuffed Lula Mae in the carrier and handed the prisoner over. "Let me know if there's anything I can do?"

She said sweetly, "Oh, but you've done too much already."

The year 1975 was notable for many things. The Vietnam War officially ended, the fifth assembly of the World Council of Churches called for "a radical transformation of civilization," and *Jaws* had theatergoers everywhere choking on their buttered popcorn. Even more frightening than a twenty-five-foot-long man-eating shark: curly perms, capes, and clogs were in. And no one looked better in them than British model and sometime actress Elysia Mason ("Easy" to her pals in the press), who chose the summer of '75 to retire from "art" films to marry wealthy American businessman, and comparative nobody, Paul Alexander.

It was not really much of a film career. Easy Mason was more celebrity than thespian. She had made a splash with such cult classics as *Die, Darling, Die* and *The Girl in the Gold Jag*, but most people knew her from her glamorous photos in British celebrity mags like *Titbit* and *TV Times* and her regular appearances on the weekly detective show *221B Baker Street*. Her romantic affairs had included eight British actors, three American film stars, two French counts, one Greek shipping magnate, one Scottish laird (Easy had referred to him as "that sheep farmer in the plaid skirt"), and one Saudi playboy. She was said to have briefly dated Prince Charles—though when asked about the royal alliance, Easy always smiled that enigmatic smile that photographed so beautifully, and said nothing.

In short, she was not June Cleaver. In fact, Elysia Mason-Alexander was not like anyone's mother—she had not even played a mom on TV. A.J. had no doubt whatsoever that she owed her existence to her dad. Which was not to say that she didn't love her mother—everyone loves their mother—but A.J. preferred to love her mother long distance. Separate continents worked best.

Rubbing the back of her neck and staring through the window of Erwin Pearl Jewelers in Terminal A at Liberty International, A.J. was reminding herself for the twelfth time that she loved her mother despite the traffic (bad), the hour (early), the lack of sleep (total), and her mood (unprintable) when there was a commotion behind her.

"Blimey, pumpkin!" exclaimed the dulcet tones of Mummy Dearest. "I almost didn't recognize you."

Elysia's reflection appeared in the storefront window like an apparition—still terrifically slim in leopard-print jeans, her hair an expertly teased, impossibly dark coil on her head. She could have been Maleficent's chic baby sister.

A.J. whirled and narrowly avoided falling over the trolley of luggage parked directly behind her. "Mother!" she exclaimed with more surprise than pleasure. "Your plane's not due for another forty-five minutes."

"I took an earlier flight." Elysia bussed A.J.'s cheek with her cool bony own. She smelled of cigarettes and Opium. She didn't smell of alcohol; that was the good news. Beneath the skillfully applied false eyelashes, her wide green eyes were clear—and questioning. "But what *happened* to you, pumpkin?"

A.J. squashed the instant rise of irritation, determined not to fall into the old pattern. "Nothing happened. I had my hair cut."

Elysia bit her lip—an appealing and much photographed expression. "By whom? The gardener? You appear to have been struck by a speeding lawnmower. Repeatedly."

"Ha," A.J. said. "You're looking well, anyway." She nodded at Elysia's leopard-print jeans. "Oh, are those coming back?"

Elysia smiled, her teeth small and white and ever so slightly pointed, catlike. "Where's Andrew, pumpkin?"

That struck a nerve, although in fairness, it was probably not intended to. "At home. His home. We're divorced, remember?"

Elysia shook her head as though this was too, *too* ridiculous, but she let it go. "Right. I suppose we'd better get this show on the road. Where are you parked?" She beckoned to a lurking skycap.

"Parking Lot A. Look, Mother . . . I think I should get up to Stillbrook as soon as possible, but you've had an exhausting trip. If you want to rest at my place for a day or two—"

"Don't be silly, pumpkin. Of course we'll drive up together. I wouldn't leave you at a time like this."

Nah, because that would be the humane thing to do.

"The thing is, you could visit with Andy. He'd love to take you to the shows and . . . um . . . try to cheer you up."

Every summer, until this last catastrophic one, Elysia spent one month with A.J. and Andy. Andy would escort them to the hottest Broadway shows, take them shopping, share Sunday evenings eating ice cream and watching sexy late night soaps. According to Elysia, this month was the highlight of her year.

A.J. added, "You could . . . talk with Andy. It might help—"

She was going to say ". . . you come to terms with our split," but Elysia cut in with a crisp, "Pumpkin, you don't seem to realize that my sister is dead. True, we weren't as close as we could have been. We weren't as close as the two of you—and Lord knows you probably wish it had been me instead of Di—"

"Mother!"

"—but that doesn't change the fact that she *was* my sister, and I'm going with you."

A road trip with crazy Mom. Who wouldn't love that?

A.J. opened her mouth, but where did she begin? It was like trying to argue with Lula Mae.

As the skycap struggled to budge the laden trolley, she fumbled in her Prada bag—a gift the Christmas before last from Andy—for her keys. "Suit yourself," she muttered, sounding like the sulky adolescent she had once been.

"Besides," Elysia added casually, "as the Bard says, 'Delays have dangerous ends.' It might look suspicious if I didn't turn up right away. I am a suspect, after all."

"You?"

"Naturally. I'm Di's next of kin. We'd quarreled bitterly. I wasn't a regular on *221B Baker Street* for nothing, you know."

"Uh, right."

Elysia reached over and patted A.J.'s cheek with her thin hand. "And don't fret, pet. Of course I'll talk to Andrew for you about this silly divorce business."

Three

The pain in her neck—that would be the *other* pain, although coincidentally *both* had started at Liberty International Airport—was getting worse. A.J. hoped she wasn't in for another bout of back trouble. This getting old thing was really a drag. Granted she was only thirty-five, but these days she felt ancient, mentally and physically. She was glad the drive to Stillbrook was relatively short, and tried to focus on the scenic wonders of Route 15 North as it narrowed from a metropolitan four lanes to a Podunk-bound two. Unfortunately the scenic wonders currently consisted of fog and rain and other cars.

Beside her, Elysia broke off the unending commentary about her plane flight—including weather, cuisine, flight staff, and apparently each and every passenger—and hitched around in her seat to stare hard out the back window of the rental car. She announced, "I think you've lost them."

"Huh?" Momentarily distracted from the shell bursts of pain flashing up and down the ridge of her spine, A.J. cautiously turned her head. "What are you talking about?"

Elysia settled back in her seat. "I assumed, from the way you're racing, that we're being followed?"

Glancing at the speedometer, A.J. eased her foot off the accelerator. "Sorry."

Elysia waved this off breezily, and A.J. was reminded of that *Twilight Zone* episode where the woman driving cross-country keeps seeing the same hitchhiker beckoning her toward a fatal accident—except in A.J.'s case the thing she was trying to outrun was seated next to her. Well, one of the things she would have liked to outrun.

"Mother," she said suddenly, "what did you mean by that crack about being a suspect in Aunt Di's murder? You weren't even in the country when it happened."

Elysia gave A.J. a disbelieving look. "You're serious? I could have hired someone, couldn't I?"

Before A.J. could respond—assuming she had an answer to that—Elysia was off and running amuck down memory lane. "You know, I remember once on *221B Baker Street*, The Shrimp, and I had to solve the murder of an Indian rajah. It turned out that the old man's nephew, who was being educated at Oxford—"

"Mother, I'm serious!"

Elysia arched affronted eyebrows. "So am *I*. I read the papers. I watch the telly. Hired killers are a fact of life. They are real. They are out there."

Something was out there, for sure.

"But what would your motive be?"

"Oh, motive!" Elysia sketched another graceful, taloned gesture.

"There has to be a motive. You're already rich."

Elysia cooed, "As the Bard says, 'You can never be too rich or too thin.'"

"The Bard didn't say that."

"I'm sure he did, pumpkin, though possibly not in so many words."

With an effort, A.J. dragged the conversation back on

track. "Andy said that you knew that I was . . ." She swallowed on the word, tried again. "That Aunt Di was leaving everything to me."

An odd silence punctuated the squeak of the windshield wipers and the whoosh of tires on the rain-slick road. "Well, I hate to break it to you, pumpkin, but I'd no idea Di had made you her heir until sweet little Mr. Meagher rang me up."

Either Andy was lying or Elysia was. It was *so* typical of her mother to force herself into the spotlight, even if it meant looking like a murder suspect.

"No one," A.J. said tersely, "is going to believe that you killed your sister for her money. I don't know how you can even joke about such a thing."

"We all have our mechanics for coping," Elysia said tartly, and that shut A.J. up, as she recalled some of her mother's other mechanics for coping. In fact, her adolescence had been spent in an agony of witnessing her mother's efforts at coping. Her father, seated next to her in that family-values train wreck, had been as much a prisoner as A.J., and it had been left to Aunt Diantha to mount the on-going rescue efforts.

Remembering her aunt's brisk but unfailing presence, A.J.s throat closed. The road ahead momentarily blurred.

"Di had her enemies. We all do. Although, frankly, my sister had more than her share. She never wasted time on tact when being ruthless would get faster results."

Thickly, A.J. said, "Andy said that the police think I'm a suspect."

Perhaps remembering a certain incident involving nude bathing and a public fountain in Rome, her mother said shortly, "Policemen have little or no imagination."

Nestled in the rolling golden hills of northwestern New Jersey and flanked by the shining Delaware River were the twenty-five square miles of deep woods and farmland that encompassed Stillbrook Township. On the outskirts of the town was a small cemetery known as the Hessian Graveyard, although it wasn't old enough to inter any fallen Hessians. It was one of those fascinating places with ornate headstones and morbid statuary of weeping cherubs and little children petting small animals. Gus Eriksson, Aunt Di's naturalist photographer lover, was buried there somewhere beneath the blanket of red and yellow autumn leaves. And now perhaps Aunt Di herself would rest there. Had Aunt Di left any final instructions about her funeral arrangements? A.J. had no idea.

She glanced at her mother as the car sped past the cemetery. Elysia shivered, staring through the windshield at the fog-wreathed trees and iron railing. For once she seemed to have nothing to say.

The town of Stillbrook was a quaint mix of carefully preserved historic homes and artsy-craftsy businesses, including everything from glassblowers to antique dealers. In the center of town was a scrupulously neat village green dominated by a large bronze statue of a World War I soldier and mule. The soldier was supposed to be a likeness of Gene Stevenson, the eldest son of one of Stillbrook's founding families, who had been killed during the war. But it was the mournful-eyed mule that had always fascinated A.J. Was the mule based on a real-life mule? Was the historical mule some kind of war hero? No one seemed to know.

"Nothing has changed," her mother said dreamily as they drove slowly down the dripping tree-lined streets. "It still looks like something out of Thornton Wilder."

"Everything has changed."

She felt her mother's stare but kept her eyes on the road.

The law office of Bradley Meagher, Esquire, was located on the ground floor of a restored gingerbread-trimmed Victorian lodged between a cheery bed-and-breakfast and a gas station/convenience store.

A.J. rang the buzzer while her mother prowled up and down the wooden porch looking about as out of place as a woman in leopard print jeans could look and still not be arrested for solicitation.

At last the door opened. A small but very fit and very tanned older man sized them up. His blue denims were slightly rumpled and his silvery pompadour stood on end—had they woken the man of law from his afternoon siesta?

"Uh, hi," said A.J. "I'm A. J. Alexander and this is—"

"Sure, and if it isn't herself!" exclaimed Bradley Meagher, Esquire, staring past A.J.'s shoulder (or possibly, given his height, under her arm). "*Easy Mason*! Saints preserve us!"

Gay, decided A.J., taking in the Palm Beach tan and the manicure. Gay and channeling Barry Fitzgerald. All they needed now was for Bing Crosby to materialize singing a show tune or two, and her life would become the macabre musical it was surely destined to be.

"Bradley Meagher, you old scoundrel," Elysia said, embracing him. She squealed as Meagher lifted her briefly off the ground. A.J. hastily stepped out of the way, but what Meagher lacked in inches he made up for in muscle.

"Me darlin' girl. You don't look a day older." He looked at A.J., who barely managed to catch herself mid–eye roll. "And here's wee A.J."

Yep, wee A.J., who was taller than both of them put together.

"Hello, Mr. Meagher." She offered her hand to forestall any attempt at levitation.

"I suppose you've come about your aunt's will."

She nodded and smiled deprecatingly, trying to convey a sort of yeah-but-we'd-have-loved-to-drop-by-anyway attitude.

"'Tis a sad affair, that's certain." Meagher ushered them quickly down a short hallway into a room stuffed with heavy old-fashioned furniture and papered with what appeared to be law degrees and honorary diplomas. There was a long leather couch covered by the spread-out funny papers. A tall birdcage stood by the street-side window. A white cockatoo, who apparently shared the same hairdresser as his owner, whistled lewdly as they walked in.

"Pretty bird!" announced the cockatoo.

"Truer words never were spoken," said the gallant Mr. Meagher. "Will you have a cuppa tea, ladies?"

"No thank you," said A.J., who planned on stopping at the Starbucks down the street as soon as they could escape.

"Ta very much," said her mother, who apparently thought they had all the time in the world.

Then of course they had to wait for Mr. Meagher to disappear for however long into the bacon-smelling halls of what was apparently his home as well as his workplace before at last returning with a surprisingly well-arranged tea tray.

Definitely gay, thought A.J. yet again, accepting her china cup and saucer.

"Hey, dude!" said the cockatoo. "Let's party!"

Mr. Meagher gave them a slightly harassed smile, flung a sheet over the bird's cage, and sat down.

"Do the police know anything yet?" Elysia asked.

"Ah, well now, *there's* a rhetorical question," the lawyer said. He seemed to be avoiding looking at A.J. "In a word, no. Of course, your sister was an outspoken woman, and there was no love lost between her and one or two others, but it's still a difficult thing to believe." He sighed. "It's a wicked world, true enough." He sipped his tea.

"You always believe you'll have more time," Elysia murmured, reading for the part of the Brave Bereaved.

A.J. set her saucer on the desktop with a clattering of china. "Apparently the police think I might be a suspect."

Mr. Meagher looked outraged. "Have they said so?"

Well, no, come to think of it, they hadn't. Andy had. His feminine intuition perhaps.

"Have they indeed, the great fascists that they are," continued Mr. Meagher, without waiting for confirmation. "And isn't it as obvious as the nose on my face that it must have been some visiting maniac who did this terrible thing?"

A.J. tried not to stare at Mr. Meagher's nose, which was, in fact, prominent.

"It's the will," Elysia said. "They appear to have wind of the will."

"Ah." Mr. Meagher left it at that. He sipped his tea.

Raindrops pricked mournfully at the windows.

"The formal reading of the will is set for Monday," he said to A.J. at last.

"Before the funeral?"

Mr. Meagher appeared slightly uncomfortable. "It's a wee bit unusual but not unheard of, and given the attention of certain parties—"

Elysia interjected coolly, "There are decisions to be made, business matters to attend to. You don't have the luxury of . . . time."

A.J. stared at her, not quite following. "I don't?"

Mr. Meagher said, "As I told your ma, there's no secret as to the dispensation of your aunt's estate, the bulk of which goes to you."

"All of it?" Maybe that sounded a little greedy; that wasn't what A.J. meant. She meant . . . *why*?

"There are a few other provisions and bequests," Mr. Meagher said, "but in essence, yes. It's all yours. Congratulations. You're one very wealthy young woman."

"I don't understand you," Elysia complained.

It was not exactly a news flash. In fact, the feeling was mutual; however, A.J. did not respond. She continued trying keys in the front door of the 1920s farmhouse that her aunt Diantha had left her. One of the keys had to fit.

She tried the next one on the bulky ring as the rain thundered down, spilling off the sloping roof of the wooden porch into the dead-looking flowerbeds surrounding the two-story house.

Elysia shuddered and turned up the collar of her jacket. "Why do you have to do this now? Wouldn't it make more sense to unpack and relax at home, and then come back here tomorrow?"

By "home," Elysia meant the farm A.J.'s father had purchased for summer vacations so many years ago. But even as a child A.J. had always felt a greater sense of belonging at Deer Hollow with her Aunt Di. At the risk of offending her mother, she couldn't resist the impulse that had her turning off the main road and driving down the muddy dirt track that led to Deer Hollow Farm. From the moment they had left the lawyer's office, the keys bestowed by Meagher weighing down her coat pocket, she'd had this . . . well, compulsion to get to her aunt's.

The key slipped into the lock. A.J. turned it and pushed the door open.

The hallway before them was dark in the gloomy afternoon light. Even so, it was familiar to A.J. The faded red Oriental runner had cushioned the footsteps of generations of Erikssons. Next to the door frame hung a black-and-white photograph of the New Jersey shoreline taken by Gus Eriksson himself in the early years of his career.

She could almost believe that Aunt Di was inside, just out of sight, ready to welcome her home.

Memories of other homecomings washed through A.J., catching her off-guard: Christmas vacations while her parents were in Europe; stopping by after school for ginger cake and the chance to pour her adolescent woes into her aunt's tolerant ear; dragging Andy for the weekend when they had first started dating in college. . . .

Stepping inside, she walked toward the double doors of the front parlor. Her eyes picked out the silhouette of a rocker and the tall outline of her aunt's maple secretary. As she felt for the wall switch, she noticed that the smell of cold and rain was as strong inside the house as outside . . . and there was something else. Something foreign . . . like antiseptic and sweat.

The next moment she was slammed into the wall and knocked down onto the hardwood floor.

Stunned, A.J. tried to process what was happening as Elysia began to scream.

Four

❧

Footsteps pounded down the oakwood floorboards. A.J. felt them vibrate beneath her hands as she painfully got to her knees. Somewhere in the distance she heard a bang and was nearly knocked back down as Elysia rushed to her rescue.

"A.J., pet! Are you all right?" Elysia's voice sounded unfamiliar—high and frightened.

"Call the cops," A.J. gasped. "I'm okay." Elysia clutched her arm, trying to help her to her feet. With her free hand A.J. grabbed at the heavy secretary, wincing at the pain radiating through the knot of nerves and muscles in her lower back. She straightened cautiously. "That son of a—" She bit off the rest of it, putting a hand to her tailbone.

"Bloody madman!" Elysia exclaimed. "*Here*, pet. Sit down." She guided A.J.'s hobbling steps to the tall rocker.

"Where did he go?" A.J. asked, letting herself down carefully. "He didn't run past you, did he?"

"He ran back into the house—"

"Mother!" shrieked A.J., jumping to her feet again. "You mean he's still in the house?"

"I'm sure he legged it," protested Elysia. She looked uneasily over her shoulder at the double doors leading into the hallway. "He must have run out the kitchen door."

"In other words, you don't know! For all we—he could be hiding in the next room listening to us *right now!*"

They were momentarily silent as the alarming possibilities sank in.

Elysia reached for the poker from the fireplace, her expression grim. "Right, then."

"What do you think you're doing?" A.J. protested, trying to grab the poker from her. Elysia waved it out of reach and nearly took out the Tiffany lamp on the nearby table. "This isn't a movie set! You can't chase after him. He might have a gun."

"You call the coppers. I'll reconnoiter."

"You'll wreck *something*, that's for sure." A.J. managed to wrest the poker from her mother's manicured hands. "Just . . . sit. Please."

Elysia looked both affronted and wounded. A.J. ignored her, clutching the poker and ducking her head into the dim hallway. There was no sign of anyone down the long corridor leading to the kitchen. To her right, the front door still stood open, rain dripping steadily off the porch roof.

Trying to sift through the terrified confusion of the assault, A.J. recalled that unnerving bang when she was trying to get to her feet. Since it couldn't have been the front door, maybe it had been the kitchen door. That made more sense. No sane burglar would hang around, right?

She listened closely. Nothing but the rain gurgling in the gutters and rattling on the leaves of the bushes surrounding the porch.

"What are you doing?" Elysia whispered from right behind her.

A.J. nearly rocketed off the floor. Elysia held what

appeared to be an old sheep's crook. Not a bad weapon, actually, although it was hard to picture a less likely shepherdess than Elysia.

Recovering her composure with an effort, she said, "I'm going to call the police."

Elysia nodded.

A.J. crept across the hall to the old-fashioned phone on the wall.

"Does that manky thing still work?" A true child of her generation, Elysia was deeply suspicious of anything over forty years old. She herself was decades past that milestone, but even now she refused to admit it.

"It used to."

A.J. dialed 911 and finally explained her emergency to the tinny-sounding voice at the other end of the line. The voice promised that help was on the way.

Spotting Elysia—sheep crook held at the ready—reconnoitering down the hallway, A.J. hastily hung up.

"Wait! What are you doing?"

"Securing the perimeter."

Too many episodes of *The Avengers*. That was the problem. One of the problems.

A.J. darted after her mother. She was just in time to see Elysia slip into the kitchen.

"Mother!" she hissed.

No response. A.J. tiptoed quickly across the hall. She reached the kitchen. No Elysia. She flipped the wall switch. Cheerful light flooded over the polished floor and beadboard cabinets. The checked navy and white tile backsplash brought back childhood memories, as did the copper canisters and the pig cookie jar on the gleaming countertop.

A slam brought A.J. back to the present. Elysia stood in the enclosed porch off the kitchen where an open door led out to the muddy backyard. The door screen swung in the wind.

"The blighter's scarpered!" Elysia sounded slightly disappointed.

"Thank God for that," A.J. said, massaging the small of her back.

She stared at the small pots of herbs growing on the windowsill over the big farmhouse sink. Diantha had planted those herbs just as she had chosen the colorful woven rugs. Her vegetarian cookbooks sat on the shelves, and there were spices in the wooden rack generations of Eriksson women had probably never heard of, but otherwise the house seemed untouched by time. The long pine table and matching chairs, the china hutch and kitchen cupboard were the furniture Gus Eriksson had grown up with. That always surprised A.J. Her aunt was such a contemporary woman, so focused on incorporating yoga into every aspect of her life, she might have been expected to dump all the antiques and bric-a-brac, but she hadn't. Everything was immaculate but comfortably shabby.

For a moment A.J. pictured Aunt Di standing at the stove cooking one of her curries and laughing her raucous laugh. It was such a hearty shout of a laugh, unexpected from someone as serious and focused as Diantha. Even people who didn't particularly like her found it hard not to smile when she let out that laugh.

Tears stung A.J.'s eyes and she turned away so that her mother wouldn't see.

Elysia closed the back door and fastened it. "Have a seat, pumpkin," she said briskly. "I'll make us a nice cuppa. That'll settle your nerves."

A.J. started to speak but was interrupted by the electronic whoop of a siren blast from the front of the house.

"Bloody hell!" Elysia's exclamation proved her own nerves were none too steady.

"That was fast!" agreed A.J.

She limped out to the front porch. A black and white

four-wheel-drive utility vehicle was parked in the drowned yard. Exhaust drifted gently across the sodden grass.

As she stared, the SUV door opened and a tall, broad-shouldered man in a yellow slicker and a rain-spattered hat got out.

"Ma'am." His breath smoked in the chill air. He touched the brim of his hat. "You've had some trouble?"

His eyes were green—startlingly green—in his tanned face. He was handsome in a rugged Marlboro Man kind of way. Handsome in a way A.J. didn't like. She didn't like big, buff, overpoweringly masculine men. She liked clever, sophisticated, sensitive men. Of course, she preferred clever, sophisticated, sensitive *heterosexual* men, but apparently one couldn't have everything.

This guy looked as though he would be comfortable in a ripped pirate shirt on the cover of a romance novel.

"Someone broke in and knocked me down," A.J. said. "We think he ran out the back."

"Did you get a look at him?" He was already moving past her, whamming open the screen door

"He was just a shadow. A . . . bulky shadow."

"But you're sure he was male?" he threw back.

Had the intruder been male? She had been hurled to the ground before she'd had a clear look. She remembered the scent of wet wool and sweat but nothing specifically masculine, unlike the sort of nice herbal aftershave this trooper was wearing. "I-I think so."

He gave her a narrow look.

Belatedly it occurred to A.J. that the cavalry had arrived awfully fast.

And he hadn't identified himself. He was obviously some kind of law enforcement—you didn't have to be a criminal to feel the lawman vibe—but he hadn't actually given her a name or a badge number or anything.

Not only that, this trooper or whatever he was, had a deep voice that was vaguely—unpleasantly—familiar.

Uneasily, A.J. followed him down the hallway, watching him track wet and mud down the Oriental runner as he made for the kitchen.

He moved quickly for a big man. And there would be no mistaking *him* in the dark for anything but male.

Down the hall, through the kitchen, and out the back porch, A.J. trailed him to the backyard. Then out through the peach trees and down the crooked stone walk, past the garden sheds and the hanging swing where A.J. had spent many contented hours reading as a teenager.

"Oi!" shrieked Elysia. "Over here!" She waved to the cop and A.J. "There are foot prints!"

"Oh my God," A.J. muttered, and the cop glanced back at her. Instantly she composed her face; she'd had a lifetime of practice, since she'd always had to cover her reactions to Elysia.

As they reached Elysia, she pointed triumphantly at what appeared to be a path of muddy footprints, already half-filled with water, leading toward the pasture.

"It looks like the perp jumped the fence and escaped across the meadow." Elysia's normally ivory cheeks were flushed, and a strand of dark hair had escaped her upsweep, giving her a slightly disheveled appearance. It reminded A.J. uncomfortably of past occasions when her mother's dishevelment had been a perilous sign of things to come. "He probably parked in the woods."

"Maybe," the cop said, noncommittally. He strode over to the crooked fence that lined the pasture.

Elysia's gaze followed him. She looked at A.J. and raised her elegant brows.

"Now *there's* a bit of all right," she murmured.

"A little young for you," A.J. said, and Elysia chuckled.

They continued to watch Mr. Law and Order as he stood, hands on hips, surveying the pasture. What exactly was he hoping for? A.J. wondered. An incriminating scrap of clothing? Betraying cigarette butts? A signed confession?

After a few moments he rejoined them. "There's no sign of anybody. I guess someone could have taken off across the pasture, but he'd have to be pretty fast on his feet." He turned to A.J. "What can you tell me about this guy who knocked you down?"

"He was big. I didn't get a good look at him."

"What about you?" he questioned Elysia. "Did you see this intruder?"

"Well, I saw *something*." Guiltily she met A.J.'s eyes. "He was just a-a shape. A hulking shape."

"A hulking shape?" the cop repeated slowly. He glanced at A.J. "A bulky shadow, you said?"

"Right." Was there something suspicious about their description? A.J. didn't understand his skeptical expression. But maybe that was how he always looked.

"Bigger than a monkey and smaller than a bear. My attention was on m-my child." Elysia managed to inject just the right amount of maternal quiver in that, but the cop looked unimpressed.

A.J. said, "You saw the footprints."

They all stared at the soggy ground. Flooded indents were all that remained of the footprints.

The cop said, "I had a quick look at some muddy prints. They weren't clear and they weren't that big. It's possible you could have made them yourself."

A.J. opened her mouth, but before she could respond, he said laconically, "By accident, I mean. Maybe you ladies were walking around out here earlier."

"We had just arrived," A.J. said. "I had just unlocked the door and stepped inside the house when he came charging out of nowhere and knocked me over."

"Anything taken?"

"We didn't have time to check," she admitted. "You got here so quickly."

Those green-green eyes flicked to hers. "Yeah, well, I was actually on my way to see you, Ms. Alexander. I'm

Detective Oberlin with Stillbrook PD. We spoke on the phone."

So she was right about his voice being familiar. He was the insensitive jerk who had given her the bad news about Aunt Di.

The rest of his words slowly registered. *He was already on his way to see her?* She recalled Andy's comments about her being a suspect. It looked as though Andy had been right.

"I remember," she replied curtly.

"Sorry for your loss." His glance included Elysia.

"Thank you," Elysia said bravely. "It was a great shock to us all."

"Murder generally is."

This guy was a real loss to the diplomatic corps.

"Your compassion means the world to us," A.J. sniped. She was not normally prone to antagonizing law enforcement, but something about Oberlin rubbed her the wrong way—from the moment she'd first heard his voice. "I take it you're not here heading up the Welcome Wagon?"

His very firm mouth twitched with something that, in a human, might have indicated amusement.

"I do have a few questions," he admitted. "Strictly routine."

"Naturally," Elysia said. "We're always happy to assist the police with their inquiries." She made it sound like the favorite part of their day—right up there with lunchtime.

"Sure," A.J. said. "Don't let bereavement, burglary, and assault cramp your style."

"Hey, if you'd prefer to talk to me tomorrow, I can wait," Oberlin shot right back.

Elysia tittered uneasily.

Before A.J. could decide on a suitable response, he added, "Why don't we step inside and see what this burglar of yours might have got away with?"

Clearly he didn't believe there had been a burglar. A.J. said shortly, "Why don't we?"

They trooped inside the house, pausing only to knock the mud off their shoes on the back stoop. Privately A.J. admitted that there was something disarming about watching a big tough detective grimly scraping the soles of his boots across a hedgehog-shaped mud brush.

Inside the porch, Oberlin removed his hat and rain poncho. He was, as A.J. had guessed, tall and leanly muscled in form-hugging Levi's and a surprisingly well-cut blazer. His hair was dark and cut short to discourage what appeared to be an unruly wave.

She watched him examine the lock on the back door. "Doesn't appear to be forced."

"Di was never one for locked doors." Elysia sighed.

"This door *was* locked," Oberlin informed her. "We were here all day yesterday. When we left, the house was secured."

A.J. and Elysia exchanged shocked looks. The police had already searched Diantha's home?

"You were here without a search warrant?" A.J. asked.

Oberlin met her gaze coolly. "We had a warrant."

She swallowed hard.

Oberlin continued through the house checking doors and windows. Everything was locked and fastened, nothing broken or forced, and from what A.J. could remember, nothing appeared to be missing.

In the room Diantha had always referred to as "Gus's study," the top drawer of the large desk had been pulled out and set on top. Stacks of letters had been set to one side.

"There!" Elysia said triumphantly. "He must have been searching the desk when we interrupted him."

Oberlin grunted. What was this guy's problem? Did he honestly think she and Elysia had faked a break-in? Why?

Or did he simply believe Diantha had been sorting through the drawer before her death? It was true that there was no indication that whoever had removed the drawer had been in any kind of a hurry.

Elysia mused, "What about that amber statue of Quan Yin? I don't recall seeing that anywhere."

But further search revealed the valuable antique statue was now in Diantha's bedroom.

"There was that painting by that deaf artist. . . ." Elysia suggested.

John Brewster Jr.'s painting of a small girl and a dove turned out to have been moved to one of the guest rooms.

"There was that French clock with the marble base and the bronze sculpture of a Saint Bernard. . . ."

"It's in the front parlor," A.J. said, heading off Detective Oberlin's exasperated reply.

It was clear that Oberlin had lost all interest in their possibly imaginary burglar. In formidable silence he followed them from room to room.

"I guess it's possible a kid could have slipped in here," he admitted grudgingly. "It's the kind of thing kids dare each other to do. Your aunt's death is no secret."

A.J. tried to think back to that frightening moment in the hall when her attacker had come out of nowhere. Could the intruder have been an adolescent? There had been a force, a solidness to him—or her—that she didn't associate with teenagers. But it was possible. She remembered doing stupid things herself on a dare.

"That's very clever, Inspector," Elysia said. "Perhaps this young delinquent planned on selling Di's valuables for drug money. Why don't we make ourselves comfy in the kitchen? We can have a nice hot cuppa, and you can ask your questions while I count the silver."

"I'm sure the silver is all there," A.J. said. Which was probably more than Detective Oberlin was willing to say for the two of them.

Elysia led the way to the kitchen, where the teapot was shrieking merrily on the back burner. A.J. sat at the opposite end of the long pine table. She found it irritating the way Oberlin's physical presence crowded her. He didn't have to be next to her. He didn't even have to say anything.

Not that he was keeping quiet. They were no sooner seated then he said brusquely, "We won't know for sure until we get the ME's autopsy report, but from the prelim it appears that your aunt was strangled late Friday night or early Saturday morning."

"Do you have a suspect?" A.J. tried to keep her voice steady.

His gaze held hers. "Right now it's more of a process of elimination, which is why it would be helpful to cross you and Mrs. Alexander off our list. Just for the record, can I ask where you were late Friday and early Saturday morning?"

"Home in bed."

"Unfortunately *that's* probably true," Elysia said. "Do you much mind soy milk, Inspector?"

"Sorry?" Oberlin looked momentarily confused.

Elysia held up a carton. "Soy milk? For your tea. Di doesn't seem to have anything else."

"Uh, sure. Whatever."

He wasn't getting away that easily. Elysia splashed milk in his cup and served it to him, eyelashes fluttering. "And the same goes for me, you know. Tucked up in my wee trundle bed. And *no one* to vouch for me."

Oberlin nodded absently, watching A.J. "And were you also sleeping solo, Ms. Alexander? On a Friday night? An attractive, single lady in Manhattan?"

Instinctively she touched her butchered hair, still damp from the rain that had washed away whatever was left of her makeup. She knew how she looked: gaunt, haggard— the only color in her face came from the shadows under her eyes. Worse, she knew how she felt. Andy's cancer patient comment wasn't that far off the mark.

But Oberlin spoke so casually, so neutrally, that for an instant A.J. didn't register just how far out of line he was. If she'd had any doubts that he seriously considered her a suspect, that sardonic comment took care of them.

"I-I have an extremely demanding job."

"She needs her beauty sleep," Elysia put in helpfully. "Every minute." She set A.J.'s cup in front of her, ignoring her daughter's stare. "There! Isn't this cozy?" Seating herself at the table, she lifted her own cup and sipped daintily.

A.J. had to give Oberlin credit. The guy knew how to focus. He said to her, "Did you get any phone calls? Would anyone be able to vouch for you?"

"No."

"Andrew must have rung you up," Elysia said. "You two talk all the time. Are you sure Andrew didn't phone late to discuss . . ." Her eyes bored into A.J. A.J. ignored the message there.

"I didn't talk to Andy," she said curtly.

"Andy being your ex-husband—Mr. Andrew Belleson?"

"Correct."

"Okay." He glanced at Elysia. "And you, Mrs. Alexander, were out of the country until this morning, is that right?"

"Er, yes."

"How would you describe your relationship with your aunt?" Oberlin said, swiveling back to A.J.

"Good."

"When was the last time you saw her?"

"I don't know. A couple of years ago. Spring. Three years ago. I think."

"My relationship with my sister was always a difficult one," Elysia said reminiscently. "We were both passionate, dynamic women. We were bound to butt heads."

Detective Oberlin appeared not to hear her. "You can't remember the last time you saw your aunt?"

Elysia leaned forward, her tone confidential. "It's because of Andrew. Di took one of her peculiar dislikes to Andrew. She was like that, you know. She would take these instant and irrational dislikes to people. Anna was like the daughter she never had, and I expect she was rather jealous of losing her."

For a moment A.J. couldn't think who Anna was. Oh yeah, *she* was Anna. And the only person in the world who called her that was Elysia—knowing full well A.J. loathed it.

"So Ms. Mason and Mr. Belleson didn't get along?"

"Oh, *nothing* like that! It's impossible to quarrel with Andrew. He's the sweetest man who ever lived. No, my point is simply that it made visits here rather *awkward* for Anna. And of course she works every *minute*. Like a navvy."

What the hell was a navvy? And did she really want to know? A.J. barely managed to control her expression as Detective Oberlin turned back to her. She wondered why he was allowing Elysia to interrupt. He was letting her blab and blab. Why? Why wasn't he interviewing them separately and formally? Did he think he could learn more this way? He was probably right.

"And your aunt never came to see you?"

"She didn't like Manhattan. She didn't like big cities."

"You kept in touch by phone or e-mail?"

A.J. hesitated. "Yes. Not regularly. We're both—we were both busy with our careers. I meant to—" Unexpectedly her voice broke.

Without blinking, Oberlin observed her struggle for control.

"So you wouldn't have any idea of problems your aunt might be having in her personal life? She never mentioned arguing with anyone, maybe some trouble with an employee or a neighbor or even a stranger?"

A.J. shook her head.

"Di was always having trouble with people," Elysia chimed in. "She . . . expected a great deal. From everyone. All the time. She was driven. A perfectionist. But she always kept her little worries to herself. I suppose that's one way we're alike—that fierce independence. Our unshakable self-reliance. Otherwise you couldn't find sisters more different."

More of her hair had slipped loose; it was really beginning to drive A.J. nuts. Elysia looked like Lady Macbeth in the last act.

"When was the last time you spoke to your sister?" Oberlin asked her.

"Two weeks ago," Elysia said promptly. "We rowed. We always rowed. *Ferociously.*"

"What did you . . . row . . . over?"

Elysia blinked. "Eh . . . it escapes me."

A.J. asked before she could stop herself, "What do you mean, it escapes you?" She felt Oberlin's gaze and bit off the rest of what she wanted to say.

Elysia said defensively, "We always rowed. Our rows sort of run together." She avoided A.J.'s eyes.

Detective Oberlin nodded and rose. "I think that's it for now. Appreciate your cooperation, ladies."

"Anything we can do, *of course*," Elysia said. "I'm sure I personally won't know a moment's peace until this *ghastly* tragedy—"

"Yes, ma'am," Detective Oberlin said. He did not exactly beat a retreat, but A.J. was careful not to step between him and the door. She understood a little of what he must be feeling. Even those who knew and loved Elysia found her occasionally . . . overwhelming.

In silence she watched him retrieve his yellow rain slicker and hat from the porch, and then followed him down the long hallway to the front door. He shrugged into the slicker while she waited, his movements unhurried, deliberate.

"I guess you'll be in town for a few days." He replaced his hat, automatically tilting the brim. A lot of guys looked silly in a hat; Andrew couldn't wear hats, not even baseball caps. Detective Oberlin wore his hat with tough-guy authority. "I'll be in touch."

A.J. nodded. She knew Oberlin was a long way from scratching them off his "list." After a moment she followed him out onto the porch, hugging herself against the cold as she watched him cross to the SUV with police markings.

He opened the car door and then hesitated. "Ms. Alexander?"

A.J. moved to the edge of the porch. "Yes?"

"If I were you I'd get the locks on those doors changed."

Five

❦

"**What** was that about?" A.J. inquired, rejoining Elysia in the kitchen.

"What's that, pumpkin?"

"That whole 'we always rowed ferociously' bit. Are you *trying* to attract police suspicion?"

Elysia's narrow brows rose. "It's much better to lay our cards on the table, don't you think? I remember in the episode 'Murder at the Peking Opera' . . ."

Don't look now: *221B Baker Street*'s Greatest Moments.

"He thinks we made up a story about an intruder to throw him off my trail," A.J. interrupted. She rubbed her forehead, trying to smooth away the ache behind her eyes. What a long and horrible day it had been. She was tired and depressed and her back hurt. Being suspected of murdering a loved one was just the icing on the cake.

Elysia replaced her teacup on the table. "He'd have to be off his twist, wouldn't he?" She glanced up with a sly smile. "He fancies you."

"Mother, he thinks I'm a cold-blooded murderess. He doesn't fancy me. Except in handcuffs."

"Ooh! Naughty."

A.J. chose to not hear that. "Anyway, he's got to be married."

Elysia shook her head. "I don't think so. No ring. And he's the ring-wearing type."

"Then he's gay."

Elysia tittered. "Pumpkin, if there's one thing I know, it's men. And *that* man definitely fancies you."

Either men had changed a lot in the years since Easy Mason was breaking hearts, or her mother was not quite the expert she imagined. Apparently Elysia had never noticed that Andy was gay, either. She still believed A.J. could salvage her marriage to a man who couldn't, to save his life, name a single player in the NFL but could recite the lyrics to every song Judy Garland ever recorded.

And now that A.J. thought about it, Detective Oberlin reminded her way too much of Nick Grant, Andy's new "partner." Grant had the same craggy good looks and overbearing masculinity. And like Detective Oberlin, Grant was in law enforcement. He was an FBI agent. No one would ever suspect that Nick Grant was gay, and no one would ever suspect Detective Jake Oberlin of being gay, but there had to be some reason a healthy, handsome thirtysomething man was not married. If he wasn't gay, he had Serious Issues.

Not that A.J. had the slightest interest in Detective Oberlin, with or without issues. One disastrous marriage was enough for any woman. And she wasn't the type to have a fling—even if she wasn't totally and completely sick of men. Which she was. Totally. Completely. So why was she even thinking along these lines?

Following her own train of thought, Elysia suggested, "You could use that, pumpkin."

"Use what?" A.J.'s gaze sharpened. "You've got to be

kidding! The last thing I need is to start another relationship, especially with . . . with—"

"Who's talking about relationships?" Elysia smiled, looking unnervingly like Snow White's royal stepmum when the mirror gave the right answer. "I don't mean you should get *involved* with that good-looking brute. Don't be silly. You and Andrew are going to patch things up, naturally, but you can use this copper's interest in you to your *advantage*."

A.J. became aware that her mouth was hanging open. Never a good look. Not for anyone. But whatever she might have answered, assuming she had an answer for the suggestion that she start brushing up her Mata Hari skill set, was lost as the front doorbell rang. From somewhere outside a dog began to bark.

"That will be the press, I suppose," Elysia murmured. "Just ignore them. They'll go away. I wonder if Di has any biscuits."

"Why would reporters be ringing the doorbell? How would they know we were here?" A.J. pushed wearily to her feet as the bell rang again. "Does Stillbrook even have a newspaper?" More to the point, did they have a good chiropractor?

"You could call it that, I suppose. I believe it's called *Our Babbling Brook*. Something terribly precious." Elysia sounded vague. "But I was thinking of the legitimate press, pumpkin. After all, your auntie was a bit of a celebrity in her own world."

Did Elysia think the folks from *Yoga Journal* were banging at the door? A.J. gave it up and made the return trek to the front door. She peered out the side window. A very short and very stout person with a dog stood on her porch.

She unlocked the door and yanked it open.

She blinked.

Apparently one of those suburban lawn gnomes had

come to life and was seeking refuge in rural New Jersey. A.J. had a quick impression of a lime green coat, red trousers, black rubber boots, and a hat that looked as if it had been fashioned from a burlap sack—although "fashioned" was probably the wrong word.

Next to the gnome stood a stocky yellow Lab, tail wagging with nonaggressive enthusiasm. The dog barked a couple of sharp "notice me" barks.

"Sorry to intrude," the gnome said in a low sexless voice.

"Monster!" gasped A.J., addressing the dog, not the gnome.

How had she forgotten about Monster, her aunt's beloved four-footed companion for the last decade?

"Oh, Monster!" Swinging wide the screen, she dropped down on her knees. Monster pushed into her arms, panting his hot doggy breath in her face, his melting brown eyes gazing trustfully into her own. His tail banged against the screen as he wagged it frantically.

"He remembers you," the gnome said approvingly.

A.J. looked up, wiping impatiently at the tears spilling over her cheeks. Was she going to spend the next week crying every time something caught her off guard? What had happened to her? "Sorry," she said. "I'm just . . . so glad to see him."

"Sure," the gnome said understandingly. "You must be A.J. I'm Stella Borin. Di's tenant and nearest neighbor. I live about a mile down the road." She waved toward the pasture and the woods beyond. "I heard you were over here, and I thought I'd bring the pooch by. I can't tell you how sorry I was to hear about your auntie."

"Thanks," A.J. replied huskily. She rose and shook Stella's hand. The woman had a grip like a stevedore. Dark round eyes studied A.J. shrewdly.

"Stella Borin," Elysia drawled from behind A.J. "Just back from Fashion Week in Paris?"

Stella eyed Elysia without favor. "I heard you were back, Elysia."

A.J. didn't remember Stella, so she had to be a relative newcomer to Stillbrook. Elysia, on the other hand, seemed to know her well enough to dislike her. Interesting. Especially since her mother didn't spend much time in New Jersey these days.

She found herself wondering how closely in touch Elysia had remained with Aunt Di. All that stuff about "rowing" and not knowing what was in Aunt Di's will. What was Elysia up to?

Monster plowed through A.J.'s arms, sidled past Elysia, and disappeared into the house.

"He's looking for her," Stella said grimly. "He's been waiting for her to pick him up all weekend."

A.J. mopped her eyes with her sleeve. "Thanks for bringing him home."

Stella shrugged. "He wasn't happy over at my place. And the cats don't like him, old gentleman though he is. Do the police have any suspects yet?"

A.J. shook her head. "I don't think so."

"It's terrible. Nothing like this ever happened around here before."

"Oh, pish! This used to be mob country," Elysia broke in. "I suppose it still is. In fact, isn't your, er, spirit guide some bloke named Stinky Malone, killed in a shootout back in the Roaring Twenties?"

"Spirit guide?" A.J. repeated.

"Slapsy Malone," Stella said a little huffily. "And, yes, he was slain in a shootout, but that was eighty years ago. This is a safe and healthy environment to raise a family. We've got excellent schools and any number of local attractions: museums, historical sites, swimming and hiking and horseback riding. We've got art galleries and a farmer's market and antique shops and bookstores and a winery and air balloons and . . ."

A.J. wasn't listening. She was remembering summers spent in Stillbrook: most of her childhood summers and one truly unforgettable—for all the wrong reasons—school year when her parents had separated. The separation hadn't lasted. Her father and mother were even more miserable apart than they were together, which was saying something. A.J. had loved the summers, but the school year was hell. She hadn't fit in. In fact, she had stood out like a zebra in a herd of Shetland ponies.

Deer Hollow Farm and Aunt Di had been her refuge.

"Are you selling real estate these days?" Elysia inquired. "A.J. won't be staying here. Her life is in Manhattan."

Stella opened her mouth but then seemed to think better of it. "Well, the pooch will be company for you," she said to A.J. "It gets lonely out here sometimes."

"She'll be staying at the farm with me," Elysia said.

"Will she?" Stella looked amused. To A.J. she said, "You'll find my number in Di's phone book. You give me a call if you need anything."

"Wouldn't you know if she needed you?" Elysia asked sweetly. "Wouldn't you see it in your crystal ball?"

Stella flashed Elysia a surprisingly black look, but the smile she offered A.J. seemed genuine.

"You come and see me, A.J. Any time you like."

"**Don't** worry, pumpkin," Elysia said as A.J. closed the door on the last glimpse of Stella Borin's Jeep taillights retreating into the twilight. "You won't have to stay a day beyond the funeral."

"The police might have a different idea." A.J. turned on the parlor light and sat down gingerly on the overstuffed sofa. Her back hurt even more than usual, and she was going to have a colorful set of bruises by morning. Her stomach was growling, but the idea of food made her queasy. What she really wanted was a long hot soak in the tub to loosen up her muscles and warm her bones. A bath and then a long deep sleep.

Down the hall, Monster could be heard walking slowly from room to room, his nails clicking on the hardwood floor.

"Oh, bother the police!" Elysia said with unexpected sharpness. "You leave the police to me."

A.J. scrutinized her mother's face curiously. "You don't think it was some random madman, do you? You think someone Aunt Di knew killed her."

Elysia blinked. "I . . . suspect no one and everyone," she said at last.

"Well, that narrows it down."

"It doesn't have anything to do with you, pet." Elysia was unexpectedly earnest. "You're going to go home and patch things up with Andrew and forget all about this appalling tragedy. I know it will take time, but it's what Diantha would have wanted."

Was it? A.J. wondered. "Actually, what I'm going to do is call a locksmith," she said, getting up off the sofa.

"We can call from the farm." Elysia trailed A.J. into the hall. She meant Starlight Farm, the property she owned on the other side of the valley.

A.J. took a deep breath. "I'm not going to the farm. I'm going to stay here tonight."

Elysia went very still. *"You what?"*

A.J. knew that tone only too well, though it was many years since Elysia had tried it on her.

"I'm going to be sleeping here." She hated the fact that she sounded defiant. As though she knew she was in the wrong—which she didn't. It felt right to stay at Deer Hollow. She felt close to her aunt here. She felt like she had come home.

"A.J., you cannot stay here."

"Detective Oberlin would have said—"

"I'm not talking legalities," Elysia exclaimed. "I'm

talking common sense. Just a few hours ago someone broke in here!"

"That's why I'm calling a locksmith. Anyway, I think Oberlin was probably right. It was probably just a kid on a dare. Or maybe even someone trying to steal a few antiques from a deserted house. I don't believe he'll come back now." She caught sight of the dog vanishing into another room off the hallway. "Anyway, Monster will protect me."

"What if it wasn't a kid or someone trying to nick the silver?" Elysia asked. "Suppose it was the person who murdered Di? Suppose he was looking for something, something that was worth killing for. Do you honestly believe an old dog and a new set of locks is going to stop him?"

A.J. had a sudden and unnerving picture of a sinister someone creeping up on the house even now. "Jeez, Mother! Do you mind?" She turned to the phone, dialing information and asking for the number of a local locksmith. While the operator looked up the number, she covered the mouthpiece. "It makes sense to stay here since I'll have to sort through all this stuff." She shrugged. "Maybe I'll find something that will help catch whoever killed Aunt Di."

She turned back to the phone as she was connected to the locksmith.

Finishing her call, A.J. joined Elysia in the kitchen, where her mother stood examining the contents of the refrigerator.

"I suppose I could manage an omelet," Elysia was saying vaguely. "If I could find something to put in one . . ."

"You don't have to cook dinner, Mother. Really."

"We have to eat."

She had a point. A.J. could feel her blood sugar bottoming out. "Green onions," she pointed out. "Mushrooms."

"Mm. Bacon or a bit of ham would be lovely. . . ."

"Aunt Di was vegetarian. You're not going to find bacon in her fridge."

"I never understood that," Elysia sighed. "I simply can't understand people who turn food into a religion. Oh, *thank God*, here's some cheese." She backed out of the fridge, balancing her eggs, mushrooms, and block of cheese.

A.J. sat at the long pine table while her mother cooked. She couldn't remember the last time Elysia had prepared a meal for her. She wasn't sure if she ever had. A.J.'s father had fixed her breakfasts when she was small; the rest of the time they'd eaten out or had delivery. A.J.'s culinary skills were primitive at best. But an adult woman in a metropolis can live quite well on yogurt, diet soda, and Chinese take-out. Once A.J. had married, Andy had done all the cooking. Andy was a wonderful cook. He was going to make some man—probably Nick Grant—a wonderful wife.

Elysia cracked eggs in a bowl with the casual flare of Andrey Hepburn in *Sabrina*. She was saying, "If we're going to stay the night . . ."

A.J. snapped back to the present. "Look, Mother," she said awkwardly. "I was planning . . . that is . . . I'd prefer to stay . . ." The expression on Elysia's face made her half swallow the rest of her words: ". . . on my own."

Elysia said nothing. Her silence did all the shouting for her.

"I just need some time to myself. I need some time to think."

"I don't see the point of thinking," Elysia said shortly. She turned back to the stove.

A.J. stared unhappily at the elegant and greatly offended line of her mother's back. She felt horribly guilty. She was supposed to, of course; that was Elysia's specialty. If only they could really talk, it would be different. But she couldn't take an evening of advice on how to win back Andy, or worse, seduce that grim-faced cop. She couldn't listen to Elysia's catty reminiscences about Diantha. She was too tired to keep her guard up, and that's what she always had to do with her mother.

She needed peace and quiet. She needed time to deal with her grief in her own way.

"I'm sorry," she said to Elysia's back. "I feel like I have to do this."

"People always say that when they simply want their own way, don't they?"

"Please don't be angry."

"Angry?" Elysia swung on her heel, smiling with ferocious brightness. "Pumpkin, if you prefer to spend the night all by yourself in this spooky old house with a maniac on the prowl, well, I've certainly never been one to interfere."

"That's true," A.J. said gravely. "And, er, thanks."

It was just after eight o'clock, and the locksmith had come and gone, when Elysia finally departed. A.J. went through the house double-checking the newly replaced locks on the windows and doors. Monster padded quietly after her, as though hopeful she could locate Diantha where he had failed.

In the parlor she stopped to examine the groupings of photos on a pie-shaped table. There were several pictures of herself at different stages growing up. She ignored them, reaching for a silver-framed picture of her aunt and Gus Eriksson. Gus had died before A.J. was born, but she felt as though she knew him from documentaries and photographs. He had been a kind of cross between John Muir and Ansel Adams. Now she realized her aunt must have been her own age at the time the photo was taken, just a year or so before Gus's death from leukemia.

Gus had one of those bony intelligent faces, not handsome, but memorable. Di had a funny smile in the photo. She looked happy and young. They had never married, but theirs was one of those never-ending loves. Di never found anyone else—and she never looked that innocent and carefree again. But she had been happy, and she had lived a long and fulfilling life, and the thought of that gave A.J. comfort. In time she would get over Andy. There would never be anyone else for her, but she would be happy, and she would live a long and fulfilling life.

Yeah, right. Doing what? Helping to arrange book signings for panicky writers? Coming up with strategies to revive interest in substandard dog food? Devising ad campaigns to convince consumers of the nutritional benefits of candy bars?

I'm just tired, she reassured herself. She'd been through a lot over the past few months. It was natural that she'd feel a little depressed, a little dissatisfied with her life. She just needed a break. Maybe a funeral on the edge of civilization wasn't the ideal vacation from her problems, but the change was bound to do her good. Give her time to sort things out.

She turned out the light in the front parlor. Monster sat by the front door, waiting patiently to go outside.

A.J. opened the door and watched him cross the porch and vanish into the darkness, his dog tags jingling. The rain had stopped. The night smelled of woodsmoke and wet earth. The moon peeped through the tattered cloud cover like a silver eye.

She had a sudden awareness of how alone she was out here. Her nearest neighbor was Stella Borin, and she lived over five miles away. A.J. had felt confident when she assured Elysia the would-be burglar wouldn't be back; now she wasn't quite so sure. What if he hadn't been looking to steal a few portable valuables? What if he had been looking for something that tied directly into Diantha's death? What if he *was* Diantha's murderer?

"Monster!" she called.

Silence.

Not so much as the twitter of a bird or the chirp of a cricket. But that didn't mean anything. The local denizens were probably all tucked up trying to stay dry.

"Monster!" she called again.

To her relief, Monster materialized on the lawn like a ghost dog. He wandered placidly back up the stairs. If there was danger lurking out there, the dog didn't seem to sense it.

A.J. locked the door and tested it.

Her back was twinging and throbbing now. She was going to have to find a chiropractor fast or she'd never get through this week. Hobbling into her aunt's bedroom, A.J. stripped the sheets from the bed and remade it with the linens from the hall cupboard.

She felt comforted in Diantha's room, remembering times as a child when bad dreams had sent her into her aunt's bed. She felt safe. She opened her suitcase and pulled out her favorite pair of Nick and Nora flannel pajamas. Navy flannel decorated with cocktail glasses; they seemed oddly festive given the circumstances, but they were warm and soft and comforting.

Too tired to unpack—too tired to do more than brush her teeth—she climbed into the wide, old sleigh bed. The rain had started again. It drummed against the roof in a soothing rhythm. Monster lay before the fireplace, snoring gently. A.J. looked at the books on her aunt's nightstand. Diantha was always reviewing books and yoga-related products for the studio gift shop. No detail of her empire had been too small or insignificant for her personal attention.

Idly A.J. studied the titles: *Light on Yoga*, the 1966 classic was one of Diantha's perennial favorites. *The Living Gita* by Sri Swami Satchidananda looked as if would be excellent for putting her to sleep within minutes. She smiled picking up the third book, *Babar's Yoga for Elephants*.

A.J. flipped through the brightly illustrated pages,

surprised into a chuckle at the pullout poster of Babar doing his yoga poses. Her eyelids grew heavy. She replaced the book on the nightstand and switched out the light.

The room was dark when A.J. woke. She knew immediately where she was; what she couldn't figure out was what had broken her sleep.

Had she heard something?

She listened uneasily. The rain had stopped again. The house creaked in the way of old buildings. Nothing to worry about there, right? She could hear Monster slumbering peacefully beside the bed.

It felt strange to lie here in Diantha's room. She remembered waking up in this house as a child, traveling the long dark hallway to the safety of her aunt's bed. That comfortable sleepy soapy smell and Diantha's sleep-husky voice. *Bad dreams, lovey?* Tears trickled down the side of A.J.'s face and slipped into her ear. She rubbed her face in the pillow.

"I wish I'd had a chance to say good-bye."

The nocturnal silence seemed profoundly empty. There was no comfort here, there was . . . nothing.

After a time she fell back into restless sleep.

Someone was coming down the hallway. . . .

A.J. woke with a start.

Had she heard something?

She listened closely.

The room felt chilly. Was that because somewhere in the house a window or a door was open?

She thought of the new locks and told herself to relax.

Of course, even if there were someone sneaking down the hall she would tell herself that there was no one here.

It could happen.

She reached across and turned on the bedside lamp.

Mellow light flooded the room, picking out the familiar furniture and photos. The carved statue of Quan Yin, Buddhist goddess of compassion and mercy, smiled enigmatically from across the floor. A.J. glanced to the side of the bed.

Monster panted softly, eyes on her.

"Hi," A.J. whispered.

His tail thumped the floor. He got up and climbed without too much difficulty onto the bed, circled once and settled into a comfortable ball against her hip.

"I don't think you're supposed to be up here," A.J. informed him.

Monster's doggy smile seemed to say he had been thinking the same thing about her. He thrust his nose under his tail and proceeded to go to sleep.

Six

The phone woke her.

A.J. rolled over and fumbled for the receiver. " 'Lo?" she croaked.

"Ms. Alexander?" The voice was male, familiar, unwelcome. Detective Oberlin.

"Do you have any idea what time it is?" A.J. snarled.

"It's . . ." He paused, apparently checking his watch. "Five after twelve."

"What?" She sat bolt upright. The overcast skies behind the drapes made it seem earlier than it was. She looked at the other side of the bed, but Monster was gone. Apparently a dog with things to do and places to go.

"God, I overslept." She swung her legs off the bed and rubbed her cropped head. "I had a horrible night—" She bit off the rest of it. What did he care whether she had a horrible night? He would just think it was a symptom of her guilty conscience.

"Any disturbances?" Oberlin asked in a politely official tone.

"No. Is there something I can help you with?"

"I'd like to come by a little later and discuss the case with you."

"There've been some developments? Have you arrested someone?"

"Not just yet," he said smoothly. "There are one or two points I'd like to go over with you. Maybe I could drop by around two?"

"Sure," A.J. said grudgingly.

"See you then," Oberlin said and rang off.

Was that a threat or a promise? A.J. climbed carefully out of the big bed. Babar had inspired her to try a couple of toe touches, but her spine seemed to have fused, and she didn't want to risk being frozen on all fours when Detective Oberlin arrived.

Hand on the small of her back, she made her way down the hallway. She found Monster lying in front of the back door and let him out for his morning constitutional.

A long hot shower helped relieve some of her stiffness. She poured some Aromafloria Stress Less bath gel into a washcloth and was soothed by the steamy scents of lavender, chamomile, and sage. Aunt Di had advocated a life of discipline and self-control, but didn't that really boil down to quality versus quantity? Aunt Di had not accumulated tons of possessions, but she had lived well. Sensibly. A.J. thought of her own overstuffed closets, the drawers brimming with cosmetics and grooming aids—half of them used only once or twice.

Speaking of which . . . She studied herself critically in the foggy mirror. Her hair really did look like hell. Maybe she could find a salon in town. They couldn't do much more damage than she already had with her trusty nail scissors. She sighed. Her skin looked dull, her eyes looked dull, her hair looked dull. Her mother was nuts; no way would anyone find her attractive right now—and that was the way she wanted it.

Dressed in jeans and a black Metropolitan Museum of Art T-shirt, she wandered barefoot into the hallway. The house was very quiet. Too quiet. Why had she thought she wanted to be here by herself? She hated living by herself.

She padded into the kitchen and nearly jumped out of her skin at the sound of frantic scratching on the back door. She hurried to open the door, and Monster calmly trotted in. Apparently a pack of wolves wasn't chasing him after all.

"You scared me!"

Monster licked his chops and gave her that sheepish doggy smile. His yellow coat was rough with wet, and he was tracking muddy prints across the wooden floor.

"Oh man," muttered A.J. And yet she welcomed the distraction of the dog. She grabbed a paper towel and wiped up the muddy prints, then rubbed it over Monster's coat till the paper shredded away to nothing.

Monster sat down at his bowl and eyed her soulfully.

"Are you supposed to eat twice a day?"

He assured her with another heavy thump of his tail that he was practically *required* to eat twice a day.

She fed the dog and then began hunting through the fridge for something she could eat. Tofu, soy milk, soy breakfast links, and more vegetables than she'd seen in the last six months. The problem wasn't that Aunt Di had been a vegetarian; the problem was that she didn't eat junk food. These days A.J. practically lived on junk food. Pop-Tarts and Yoo-hoo had become staples. She didn't know if her system could survive a sudden return to healthy eating.

Opening cupboard doors, she examined beans, cereals, lentils, semolina flour, and—oh good!—peanut butter. Peanut butter and jelly: one of her favorite childhood breakfasts. She'd forgotten that she used to love breakfast.

She had a sudden memory of lazy Saturday mornings with Andy: lying in bed eating fresh croissants and drinking espresso, reading the papers, listening to music, talking. A lot of talking. Now she knew why. Oh, and those wonderful, long back rubs. Andy would have made one heck of a masseuse. All those leisurely, relaxing massages that never went anywhere. She had thought it was a sign of his extraordinary sensitivity and understanding. Now she realized it was lack of interest.

Her appetite gone, A.J. settled on coffee. Thank goodness Aunt Di hadn't come up with some healthy alternative to java.

She drank standing over the sink, staring out the window. The rain had stopped but the skies were leaden. The line of trees across the meadow looked drab and barren, stripped by yesterday's storm of their fall foliage.

Had Aunt Di ever been lonely out here? But Aunt Di had always seemed too self-sufficient and tough to experience an emotion as feeble as loneliness.

Finishing her coffee, A.J. placed her cup in the sink and walked to the back door. She removed Aunt Di's green waxed jacket from the hook on the back porch and stepped out for a quick walk. The air was crisp and stung her cheeks, but it smelled rain-washed clean. Monster trotted a few yards ahead, stopping along the way to investigate a particularly inviting bush or tree.

She wondered what "one or two points" Detective Oberlin wanted to discuss. Had there been any developments overnight? It didn't seem likely if the police were focusing their suspicions on her. It was unbelievable to A.J. that anyone could think her capable of murder. Of course, policeman had to have suspicious minds; it was probably a job prerequisite.

But there had to be other people who might have something to gain by Aunt Di's death. And even if they didn't have something to gain, Aunt Di was the sort of person you either loved or hated.

Up ahead, Monster suddenly froze and pointed, head high and tail outstretched.

A.J. stopped walking and stared. To her relief a deer

stepped out of the treeline and picked its way across the meadow.

She relaxed and called to the quivering dog. After a reluctant moment or two—apparently he hadn't yet fully embraced the vegetarian philosophy—Monster snapped out of his trance and trotted after her.

Arriving back at the house, she was less than thrilled to see the police SUV parked in the front yard. Detective Oberlin stood on her front porch. Monster wagged his tail, which showed what a bad judge of character he was.

A.J. took a deep breath. She remembered one of Andy's favorite quotes from *Book of Five Rings*, which according to him was the quintessential business strategy book: "In battle, if you make your opponent flinch, you have already won." She had to make sure Detective Oberlin did not make her flinch—or, at least, did not see her flinch.

"Hello," she called.

He turned and raked her over with those disconcertingly green eyes. She wondered if he wore colored contacts, though he didn't look like the kind of guy who wasted a lot of time worrying about his looks. He probably didn't own a grooming product. He probably thought soap *was* a grooming product.

"Ms. Alexander. I was wondering if you planned on standing me up."

"Why would I? I want to hear what you've done to solve my aunt's murder."

Oberlin's eyes narrowed, and A.J. felt a spark of triumph.

She mounted the stairs, brushed past him, and unlocked the house. They all trooped inside.

"It looks like more rain is on the way," she was saying when she heard a scuffling sound behind her. She glanced around. Detective Oberlin was occupied in shoving Monster away. The dog landed on its haunches.

"What are you doing?"

To her surprise, the detective's cheeks reddened. "Nothing. Your dog is . . ."

He didn't finish it.

Okay. That was a little weird.

A.J. led the way into the parlor. Detective Oberlin took one of the large overstuffed chairs by the fireplace, and Monster sat down in front of him, eying the cop expectantly.

"Monster, go lie down," A.J. ordered, taking the chair across from Oberlin.

Monster gave her a guilty look and came over to settle on her feet.

Detective Oberlin cleared his throat.

"It looks like your aunt was strangled between four thirty and six a.m on Saturday morning. We're theorizing it was around five because Suze MacDougal, the student who found your aunt, arrived at the studio at six fifteen for the Sunrise Yoga class. Suze didn't see anyone, the place was deserted."

"Could this Suze have had anything to do with my aunt's death?"

"We've ruled her out as a possible suspect."

A.J. nodded. She wanted to ask why, but she knew he wasn't about to explain to someone who *was* a possible suspect.

"Your aunt was strangled with a yoga tie, which indicates that the murder was not premeditated."

"What does that mean?"

"Premeditated? It means that the murder wasn't pla—"

"I know what premeditated means," A.J. interrupted. "What does it mean to *you*?"

Instead of answering he said, "Your aunt doesn't appear to have struggled or tried to defend herself. Even assuming that she knew and was not afraid of her attacker, once that tie was slipped around her throat she should've started fighting back."

"You're assuming that she knew her attacker?"

"It seems likely. Motive generally presupposes prior knowledge of the victim."

"But every crime has a motive, right?"

His eyes narrowed. "Right."

"So what you really mean is you're assuming a particular motive is involved here. You don't think it could have been some random attack?"

He said tersely, "No. She wasn't sexually assaulted—" He caught A.J.'s expression and said, "Sorry. You asked; I'm explaining why I don't think this was a random attack. Nothing was taken from the center, there was no vandalism. It's possible that your aunt surprised an intruder, but then why didn't she fight back."

It wasn't a question, and A.J. didn't have an answer. It didn't make sense to her either.

"There's something else. Whoever killed your aunt arranged her body in a yoga position called Corpse Pose."

Corpse Pose. *Savasana.* The final resting pose of a satisfying yoga session. It wasn't a complicated position; it would take virtually no strength at all to arrange a body thus, but arranging the body into that final position surely indicated familiarity with yoga. Aunt Di's killer was either a student or an instructor—or someone who had wanted to have the last terrible word.

She said huskily, "Somebody has a sick sense of humor."

"Yeah. But that sense of humor is one more indication that your aunt wasn't killed by a stranger. She knew her killer. Her killer knew her. Her killer knew yoga. Her killer may not have gone to the studio planning to commit homicide; maybe they argued and things got out of hand. But, again, if they had something to argue about, they knew each other."

It wasn't *CSI*, but he did have a kind of ruthless logic.

"Haallooo the house!" trilled a familiar voice from down the hall.

Oberlin raised his head. "What the hell's *that*?"

"The house is haunted," A.J. said sweetly.

He bit off what might, under other circumstances, have been a laugh.

"We're in here!" called A.J.

Elysia's heels could be heard tapping down the hallway. She sauntered through the doorway like Maggie the Cat making her entrance. Today's ensemble was Elysia's idea of country living: stilettos, stovepipe jeans, and a long white fur jacket.

"Hullo, pumpkin. Hullo, Inspector . . . I'm sorry, what was your name?"

"Detective Oberlin, ma'am."

"Oh, don't call me madam," Elysia returned merrily. "I'm just one of the girls!"

Detective Oberlin's expression was priceless. He recovered instantly, but it took all A.J.'s willpower not to give in to a nervous giggle. "Detective Oberlin has been explaining why he believes Aunt Di must have known her killer."

"A safe assumption in a village the size of this one." Elysia sat down in one of the overstuffed chintz-covered chairs and ostentatiously lifted one leg over the other. She had wonderful legs, no doubt about it.

Detective Oberlin, however, seemed impervious to any and all feminine charms. He said, "Can you think of any reason someone might want your aunt dead?"

"No."

"What about boyfriends? Lovers?"

"I'm afraid you're way off the scent there, Inspector," Elysia answered. "My sister had one great love of her life, and that was Gus Eriksson."

"The naturalist?"

"He's better remembered for his photographs, but yes. Di inherited this farm and half the county when Gus died." She added pointedly, "Of leukemia, in case you're wondering."

He ignored the jibe. "That was over forty years ago, wasn't it?"

"It doesn't matter if it was a hundred years ago. Di never got over it. There was never anyone else for her. She lived like a nun."

"A nun?" he repeated mildly.

"Well, one of those New Age nuns, I suppose. Anyway, the point is that Di did not have a lover or a boyfriend."

He turned to A.J. "Your aunt was an extremely wealthy woman. Do you know who inherits her money?"

A.J. hesitated. He waited, his gaze level.

"We stopped at my aunt's lawyer when we arrived in town yesterday. Mr. Meagher told me that I inherit the bulk of my aunt's estate."

"You're claiming that you didn't know?"

Well, if she wanted to belabor the point, Andy had told her first, but she knew that wasn't what Oberlin meant; he meant had she known about her good fortune long enough for it to provide a motive for murder. She said steadily, "I didn't know."

She could hear the clock ticking in the disbelieving silence that followed her words.

"It was certainly a shock to *me*," Elysia put in. "The last time the subject of wills came up, *I* was my sister's beneficiary."

"And when would that have been, ma'am?"

Elysia looked vague. "Difficult to say. . . . Hmm. Nineteen eighty . . . four perhaps?"

Just for a moment A.J. thought Oberlin was going to roll his eyes. Of course, he was much too uptight and serious of a cop to go in for eye rolling. He stared at Elysia for a long moment, then gave a slight nod as though she had confirmed one of his darkest suspicions.

Buddy, you ain't seen nothing yet, A.J. thought. Even she was beginning to wonder at Elysia's efforts to push herself into Oberlin's investigation. If it were anyone else's mother, A.J. might have suspected Elysia of trying to, well, protect her daughter. This being Elysia, A.J. tended to believe she was merely angling for a larger role.

Oberlin rose. "Okay. Thanks for your time. You'll be staying for the funeral. What are your plans after that?"

"I haven't made any yet," A.J. replied.

"Make sure you let me know before you leave town."

He went out. Monster lifted his head with sudden interest. After a moment, the dog rose and trotted after the man.

A.J. was changing for their four o'clock appointment at Mr. Meagher's office when the phone rang.

"I've got it!" she yelled.

"How are you?" Andy asked when she picked up the phone.

"Fine. How's Lula Mae?" A.J. glanced down the hall where Elysia was apparently conducting an impromptu cupboard inspection. She could hear the cabinet doors squeaking open and squeaking closed.

"Fine," Andy replied. "I'm fine, too. Thanks for asking."

A.J.'s blood pressure shot up like Old Faithful at showtime. "Look, I'm glad you're fine, okay? I'm glad you and what's-his-name are having a gay old time with my cat while *I'm trapped here on the edge of the world under police surveillance with my crazy mother*!" She hissed the last part like a stage villain acting out for the back row.

A long silence followed. A.J. drew a shuddering breath.

Andy said at last, "She's my cat, too."

She began to laugh. It really wasn't that funny, but for a few moments she wasn't sure she could stop. When she got control of herself, Andy said, "It's going to be okay, sweetheart. You didn't do anything. Nick says the cops are just—"

"I don't care what Nick says!" The thought of Andy discussing her, discussing her plight with his new partner was unbearable. She forced her voice to a lower octave. "They don't have any other suspects. I'm *it*!"

"It's early days yet. They're still gathering evidence."

A.J.'s eyes flashed to the kitchen doorway. No sign of Elysia, but it sounded awfully quiet in there.

"I watch *48 Hours*. I know how important the first few days are in solving a homicide. They aren't looking at anyone else. They think *I* killed Aunt Di. Which means that, with every passing hour, the real killer is getting further and further beyond their grasp."

Andy made shushing sounds. A.J. was painfully reminded of all the times he'd comforted her in the past. It took a lot to make Andy mad. A.J. had always been the high-strung one, the hot-tempered one, but Andy knew how to calm her down. He could always make her laugh, and failing that, he knew just what little treat or trinket would snap her out of her moods. He understood the medicinal properties of chocolate and ice cream and hugs. She would have given anything for a hug from him now, but now it wouldn't be the same.

It would never be the same again.

Into her dreary thoughts, Andy asked, "Have you hired a lawyer yet?"

"No." She swallowed hard. "Not really. We're going to see Mr. Meagher in a little while. He's—was—Aunt Di's lawyer. He's handling her will."

"That's not what I mean."

"I know what you mean. I'm afraid it will look . . . guilty."

"You need to hire a lawyer."

"They haven't openly accused me, let alone charged me. They're still being very polite."

"Listen to me. They've subpoenaed our business records. They've probably subpoenaed your bank records."

A.J.'s heart was pounding so hard she could hardly hear over it. For a moment she felt light-headed.

"Do you hear me?"

"Yes."

"I'm not saying this to panic you, sweetheart. Nick says—"

She controlled herself with an effort. "Andy, please. Don't quote Nick to me, okay? I don't care if he has fifteen years of law enforcement. I don't care how decorated he is, or how many murders he solved or people he arrested. I don't care what he thinks, and I don't want to hear what he said. As far as I'm concerned, he doesn't exist."

She knew him well enough to know that his silence meant he was both hurt and angry. She knew that, and yet she hadn't known the most fundamental thing about him.

Those seemingly never-faraway tears stung the back of her eyes as she hung on to the phone waiting in painful silence.

"Okay," Andy said finally, quietly. "Just don't put it off too long."

Seven

⌦

"**Was** that Andrew?" Elysia asked, setting a plate of granola cookies on the table. "Is he on his way?"

A.J. sat cautiously on one of the hard-backed kitchen chairs and stifled a flare of bad temper. She told herself she was annoyed that her mother was in the kitchen taking charge, but that would be really unreasonable, since a plate of cookies and a pot of tea hardly equaled a domestic coup.

"On his way where?"

"On his way here, of course." Elysia sat down and selected a cookie, her long lacquered nails grasping like pincers. She smelled of cigarettes and the cold outside, and, illogically, that irritated A.J. all the more.

"Mother, we're divorced. No, he's not on his way."

Elysia's brows drew together. "Why in the world didn't you ask him to come? Can't you see that's why he called?"

"He called to tell me that our business and bank records have been confiscated by the police."

Elysia waved that minor detail away. "I know men. Andrew needs an excuse to—"

"Mother, Andrew is *homosexual*. He left me for another man."

There. She'd said it. It was out. Like Andy.

Astonishingly, Elysia laughed. "Crikey, pumpkin. Just because a man experiments a bit doesn't mean he's homosexual. All sensitive, sophisticated men occasionally experiment."

Experiment? She pictured Andy in a lab coat whipping up Love Potion Number Nine in a cocktail shaker.

"It wasn't an experiment. He's in love with this man. He broke up our marriage over it."

"*He* broke up your marriage?" Elysia questioned gently. "Are you sure you didn't force the issue? I know how demanding you can be, Anna. How difficult it is for you to forgive imperfection."

What happened to all the oxygen in the room? For a moment A.J. couldn't seem to get her breath. But maybe that was just as well because if she could breathe, she'd be screaming. Her hands clenched on her teacup so hard she thought she'd snap the handle.

And yet, when she finally squeezed the words out, she sounded quite pleasant. "I don't want to discuss this with you."

"It would help you to talk," Elysia said earnestly. "It's not good to keep these feelings bottled up inside."

A.J. bit back a laugh. Keeping feelings bottled up reduced the number of homicides, but it would be better not to joke about that.

Elysia sighed and shrugged. "You've always been closed. Even when you were a child. Except with your father of course. And your aunt."

A.J. popped a cookie in her mouth and ground it up in silence. She swallowed and thought all those little flakes and nuts were going to choke her. She had to get some real food right away. Something with refined sugar and a high fat content.

Elysia glanced at the clock on the wall. "I suppose, if you won't talk to me, we should be on our way to Mr. Meagher's." She sounded sad but bravely resigned to her fate.

Once in the car, though, she cheered up. There was nothing like the opportunity to critique other drivers to put Elysia in a good mood. They zipped along the country lane, passing parkland, lakes, horse ranches with glossy-coated thoroughbreds grazing in green fields, and even an emu farm.

Elysia downshifted around a lumbering tractor, and a few minutes later they blazed into the outer town limits.

It was rush hour in Stillbrook. A few pedestrians strolled along the sidewalks with shopping bags, and three cars sat at the stoplight. Elysia parked along the street with her usual frightening efficiency. The air smelled deliciously of hamburgers as she and A.J. left the car and walked across to the lawyer's office.

A.J. rang the bell and was a little surprised when the door was answered by a young girl with long dark hair and green eyes so pale they looked gray. She was strikingly pretty but anorexic thin, and her nails, when she gestured for them to follow her, were bitten to bloody quicks. Her eyes were red-rimmed as though she had been crying. It was hard to picture Mr. Meagher bullying his office staff, but maybe he was tougher than he looked.

"Everybody's downstairs," she told them in a tear-roughened voice.

A.J. and Elysia exchanged glances. A.J. had been assuming this meeting would be a mere formality between herself, her mother, and Mr. Meagher. But, as Detective Oberlin kept pointing out, Aunt Di had been a wealthy woman. It wasn't unreasonable that she might have made several bequests.

Sure enough, when they reached the office downstairs, the room was full of people. Mr. Meagher was dressed in a snazzy dark suit with a red paisley tie; his silver pompadour was neatly brushed. The funny papers from the other day were gone, and there was no sign of the cockatoo or its cage anywhere.

"Ah, ladies. Perfect timing," he greeted them, stepping forward to shake hands. To the strikingly pretty young girl he said, "That's all for today, Chloe. Thank you."

The girl murmured something inarticulate and vanished down the hallway.

Mr. Meagher quickly did the honors. "Might I introduce you to Lily Martin?"

Lily Martin was forty-something, small and lean, with a severe black bob and brown eyes set beneath defiantly thick eyebrows. She wore a black turtleneck, black Capri pants, and a small black beret. She was not pretty but she had presence.

"Lily was Diantha's right hand at the studio," Mr. Meagher informed A.J.

Lily raised one thick eyebrow. "I'm the number one teacher at Sacred Balance Studio," she said.

Since Diantha had been the number one instructor at Sacred Balance, this staking of territory seemed both unnecessary and unfeeling, but A.J. murmured something noncommittal and briefly shook the other woman's hand.

"And this is Michael Batz." Mr. Meagher indicated a very tanned young man with a mop of golden Raphaelesque curls.

"Hi," said Batz. He immediately sat down again, as though he feared someone might snatch his seat. A.J. put him somewhere in his late twenties. He was medium height and muscularly built with small and rather graceful hands.

"I think we've met," Elysia remarked. "You're the athlete, aren't you?"

Batz nodded. That seemed to be all the explanation they were going to get for his presence; Mr. Meagher turned to the remaining person.

"And I think you both know Stella Borin."

Stella, her hair in tight wiry ringlets and wearing a shapeless black and forest green jumper, nodded gravely.

A.J. and Elysia took their seats in the chairs that looked as though they had been misappropriated from a dining table. Mr. Meagher made his way behind his enormous desk.

He cleared his throat. "Last will and testament of Diantha Naomi Mason, deceased. Filed August 29. . . ."

Lily sighed, either from relief or impatience. Elysia directed a chilling look her way, but the younger woman didn't so much as turn her head. She really didn't fit A.J.'s picture of a yoga instructor; she looked as if she should be reciting bad poetry in a smoky Bohemian club.

"I, Diantha Naomi Mason, a resident of Warren County, New Jersey, being of sound and disposing mind and memory and over the age of eighteen years, and not being actuated by any duress, menace, fraud, mistake, or undue influence, do make, publish, and declare this to be my last will, hereby expressly revoking all wills and codicils previously made by me." Mr. Meagher paused to peer over the tops of his spectacles.

Elysia smiled at him; he beamed back and then awkwardly cleared his throat.

"Ahem. 'Executor: I appoint Bradley P. Meagher, attorney at law as executor of this my last will and testament. My executor shall be authorized to carry out all provisions of this will and pay my just debts, obligations, and funeral expenses.' "

Not a word from anyone. In fact everyone seemed to be holding their breath, and yet surely they knew the dispensation of the will? The cops knew. It didn't appear to be a secret.

"Bequests. I will, give, and bequeath unto the persons named below, if he or she survives me, the property described below. To my sister Elysia Esther Alexander,

John Brewster Jr.'s painting of a girl with dove, our shared family photo albums, the silver framed photos of our parents, and the McCoy Mammy biscuit jar."

Elysia delicately touched the corners of her eyes with a lacey handkerchief that had apparently materialized in her hand.

"To my neighbor and good friend Stella Borin, the iron doorstop in the shape of a cat which sits by the front door, and the deed to Little Peavy Farm."

Elysia sniffed. Once again A.J. wondered what the history was between her mother and Stella.

"Oh, bless her heart!" breathed Stella. "The *dear* woman."

"She was that. Ahem. 'To my student and dear friend, Michael Joshua Batz, one hundred thousand dollars to be spent on training, fees, etc., for the 2012 Olympic Games, provided that he continues to meet the criteria as given to my executor in a special codicil.' "

"*Good God,*" Elysia murmured. One thing no one would ever accuse Elysia of was being repressed—but A.J. kept trying. She nudged her parent in the ribs.

"What does that mean? What codicil?" Michael Batz looked more bewildered than pleased.

"We will go over the provisions of the codicil in private," Mr. Meagher said, glancing up over the top of his spectacles.

Michael nodded quickly.

Out of the corner of her eyes A.J. could feel Elysia's eyes on her face. She turned her head and Elysia nodded infinitesimally toward Lily.

Lily was so rigid, she appeared to be trembling. The knuckles of the hands knotted in her lap were white.

What was she expecting?

The deed to a farm, a hundred thousand dollars? Either of these might be sufficient motive for murder.

"To my fellow student of the Four Noble Truths and

traveler on the Eightfold Path, Lily Martin. Five hundred thousand dollars and twenty-five percent shares in all stock resulting from development of Sacred Balance subsidiary product lines including Sacred Balance Organic Foods, Sacred Balance Clothing Line, and Sacred Balance Skin and Body Care. Finally, it is my sincere wish that you continue as lead instructor and joint manager at Sacred Balance Studios for as long as you choose, working to guide and teach my—"

"Wait!" Lily stood up. She was shaking visibly now. "What about the studio itself? What about Sacred Balance Studio?"

Mr. Meagher scowled, his Irish accent pronounced. "If you'd be so kind as to let me continue. . . ."

Batz put a hand on her arm and she sank back into her chair. She swallowed hard a couple of times like someone who suspects they've been poisoned.

Mr. Meagher cleared his throat again. ". . . working to guide and teach my principle heir. *Namaste*."

"*Namaste*? Who the devil is *Namaste*?" Elysia whispered, glancing around the room.

"It's a salutation," A.J. whispered back.

"Oh." Elysia's cheeks grew slightly pink.

"I give, devise, and bequeath all of the rest, residue, and remainder of my estate, of whatever kind and character, and wherever located, to me dearly beloved niece Anna Jolie Alexander."

It was not unexpected, yet A.J.'s breath caught as her aunt's touching words and generous act hit home, renewing her grief.

"That's not *possible*." Lily stood up, shaking off Batz's restraining hand. "She said the studio was mine. Di *always* said Sacred Balance would be mine one day." She turned to Batz. "You heard her. Everyone heard her. Everyone knows the studio is mine now."

Batz said awkwardly, "Yeah, it's pretty much common knowledge." He looked at A.J. and looked away.

"Nevertheless," Mr. Meagher said crisply, "Ms. Mason was most clear in her bequests, and if I may say so, most generous."

Lily was shaking her head, denying this, denying everything. "That will is wrong. That will is a forgery. Di wouldn't make a mistake like that."

"Be careful, young woman." Mr. Meagher's kindly rather foolish face was suddenly grim. "This will was properly drawn, signed, and witnessed. There's no funny business about it."

"I don't care! I don't believe this is what Di wanted or intended, and I can find a dozen witnesses to support that." She whirled on A.J. "Don't get too comfortable, because I intend to have this will broken. And if I can't have the will broken, I will sue your ass for ownership of that studio."

Eight

⤙⤚

The office shook with the force of the door slamming shut in Lily's wake. Mr. Meagher began to splutter into the shocked silence.

"I don't know that yoga is doing her a lot of good," remarked Elysia to no one in particular.

Michael Batz said, "She's pretty upset. They were like sisters, you know."

"Were they?" Elysia said pleasantly. "How painful this must be for her."

Stella Borin let out a crack of laughter. Batz flushed. "I just mean . . ."

Somewhere nearby—possibly in the adjoining room—a voice squawked, "Let's party!"

Mr. Meagher quit spluttering and yelled, "Pipe down, you feathered fiend!"

"Hey, dude!" came the reply.

Apparently deaf to this exchange, Elysia said to Batz, "No one could be more exasperating than Diantha. And no one could be more pigheaded once she made up her mind."

I can think of someone, A.J. thought, but she refrained from comment.

"Will the will hold?" Elysia asked Mr. Meagher. He had started for the door to the next room with the air of one planning to throttle its inhabitant, but he paused.

"That it will. But she could still tie us up donkey's years in probate."

"Feel free!" called the voice from the next room. "Hey, dude!"

"It's baiting you," Elysia soothed as Mr. Meagher's hands twitched spasmodically.

"Eh, yes. Ahem." He smoothed his silver crest with both hands. "That reminds me," he said to A.J. "Your aunt left a letter for you."

He returned to the desk, opened a drawer, and drew out a long buff envelope, which he handed to A.J. She stared down at it. In her aunt's bold hand was the name "A.J."

"Thank you," she managed, and tucked the envelope in her purse. She couldn't read it now.

"Um, how long till we get the, uh, money?" Michael asked.

Even the cockatoo seemed silenced by that one. Meeting the disapproval in the eyes around him, Michael faltered. "It's just, you know, my training expenses and everything."

Stella made a disgusted sound, and he flushed. "Look, Di wouldn't have wanted me to lose my focus. Or my momentum. She understood what it was all about."

"We'll discuss it when we go over the terms of the codicil," Mr. Meagher said.

"When can we get together?"

Mr. Meagher wandered back to his desk and flipped through his day planner. "I have room on Thursday. . . ."

"Anything sooner?" Batz inquired. "I'm kind of on a tight schedule." He offered a smile that probably went over well with impressionable females.

Mr. Meagher was not an impressionable female. He pursed his mouth as though he'd just swallowed vinegar and said finally, "I suppose I might be able to work you in tomorrow afternoon after regular office hours."

"Great! Thanks, man. So I'll see you around five?" Batz headed for the door, but the chill in the room finally seemed to penetrate his thick hide. He hesitated, glancing back at the others. "Well," he said uncomfortably, "nice meeting you all."

Lukewarm responses all around. Batz offered a sickly grin and banged out of the office.

Mr. Meagher muttered something to himself and scribbled into his day planner.

Stella Borin was shrugging into her coat, a purple wool monstrosity with a black faux fur collar. She offered a calloused hand to A.J. "I hope you don't mind about the farm?"

"You're welcome to it," A.J. said—and meant it. She was moved by the generosity of her aunt's bequests, although she felt slightly numb in the wake of Lily's reaction and the realization of how much property had been left to her. "What I can't figure out is why she left me the studio. I can't comanage long distance. Not to mention the fact that I've forgotten practically everything I ever knew about yoga."

She had a sudden memory of her aunt, tall and lithe in black leotards, smiling down on her as she earnestly tried to balance on one chubby leg in tree pose. How old had she been? Five? Six? She remembered the intense blue of her aunt's eyes. When Diantha laughed, she wrinkled her elegant nose like a little kid—an unexpectedly endearing trait.

"She must have had her reasons," Stella said. She had that funny knowing look in her eyes again.

"No doubt she spoke to someone on the astral plane," Elysia interjected smoothly. "But we mustn't keep you, old thing. I'm sure you have pigs to feed or cows to milk."

A.J. shot her mother a look, but Stella didn't seem to take offense. "You're right, Elysia. The work never ends on a farm. Sunrise to sunset."

"It sounds like a musical—with chickens."

Stella's cackle was reminiscent of chickens, too, as she headed for the street entrance of the lawyer's office.

As the door closed behind her, Elysia said, "You certainly can't allow *that woman* to take over the studio."

It was clear she didn't mean Stella.

"Well, the will was obviously a shock to her," A.J. said. She glanced at Mr. Meagher. "If it's true that Diantha originally planned to leave Lily the studio, she must have changed her mind quite recently."

"The will was drawn up and filed in August of this year," Mr. Meagher replied, although it really did not answer A.J.'s question.

"Do I own the property free and clear? I mean, once probate is settled, can I do what I want with the farm and the studio and the subsidiary businesses?"

"It's a privately held company, me dear. Stock shares are divided between the twenty-five percent held by your ma, twenty-five percent held by Ms. Martin, and the remaining fifty percent held by you."

A.J. glanced at her mother. "I didn't know you owned stock in Sacred Balance."

"I'd forgotten," Elysia admitted. "It's not as though we held board meetings."

"Is it . . . a lot of money?" A.J. asked Mr. Meagher. She knew the answer, of course, but she was still apprehensive about attaching an actual number to her inheritance.

"Between the Eriksson real estate, the studio, and its subsidiaries, you're roughly worth in the neighborhood of eighteen million dollars."

A.J. gulped.

"That's a lovely neighborhood," Elysia remarked. "You'll enjoy living there."

Andy had said something of the kind, but A.J. hadn't quite believed him.

"Gosh," she said. Inadequate, definitely, but she seemed to have run out of words.

"You're a very wealthy young woman," Mr. Meagher said, maybe thinking she had missed the point.

"I guess so." She knew she was disappointing Mr. Meagher, but she couldn't help thinking that this was bound to look as though she really did have a motive for murder.

"Of course with great wealth comes great responsibility."

That's what I'm afraid of, A.J. thought.

Mr. Meagher gave another of those polite coughs that seemed to be part of his stage craft.

"One hesitates to bring up sensitive subjects, but . . . do you have a will, my dear?"

It was nearly dark when A.J. and Elysia left the lawyer's office after briefly discussing drawing up a new will for A.J.

"We could stop for dinner," Elysia suggested, buttoning her fur coat against the burger-scented chill of the evening. "The Happy Cow Steak House is just up the street."

A.J. was thinking she could use a drink—not that she would have said such a thing in her mother's presence—but she hadn't eaten anything all day beyond one granola cookie, which was probably the real reason she felt so shaky and disconnected. Dinner was probably a good idea before she jumped back into the car with Speed Racer.

"We should probably eat vegan in honor of Aunt Di." She was mostly thinking aloud, and not really serious, but Elysia stared at her.

"Pumpkin, I know it's a lot of money and you're feeling overwhelmed, but please don't turn into one of those peculiar women out of some sense of misdirected grief."

"What do you mean by 'peculiar women'?"

"Don't start smoking clove cigarettes and forgetting to shave under your arms." Elysia said this promptly, as though she'd been worrying about it all day.

"Don't worry," A.J. said. "If I feel the desire to throw my razor away, I'll call you first."

"I suppose you're making fun of the sponsor system," Elysia said. "But you can't argue with the results."

"What? I'm not doing any such thing," A.J. protested. She wasn't about to laugh at AA or the results they achieved, but Elysia waved this off as though apologies were unnecessary and stalked off down the street.

The Happy Cow Steak House was a white two-story Victorian with flowering window boxes and a giant placard sign of a blue and white cow grinning with misplaced optimism. The parking lot looked promisingly full of cars and trucks.

Inside, the restaurant looked like a very nice bordello: red plushy carpet, red velvet wallpaper, and dark paneling. The shapely waitresses all wore tiny red outfits with white aprons, making them look like French maids who had wound up in hell. Glenn Miller played in the background.

A.J. and Elysia were escorted to one of the deep comfortable leather booths. As they passed through the crowded dining room, A.J. felt someone watching her.

She glanced around and spotted Detective Oberlin at a table with another man. Oberlin watched her unsmilingly as the other man talked.

A.J. looked away, realized it was too late to pretend she hadn't seen him, and looked back offering a polite nod. Well, it was probably more curt than polite, but at least it was a nod.

Oberlin nodded back. Equally thrilled.

Sliding into the booth, A.J. accepted the menu the hostess offered and then glanced back at Oberlin. He was still staring, although he glanced away as their eyes met.

A.J. surveyed his dinner companion. Not a cop, she thought. He was younger than Oberlin, and he looked too soft. Gentle. In fact, he sort of reminded her of Andy. Not in looks: Andy was tall and slim and elegant; this man was cute in a chubby teddy bear way. He gestured animatedly, apparently telling a joke, and he was not wearing a wedding ring.

Ah ha, A.J. thought. I knew it. *Gay.*

"What *are* you staring at?" Elysia inquired.

"Detective Oberlin is here."

"Is he? On his salary?" Elysia raised her pencil-thin brows. "Well, perhaps he's on the job. After all, this is a popular spot."

That was certainly true. Either people came from miles around to eat at the Happy Cow Steak House or they injected some addictive substance in the nightly special. A.J. realized from the glances of other diners that Oberlin wasn't the only one who had made note of their arrival. Over the top of her menu she watched people nodding their way, leaning across to whisper. It reminded her of just one of the things she didn't like about small-town living.

A waitress appeared at their table. "Cocktail, ladies?"

A.J. hesitated.

"Mineral water with a twist of lime," Elysia said.

"Diet Coke," A.J. said.

The waitress nodded and stalked off.

"Why didn't you order a real drink?" Elysia asked.

"I didn't want one."

"After the day you've had?" Elysia's laugh was disbelieving. "Look, pumpkin, I'm not going to tumble off the wagon because you have a drink in front of me."

"It has nothing to do with that. I don't feel like drinking."

"Do you realize, with the exception of your wedding, you've *never* taken a drink in front of me?"

"Well, I guess I just haven't been thirsty," A.J. said. "Could we not talk about this here?"

"Are we ever going to talk about it?"

"Hopefully not. There's nothing to talk about." Detective Oberlin's companion had apparently reached the punch line of his long story, and Oberlin was laughing. Weirdly, A.J. could pick his laugh out over the din of voices, canned music, and forks on plates.

She glanced back at Elysia and was startled at her mother's expression. Elysia looked . . . sad.

Feeling uncomfortable, A.J. returned her gaze to her menu. "So what do you recommend here?"

"Everything's good," Elysia said dismissively. "I like the veal."

A.J. thought of poor little calves crated in total darkness and fed drugs and an inadequate diet. Not that A.J. was going to win any prizes from Animal Rights International. She wore leather and she loved Taco Bell. Those two things alone probably doomed her.

When their waitress appeared with their beverages and a basket of rolls, Elysia ordered the veal, apparently without a twinge of conscience. A.J. settled for grilled steak with blue cheese.

"So what's the story with you and Stella?"

"Story?" Elysia's mouth curved, showing her little white teeth.

"There's obviously bad blood between you."

Elysia laughed a tinkling laugh. "Nothing terribly dramatic. I don't much care for charlatans."

"I'm not following."

"I do hope not. Your aunt, on the other hand, did follow. Or, at least, she appeared to." She reached for a roll and tore it open with unnecessary force. "As the Bard says, 'All sorrows are less with bread.'"

"I don't think the Bard—"

"I'm quite sure he did."

A.J. gave it up and reached for a roll of her own. There was certainly something comforting about carbs, whether the bard knew it or not. They chatted inconsequentially and ate their bread. Elysia finally voiced what was on A.J.'s mind. "What are you going to do about Lily Martin?"

"I don't know. Aunt Di wanted us to work together. I guess that's what I'll try to do."

Elysia was already shaking her head at the folly of this.

"I have to try," A.J. said. "I don't know that legally I even have a choice."

"Legally." Elysia lifted a bony shoulder, shrugging off the tiresome idea of legalities. "There are ways to convince Miss Martin that she would be happier elsewhere."

"Mother," A.J. said warningly. She had a sudden vision of her eccentric parent lacing Lily's soy latte with ipecac.

Elysia's smile was malicious although her eyes were wide with injured innocence. "Pumpkin, you know I would never dream of interfering."

"Maybe I do need a drink," A.J. muttered. To her surprise, Elysia giggled.

It occurred to A.J. that this was one of the only meals she could remember sharing just with her mother. For years Andy had served as a kind of buffer between them. A.J. had spent very little time alone with her mother since she'd reached adult status. That would be A.J.'s adult status, although maybe Elysia's, too, come to think of it.

A.J.'s eyes seemed drawn back to Oberlin's table. He was staring their way again, though nodding in absent agreement to whatever his friend was saying.

The waitress arrived with their dinners.

Elysia was right, the food was excellent. A.J. hadn't realized how hungry she was. It helped that the steak was perfectly prepared, topped with tangy blue cheese crumbles, and rested on a bed of grilled onions. Delicately seasoned vegetables accompanied mashed potatoes—although she didn't remember asking for mashed potatoes—which were a buttery whipped delight.

A.J. let herself sink into a food delirium. When she surfaced the waitress was asking about dessert.

"I don't think so." Once her stomach had time to process what had happened, there was liable to be a terrible price to pay.

"Oh, live a little," Elysia said breezily. "I'll have the crème brule."

What the heck, thought A.J. She didn't inherit a fortune every day. "Lemon meringue pie," she said, and earned an approving smile from her mother.

Was that all it took? She felt oddly pleased with herself.

The waitress brought coffee, and they ate dessert in an unexpectedly comfortable silence. The woman on the piped-in music warbled "Murder, He Says." The entire evening began to seem a little surreal.

Eighteen million dollars?

When at last they finished, Elysia insisted on paying the bill, and A.J. was tired enough—drained enough—to let her do so without comment.

They walked out past Detective Oberlin's table, where the check sat unpaid and his friend continued to chat unchecked. This time A.J. felt justified in pretending she did not see the detective.

Out on the sidewalk the lamplights shone brightly, glittering on the muddy pools in the street. The tang of woodsmoke and fried food hung in the air. Elysia's Land Rover seemed a very long way away. Automobiles passed at a leisurely pace, sending the oily rainwater into night. Elysia started across the street, nimble as a mountain goat in her stilettos, and A.J. followed.

The car seemed to come out of nowhere. One minute the street was clear, and the next, a light-colored tank was barreling down on her.

Nine

⚓

Midway across the road, A.J. froze for one startled and undecided second.

Elysia shrieked a warning.

Already A.J. was throwing herself into reverse. She did a kind of stumbling panicked backpedal, hit the curb, and crashed down, arms flailing for something to grab on to. The Hummer roared past in a wave of exhaust and rainwater.

For a shocked moment A.J. lay on the sidewalk wondering if she'd finally had it. After the initial disastrous contact of soft body on sidewalk, she wasn't feeling much of anything—that might be good, though. Above her the streets lamps were doing an unpleasant whirly thing.

"Oh my God, oh my God, oh my God," Elysia was saying, clopping back across the street.

"Jesus Christ!" exclaimed Detective Oberlin.

It was like a religious revival, A.J. thought. She blinked up, trying to focus, and Detective Oberlin's face swam into her line of vision. He was joined by Elysia, and then the alarmed face of his dinner companion.

"Wow," said Oberlin's friend—apparently an atheist.

Oberlin knelt down next to A.J., which she found oddly embarrassing. She tried to sit up, and he put an unexpectedly gentle hand on her shoulder.

"Just lay still, Ms. Alexander." He got out his cell phone and began dialing.

"Oh, pumpkin," moaned Elysia.

"D'you mind not calling me that?" A.J. requested, momentarily distracted.

"But you *are* my pumpkin," Elysia said. "You're my little pumpkin."

Detective Oberlin was requesting an ambulance. A.J. gathered her wits and made another effort to sit up. She bit back a yelp as Oberlin slipped a supportive arm around her shoulders. It wasn't the pain of her back; *that* felt pretty much like normal, other than the fact that her spine seemed to have been replaced with barbed wire. It was the alarm of being in this guy's arms—arm.

"Listen, you need to keep still," he said. "You could have a concussion or a spinal injury."

"Oh God, oh God," Elysia said.

"Oh wow," said the atheist.

"I'm okay," A.J. said, wincing as she felt the back of her skull. "Really. I don't need an ambulance. I was just stunned for a minute."

"I saw it happen," Oberlin said. "You took a hell of a knock on the head."

"My least vulnerable area," A.J. assured him. She studied her fingers. No blood, thank goodness. "I think my coat absorbed most of the fall."

She loved this coat. It was a Jil Sander cinnamon leather and shearling design; it had been a Christmas gift from Andy three years ago. She hoped her unscheduled splash down hadn't ruined it, although better the coat than her.

Oberlin was still hesitating, and A.J. said again, "No ambulance. I just want to go home and go to bed."

He nodded curtly, canceled the ambulance, and began dialing again. "I guess you didn't get a license number?"

"You're kidding, right?"

"How many yellow Hummers can there be in this county?" Elysia asked.

"Good point. You're sure it was yellow? It looked white under the lights."

"It was yellow. I'd stake my reputation on it."

Her reputation as what? A.J. wondered. TV sleuth or innocent bystander?

"Hey," said the young teddy-bear-looking guy, "aren't you Easy Mason?"

Elysia, tying a silk scarf over her hair, paused and preened. "Well! How nice of you to notice."

"I heard you lived around here, but I never dreamed . . ."

Okay, now A.J. knew for sure that he, at least, was gay. Easy Mason was practically a gay icon, a scary cross between Joan Collins and Margaret Thatcher. Normal red-blooded American men did not have a clue who Easy Mason was.

"Yeah, dispatch," Oberlin was saying, "I've got an attempted hit-and-run—" He rose and moved off a few steps.

A.J. drew in her legs, preparing to stand. Two pairs of helping hands reached out. A.J. grabbed for her mother's hand and for the young guy's hand as she struggled to her feet. It wasn't graceful, but she was standing again, and that was good news.

"I've seen all your movies. I've got the limited release letterbox edition of *Girl in the Gold Jag*, and I've even got a bootlegged copy of the first season of *221B Baker Street*."

"Quiet, please," Oberlin requested. He proceeded to give a description of the Hummer. "Nothing on the plates," he said. "Tinted windows. I couldn't see the driver."

A.J. realized she was shaking and it wasn't just due to the cold and wet. Detective Oberlin finished his phone conversation and turned to her. "You're sure you don't want to take a guess as to who was driving that vehicle?'

"You said yourself the windows were tinted. . . ." The significance of his question sank in. "You mean you think—? But it had to be an accident!"

His eyes glittered like emeralds in the faded light. They met hers gravely. "I happened to be staring out the window when you started across the street. That Hummer accelerated toward you."

A.J. swallowed hard. "But that doesn't make sense."

He shrugged. "That's the way it looked to me."

A.J. looked to her mother for confirmation. "I was watching you, pumpkin. I didn't see the Hummer until it was too late." Elysia shuddered at the memory.

"You have any enemies, Ms. Alexander? Annoy anyone lately?"

She thought instantly of Lily and wondered if Oberlin knew about Lily's reaction to Diantha's will. But Lily hadn't threatened to kill her; she'd threatened to sue her. Talk about ironic: try the idea of killing someone over a yoga studio.

She saw Elysia's lips part, and said hastily, "I'm sure this was just a coincidence." She threw her mother a warning look.

"Coincidence?" Oberlin seemed to go on alert. "So someone did threaten you?"

"No. Of course not. I think Lily Martin was upset that I inherited my aunt's yoga studio. She talked about suing me, but I think it was mostly . . . shock."

"It's worth checking out," Oberlin said grimly.

Into the silence that followed his words, Elysia said briskly, "Well, let's get you home, pumpkin."

"Is there anything else?" A.J. asked Oberlin.

"That's it. For the moment."

"It doesn't make sense. Why would anyone try to run me down?"

A.J. didn't realize she had spoken the words aloud until Elysia said carelessly, "Policemen see crimes and criminals everywhere. Accidents happen every day."

As though illustrating her point, the lights changed at the intersection and Elysia put the pedal to the metal as though the flags had just cut the air at the Indy 500.

Over the screech of tires, A.J. said, "Yeah, but it's quite a coincidence that a couple of hours after inheriting Aunt Di's fortune, someone tries to run me down."

"You can hardly suspect *Andy*."

A.J. stared at her mother. "It never—why would you even suggest such a thing?"

Elysia looked, for once, momentarily flustered. "Why, I . . . Andrew is your heir, isn't he? At least until you rewrite your own will. If one were to be cold-bloodedly logical about the entire matter, I suppose Andrew has an excellent motive—one of the best."

No, that was even crazier than the idea that someone might have deliberately tried to run her down.

"Is that the world according to *221B Baker Street*?"

Elysia said a little haughtily, "Perhaps my years of sleuthing have jaded my view of human nature, but no one knows better than I that Andrew is incapable of hurting another person."

A.J. opened her mouth then closed it. "I suppose I do need to make a new will."

Elysia made a disapproving noise but didn't reply. They were flashing past the little shops and stores, most of them now closed for the night. As they neared the edge of town, A.J. spotted a gas station and mini-mart.

"Can we stop for a minute? I've got to get some things."

Elysia pulled into the small parking lot, and A.J. hobbled into the store, ignoring her body's protest. She only hoped her aunt had some kind of sore-muscle pain reliever; her body didn't yet realize the extent of what it had to protest.

"If you were still hungry, pumpkin, you need only have said so," Elysia murmured, watching A.J. pile squeeze cheese and crackers, frozen yogurt, cherry Pop-Tarts, Ding Dongs, Yoo-hoo, a bag of lettuce and a carton of milk just for form's sake, pizza rolls, microwave popcorn, and Doritos into the plastic basket.

"I'm just picking up some staples."

"Were you planning on spending your entire inheritance in this store?" Elysia asked a few minutes later when the shopping spree showed no sign of stopping.

A.J. ignored her, lugging her basket through the aisle and heaving it onto the counter. The clerk studied the gaily colored packages of processed food and raised an eyebrow.

"You're the niece of that yoga lady, aren't you?"

Surprised, A.J. nodded. "Did you know my aunt?"

"Knew *of* her. Everyone knew of her. Always butting into everyone else's business. Always giving her opinion where nobody asked for it." The woman rang up the junk food with practiced speed.

A.J. flushed. "My aunt spoke up for what she believed in. She tried to help people."

"The best way to help people is to mind your own business."

"Save your breath, pet," Elysia drawled to A.J. "There's no point arguing with savages."

"Savages!" exclaimed the woman. "Savages." She shook her head and thrust the plastic bags at A.J. "You talk to some of the farmers around here. See how much help your aunt was to them."

In silence, A.J. and Elysia got back in the car and sped along the road to Deer Hollow.

Elysia said at last, "This is an unpleasant and uncivilized country."

"One person's opinion." A.J. wasn't sure if she meant the clerk at the convenience store or Elysia. "Do you know what she meant about the farmers?"

"No idea." Elysia jerked her pointed chin at the back seat laden with groceries. "Anyway, I'm not sure what all this laying in of provisions is in aid of. You can't still be planning to stay at Deer Hollow."

"Of course I'm staying there. The farm is my home."

"Pumpkin, did you happen to hit your head when you fell? Because that is a bloody daft idea. Your home is in Manhattan."

"I just mean temporarily," A.J. said. She felt guilty saying it, and she wasn't exactly sure why.

"Why in the world would you want to stay in that drafty old hole when you could stay with me? We could have such fun." Elysia sighed, recalling sentimental memories of mother-daughter events that existed only in her imagination. "We could have a-a sort of slumber party."

Now that really *was* a frightening idea. Mud packs and the exchange of midnight girlish confidences with Elysia?

"I have to sort through all Aunt Di's things. It makes sense to stay at the farm. I can work late at night and start early in the morning."

"You can still stay late and drive over early in the morning from Starlight Farm."

The problem was—had always been—that A.J. could not out-argue Elysia. Her mother just kept coming up with reasons why A.J. needed to do exactly what she wanted. She had an inexhaustible supply of them for every occasion. A.J. strained for patience. "Mother, I *want* to stay there."

She sounded like one of those old TV commercials: *Mother, please! I'd rather do it myself!*

"I see."

"I" and "see." Could there be two more dire words in the English language?

The shining road spooled before them, the moon glinting between the rooftop of trees. White tree trunks flashed past, the occasional red gleam of eyes flashing in the underbrush.

Elysia didn't speak another word on the drive home, and although it was not a long drive, it felt like forever before they pulled into Aunt Di's drive and parked beneath the trees.

"Will you be all right?" Elysia asked. "Not that you would know."

"I'll be fine." A.J. got out and reached for her groceries. They weighed a ton. And so would she if she ate all of it.

"Good night, Mother. Thank you for dinner."

"I'll call you in the morning," Elysia said. "I hope you'll still be alive."

"If I'm not, just leave a message."

A.J. climbed the porch and let herself in. Monster greeted her at the door. She did a quick reconnoiter—to use Elysia's term—of the rooms and waved the all clear. The blue and white Land Rover snarled disapproval, and then Elysia backed up the vehicle and took off down the dirt road.

A.J. sighed, staring after the red taillights. It was hard to imagine anyone less suited to a Land Rover, but perhaps her mother had played Lady Explorer in a film.

A.J. fed Monster and ran herself a very hot bath. She soaked her aching muscles until the water began to cool, and then she toweled off and examined the cupboards, finding something called Tiger Balm.

Liberally coated in oil, and smelling strongly of camphor, A.J. headed for the kitchen. She microwaved a packet of popcorn and went into the parlor to start a fire. She was tired but restless, and the silence was beginning to claw at her nerves. It was a pity Aunt Di hadn't invested in a small television for the front room. A canned laugh track would have helped right about now. She remembered her brave words of wanting to sort through Diantha's belongings, but the truth was, she wanted to postpone that task for as long as she reasonably could.

As she sat there watching the fireplace flames dance, she remembered the letter from Aunt Di that Mr. Meagher had given her.

She retrieved it from her purse and ran the edge of her thumb under the heavy cream flap. Just for an instant she thought she caught a whiff of Aunt Di's fragrance, that light blend of green tea soap and Japanese flowers. It was a scent straight from her childhood.

She unfolded the thick paper and stared at the black symbols on the cream stationery. She had to blink a couple of times before the symbols became words.

Dear A.J.,

The women of our family all share one trait: it's difficult for us to talk about the things that matter the most to us. You were born at six o'clock on a rainy London night, and from that moment, you became one of the things in my life that means the most to me.

Time and distance doesn't change that because the time and distance between us is a matter of minutes and miles, never of the heart.

In every way that matters, you are my daughter, and it is only right that I leave whatever legacy I have to you.

I hope that this door opens when you most need it, A.J. I hope that you will welcome this opportunity without regret or guilt, for those are useless emotions. I know that you will always face the future with courage and grace.

There was a story you loved when you were little. Fairies attend the baptism of a little princess and bestow blessings on her: beauty, wealth, charm, the usual.

The blessings that I would bestow on you are a joyful spirit and a heart at peace. I can't wave a magic wand over your head, but I can open this door.

Be happy, darling girl.

Love, Aunt Di

A.J. blinked hard but the tears would not be stopped. She let them spill, her aunt's words disappearing in the dazzle of firelight and shadow.

Ten

The sun was shining when A.J. woke. She was astonished to see that it was only eight o'clock. She had slept so deeply and dreamlessly she expected to see the clock hands pointing to noon.

The aches and pains of the previous night were noticeably missing. For a few moments she simply lay there blinking in the sunshine, listening to the sweet trill of birds outside the window. While she couldn't exactly say that she had achieved the kind of peace that Aunt Di had wished for her, she did feel calmer than she had in days, weeks, maybe even months.

Even the memory of Lily's anger, her own brush with death, and the knowledge that Detective Oberlin thought A.J. might have something to do with her aunt's murder left her strangely untroubled. In fact, the only thing that really bothered her was the memory of Elysia tearing off into the night in her Land Rover.

The women of our family all share one trait: it's difficult for us to talk about the things that matter the most to us.

It was early enough that she could still drive into Still-brook, pick up a peace offering in the form of the German pastries that Elysia was so fond of, and drive out to Starlight Farm. She considered this plan for a sun-dappled moment and realized that she really did want to make peace with her mother. Last night had almost been . . . well, moments of it had almost been . . . nice. Or at least less maddening than most of their other mother-daughter outings.

Driving into town, trailing a dawdling school bus down the wide country lane, A.J. noticed for the first time what a pretty, quaint place it was. It was so pretty that she hardly even minded moseying along behind the school bus.

She parked and went into the former German bakery, which had been repainted and renamed Tea Tea! Hee! It was still crowded at nine o'clock on a Tuesday morning. A.J. got in line and told herself that she was imagining that everyone else was looking her up and down.

"You're Diantha Mason's niece," the man behind the counter said when at last it was A.J.'s turn.

She nodded, remembering the woman at the convenience store.

"Shame," he said obliquely.

She purchased her pastries and a cup of coffee and started for the door.

"A.J., is that you?" A very pretty blonde about A.J.'s age was smiling at her from the waiting line.

A.J. smiled back uncertainly. "Do I—?"

"Nancy Moore. We went to school together." The woman offered a hand, and A.J. shifted pastries, coffee, and purse to shake it.

"Nancy Moore?" Surely this slim, lovely woman who looked like an aerobic instructor couldn't be her old plump and self-conscious pal?

"Well, it's Nancy Lewis now. Dr. Lewis, in fact." Nancy smiled self-deprecatingly. "I moved back here after medical school. Believe it or not."

"Why wouldn't I believe it?"

Nancy looked puzzled. "Why, because that's all we ever talked about. Getting out of this place. 'Stillborn,' you used to call it. Of course, you did get out a year later when your parents got back together."

For a moment it was as though they were discussing a mutual and nearly forgotten friend. A.J. never thought about that time in her life. Actually, she had pretty much blocked out a good decade of her life, but that year in particular had been consigned to the attic of her brain. In the end, Elysia had finally agreed to seek help for her drinking, and A.J.'s parents had reunited. They had moved back to New York. One big happy dysfunctional family again.

"I was so sorry to hear about your aunt," Nancy was saying. "She was such an amazing woman. She was the kind of woman you read about in books."

"Thank you." A.J. was touched. "I have to admit public opinion seems a little divided."

"Just talk to the parents of some of the kids she helped. I don't think Chloe Williams would be here today if it wasn't for Diantha. Your aunt truly made a difference in this community."

A.J. remembered the startlingly pretty girl who had opened the door to them at the lawyer's office yesterday. She thought of the bitten nails and dark shadows under the lovely eyes. "Chloe Williams? Does she work for Mr. Meagher?"

"That's right. Do you remember Dan Williams? Chloe is his daughter."

A.J. nodded politely, although she couldn't remember Dan Williams. With the exception of Nancy, she couldn't remember almost any of the people she had gone to school with that dreadful year. Maybe she had deliberately blocked it out.

Nancy dropped her voice. "Dan committed suicide last year. Business was bad and he was suffering from depression. Anyway, Chloe went into an emotional tailspin. She changed from a pretty, popular, outgoing kid on the honor roll to—well, she developed a really serious OxyContin addiction. In fact, she only got out of rehab four months ago. Diantha took her under her wing, and the kid has made amazing progress. I think Di literally saved Chloe's life."

Some tight knot in A.J.'s gut slowly eased. "Thanks for telling me," she said.

"Di could be difficult, no doubt about it, but if you talk to the parents of some of our troubled teens, she's eligible for sainthood. Although I'm not sure they have saints in yoga."

They laughed and shuffled forward a few feet with the rest of the line, where it seemed everyone was making a supreme effort to pretend they were not listening in.

"So how are things with you?" Nancy inquired, her hazel eyes curious. "You're married, I know, and you're some kind of hotshot marketing consultant, I hear."

"Divorced," A.J. admitted.

Nancy made a face. "Me, too. Any kids?"

"No."

"That's not necessarily a bad thing." Nancy laughed. "Although I wouldn't trade Charlayne for all the Prada bags in New York." Her gaze lit unconsciously on A.J.'s purse. "I'm sorry you missed her. I just dropped her off at the studio."

"The studio?"

"Sacred Balance. The school coordinates certain PE electives with the studio."

A.J. stared at her. "The studio is open?"

"Well, yes." Nancy looked uneasy in the face of A.J.'s anger. "Shouldn't it be?"

"Aunt Di isn't even buried!"

"Oh. Well, to tell you the truth, Di would probably—"

But A.J. was already out the door and on her way to her car.

The new Sacred Balance Studio was a far cry from the original building, an old warehouse on Seventh Street where Diantha had first set up classes nearly twenty years earlier. Not only was this location on the edge of town scenic and lovely, but the building itself was also amazing. The architecture was clean and modern, with lots of reflective windows that caught the glinting gold of leafy branches shaking in the wind, the lazy glide of fleecy clouds, and the azure skies overhead.

The parking lot was half-full with several cars and two school buses. Women wearing yoga clothes and carrying gym bags walked to and from the entrance.

A.J. parked and marched swiftly up the walk, past the beds of mostly browned flowers and evergreen shrubs. A squirrel, cheeks stuffed with nuts, scampered along the top of the short stone wall. A brass placard proclaimed *Sacred Balance*.

It must be really beautiful in the spring, A.J. thought. Too bad she wouldn't be here then.

She pushed through the glass doors. The lobby was a large airy room with giant black-and-white vintage posters from the 1960s, potted plants so perfect she thought they must be fake, and a soothing color scheme of linen, cream, and bisque.

A short girl with spiky yellow hair and huge blue eyes stood behind the front desk.

"Oh," she said, spying A.J. "Uh, hello. You're Ms. Alexander, right?"

"That's right," A.J. said crisply. "Where's Lily Martin?"

"Uh . . ." The girl looked sideways at a tall, handsome,

silver-haired man with a clipboard—clearly another instructor.

The man picked up his cue. "Simon Crider," he said, offering his hand. "I teach the Beginner and Senior classes. Perhaps your aunt spoke of me?"

"Yes," A.J. lied—force of professional habit. "It's a pleasure to meet you."

They shook hands. His grip was cool and perfunctory.

"I can't tell you how devastated we all are." Crider nodded toward the girl behind the desk. "This is Suze Mac-Dougal. She answers the phones, schedules appointments, and generally keeps us all on track."

More hand shaking. "You're the girl who found my aunt's body," A.J. said.

Suze blanched. "Yes. I'm soooo sorry. Di was soooo amazing. She was like . . . like . . ."

"A force of nature," Simon supplied. And then before A.J. could ask Suze anything else, he said, "You wanted Lily? She's upstairs with Yoga for Young Adults. We might be able to catch her before class starts."

"How long have you been an instructor here?" A.J. asked as they walked. Despite the anger that had fueled her drive over there, A.J. found—almost against her will—the atmosphere of the studio soothing. Initially she had wanted nothing more than to tear into Lily, but now she found herself genuinely interested in Simon's response.

"Seven years. I moved to Stillbrook a few months after my wife died."

He was a handsome man, just a few years younger than Diantha, and they obviously had some key things in common. For the first time A.J. wondered if her aunt could have been involved with someone after Gus died.

She followed Simon past a gift shop. He gestured toward a corridor off the main hall. "The instructor offices are down here."

"How many instructors are there?"

"There're just the three of us now. Lily, myself, and Denise Farber. Denise teaches Pilates mostly, but she's been helping out with the yoga sessions. Di was talking about hiring another instructor or maybe two. We're growing fast." He glanced sideways at A.J., and she understood his doubt: they must all be wondering about the fate of Sacred Balance. That was one reason why A.J. had wanted the studio kept closed until she'd had the opportunity to meet with the staff herself; she didn't want rumors or speculation.

Taking his role as designated tour guide seriously, Simon said, "On the first level we've got the front lobby, gift shop, instructor's offices, and . . . one studio. We mostly use it as a stretching room."

His inflection was odd.

A.J. asked, "Was that the room where—?"

"Yes."

They continued upstairs. A.J. could hear the sounds of voices from down the hallway. Agitated voices.

"On this floor we've got the two main studios. Upstairs is the massage room, the showers, library. . . ."

"Showers upstairs?"

"Uh, yes."

"Upstairs?"

"Di liked the idea of big windows and lots of light—"

"In a shower?"

"Di had a vision—"

"And so does anyone walking in the woods." A.J. followed the sounds of raised voices. "What's down here?"

"Uh, Lily's working with the kids."

Working them up into a frenzy, apparently. Then A.J. told herself to be fair. She hadn't seen Lily at her best. There had to be some reason Diantha had promised her the studio.

And some reason she changed her mind, a tiny voice chimed in.

As they approached the open double doors, A.J. could

hear Lily's slightly harsh voice. "I don't know, Chloe. Maybe the station manager thought it would be in bad taste. Maybe Di's niece asked them to pull the *Organic Living* spots."

"Why would she do that?"

A.J. looked inside the room. The dark-haired girl from Mr. Meagher's office was speaking. Jeez, the kid was thin. She looked like Kate Moss after a hunger strike. The crying jag had apparently turned into full-time employment: her face was blotchy, eyes swollen and red. The other kids stared at her with less sympathy than curiosity.

"Who knows?" Lily responded to that high, wavering voice. "What I do know is we have to keep our focus. That's what Di would want. Let's start with the basic stretches."

"Do the police know who killed Di?" That was one of the few boys in the class.

Lily put her hands on her hips, her impatience clear. "I don't know."

"How do we know he won't come back?" This from a tall redhead in black yoga togs.

"Who?" Lily asked.

"The killer," a pouty-looking blonde girl said, her tone as impatient as Lily's own.

"I don't—" Lily bit back her immediate response. "There is absolutely no danger to anyone. This terrible thing had nothing to do with the studio." She snapped her fingers like a hypnotist trying to break a trance. "Okay, people, let's focus here." She caught sight of A.J. and Simon Crider. Her pointed face grew even tighter. Probably as tight as A.J.'s felt.

A.J. beckoned to her. Lily stared at her and then said to the boy who had spoken up, "Stu, close the doors please."

A.J. opened her mouth and then shut it. She and Simon stepped back as the boy sprinted over and pulled the heavy doors shut in front of them.

"Excuse," he said with an apologetic glance.

"Okaaaay." A.J. said as the doors clanged with finality.

"Well!" Simon said hurriedly. "It looks like they were running a little behind schedule. The class lasts for forty-five minutes. You can speak to Lily then, if it's convenient."

"Oh, I intend to," A.J. said.

Her tone must have registered, because he said uncertainly, "Sure. Of course. In the meantime, if you'd like to wait downstairs in the lobby?"

Apparently Lily hadn't communicated to the staff that A.J. now owned the studio, nor was this the way A.J. wanted to introduce herself.

"Would it be all right if I waited in my aunt's office?"

Simon glanced instinctively at the closed doors of the yoga studio. After some hesitation he shrugged. "I don't see why not. She was your aunt after all."

They went back downstairs, and Simon unlocked Diantha's office then reached in and turned on the light. "It was nice meeting you, Ms. Alexander. Maybe we'll see you again before you leave?"

"Maybe so," A.J. returned, shaking his hand farewell.

Alone again, she examined the office. Unlike Deer Hollow, Diantha's office was organized, modern, and minimalist. There was a beautiful but functional pale wood desk and two coordinated chairs. Matching bookcases lined one wall. This space better reflected the woman, A.J. thought, and yet she supposed it was significant her aunt had never changed the farmhouse. Perhaps she simply couldn't be bothered.

She studied bookshelves lined with videos, DVDs, and books on yoga and spiritual matters. There was a miniature fountain in the corner, with water pouring over shiny stones in soothing endless repetition. Chair, desk, everything was set up with attention to functionality and ergonomics.

A.J. sat down at the desk and studied a picture of herself

with her aunt on her wedding day. She wondered what Diantha had thought of the messy end of A.J.'s marriage; she had been too ashamed to tell her aunt about it, but knowing Elysia, her failure would have been communicated loud and clear. Somehow she had a feeling Aunt Di would not have been totally surprised.

"Boy, I'd watch where you stick your feet. There was a timber rattler coiled up there a few weeks ago."

A.J. jerked her feet back. Suze MacDougal stood in the doorway. She was smiling, so maybe she was kidding.

"Are you serious?"

"Yeah. We're right on the edge of the woods, so we've got to be careful about keeping the perimeter doors closed."

"There was a live rattlesnake under this desk?"

Suze nodded again.

"What happened to it?"

"Di scooped it up in a trash bin, carried it out to the woods, and released it. Can I get you anything?"

A.J. quit rubbing her ankle, which had suddenly developed creepy-crawly syndrome, and pointed to the teapot on the hot plate. "Water?"

"Sure! Be right back." Suze took the pot and was back in a couple of minutes. She handed A.J. the full teapot and sat down in the extra chair, perched on the edge ready to return to her post if duty called.

"Gosh, I was sooo sorry about your aunt. She was the most wonderful person. She was like . . . like . . ." Suze apparently still hadn't worked out exactly what Diantha was like.

A.J. put the pot on the hot plate. "Thank you." She studied the younger woman. She could see Suze was bursting to talk. "It must have been awful. Finding her, I mean."

"I didn't know she was dead at first," Suze said. "She was lying there on her mat—"

"In the stretching room down the hall?"

Suze nodded. "And I didn't really look at her too closely, you know? I didn't want to be rude. But after a while I kind of noticed that she wasn't moving. I got up and I could see from her face that she . . . Her eyes were open and kind of . . . staring."

A.J. closed her own eyes, and Suze said hurriedly, "Gosh, sorry. There was this thing tied around her neck. It looked like a yoga tie."

"A yoga tie?"

"You know, a prop for the workout. Like a block or a mat or . . . a tie."

"Did you recognize the yoga tie?"

"It was green. That's all I noticed." The enormous blue eyes were curious. "The police asked that, too."

"You didn't see anyone that morning? You didn't hear anything?"

"No. The only car in the lot was Diantha's. And it's kind of a walk from town."

"Had Diantha argued with anyone recently?"

"Well, I mean, she *was* Diantha."

"Really argued. Bitterly."

Suze said uncomfortably, "I don't know."

"It could be important," A.J. pressed.

"Things were kind of . . . weird that week. Everyone was sort of testy. Di was snapping at the kids, which really wasn't like her. And she and Lily had a couple of run-ins."

"About what?"

Suze lifted both shoulders. It was an exaggerated shrug like a cartoon character.

"And she and Michael had a big blowup."

"Michael?"

"Michael Batz. He's a student here. Well, he's really a runner, training for the Olympics. He was sort of Di's . . . protégé, I guess. She was helping him with diet and special workouts and stuff."

A.J. considered this silently.

Suze jumped up. "Shit, er, shoot! The kids are *out*!"

She sounded like a zookeeper noticing the cages had been left unlocked. A.J. followed her into the main lobby, which was now full of teens and college-age students pulling shoes from cubbies, joking with each other. Lily was coming down the stairs talking with the still distraught-looking Chloe. Had anyone thought about getting this kid grief counseling, or did they imagine a few limbering exercises would set her straight?

"I want to talk to you," A.J. said, moving through the crowd toward Lily.

"I don't have time for you right now," Lily said icily. "Call for an appointment." She patted the dark haired girl's shoulder. "Go back to school, Chloe. We'll talk later."

All A.J.'s good intentions of keeping it calm and professional evaporated in the face of Lily's insolence. "Who the hell do you think you are, lady? And what do you mean by opening this studio so soon after Diantha's death?"

She had to speak up in order to be heard, so her voice came out sounding much harsher than she had intended. The kids fell silent; there were a couple of nervous snickers. Simon Crider appeared in the hallway outside his office, clipboard still in hand. Maybe he would bop her over the head with it if she went too far.

"I think you'd better go," Lily said, suddenly all quiet poise and dignity.

"If anyone goes, it will be you," A.J. said. "Or have you forgotten who owns Sacred Balance now?"

There was a collective gasp as in a movie scene. Lily's face flushed red and then went bone white.

"I haven't forgotten anything." She was trembling as she had in the lawyer's office. And now A.J. recognized that emotion for what it was: not fear, nor anxiety, and certainly not nervousness. It was rage, pure and simple. "I haven't forgotten that I'm the one who worked side by side with Diantha to make this studio a success. I trained for years, and everything I've got, I earned. What have you earned? You didn't even come to see her."

No one spoke or moved or seemed to breathe.

Lily said fiercely, "Diantha promised the studio to me. Ask anyone here. Go on, ask them." She gestured angrily to the mesmerized crowd. "They all know Diantha intended the studio to be mine one day. Their loyalty is to *me*, because without me there is *no* Sacred Balance Studio."

There was only one answer to that. It wasn't kind, but A.J. said it anyway. "And yet, Diantha left the studio to me. She must have had a damn good reason."

The girl, Chloe, who had stood frozen through this exchange, suddenly gave a sob and pushed through the ring of bystanders. No one but A.J. seemed to notice as she shoved through the glass doors and went running down the walkway to the parking lot.

Lily gave A.J. a withering look. "*You?* What do you know about running a business? What do you know about running a yoga studio? What do you know about yoga for that matter?"

"I guess I'll learn."

"Don't bother. I meant every word I said yesterday. I'm going to sue you for ownership of this studio." Lily turned and stalked toward her office.

"Lily," Simon Crider said.

She ignored him, going into her office and slamming shut the door.

"Is it true?" Simon asked A.J.

"Yes, it is."

The staff looked stricken. This was probably like a second death for them, A.J. realized.

"Cool!" said the pouty blonde student A.J. had seen earlier. "I think it's great news! It's about time something happened to shake things up." A couple of the others nudged her and made shushing sounds.

"Murder isn't enough for you, Jennifer?" the male student Lily had addressed as Stu said.

The blonde gave him a level look and raked her manicured hand through long silky hair. "Di always told us to speak our minds."

"Yeah, and look what happened to her," someone muttered.

There was a funny silence, and then everyone was very busy again. While the kids finished changing shoes and grabbing their gear, A.J. studied her staff. Suze looked wide-eyed, Simon somber.

"I'm sorry," A.J. said after the last of the young adults had filed out with a reluctant over-the-shoulder glance or two. "I had planned to announce the changes at a meeting later this week. I haven't had time myself to think what this means."

"Are you going to keep the studio open?" Simon asked.

"Yes." A.J. didn't hesitate.

He didn't look as comforted as she'd hoped. But then the negative energy emanating from behind Lily's closed door was like radioactive fallout.

A.J. said carefully, "But I feel the studio should remain closed for the next few days. Until I've had a chance to meet with you all. Until after the funeral."

"Lily won't like that," Suze said uneasily.

"That's unfortunate." A.J. knew she had to work to repair the very bad first impression she had made. As much as she personally disliked Lily, the yoga instructor probably had the loyalty—and sympathy—of every staff member. "I know this is hard on her. Hard on all of you. I'll try to make it as painless as possible."

Neither Simon nor Suze said anything.

A.J. said to Suze, "Would you mind putting up a sign saying that the studio is closed for the next four days?"

"Sure!" Suze ducked behind the counter and reappeared with felt pens and paper. She began to scrawl huge letters on the paper.

Into Simon's funereal silence, A.J. said, "I'll be in touch within the next day or so."

He nodded.

Her work done—and the destruction of everyone's day complete—A.J. retreated to the parking lot and her car. She let herself in and sat for a few moments breathing heavily, as though she'd run a mile.

Then she started the engine and began to drive.

She needed to talk to someone. Anyone. She glanced at the bag of forgotten pastries on the seat next to her.

Elysia.

She could talk to Elysia. She pulled to the side of the road, turned, and headed back across the valley.

Oh God, she was running home to her mother.

Eleven

❧

"**You** think Lily Martin killed Diantha?"

A.J. nearly choked on her pastry. "I didn't say that."

"But you think it." Elysia had on her Master Detective expression. "And it makes perfect sense. She certainly had motive."

A.J. was feeling a lot calmer after the scenic drive to her mother's farm. On impulse she had stopped by Deer Hollow to pick up Monster, and the dog had thoroughly enjoyed his trip, head stuck out the window as he sniffed and sneezed into the breeze on the drive through beautiful green rolling hills, past old farmhouses and new horse ranches, over one-lane bridges that spanned the shining Delaware River.

"I'm sure other people had motive as well. According to Suze MacDougal, Diantha fought with Michael Batz the week before she died."

"Oh, that boy couldn't hurt a fly." Elysia tossed Monster a bit of pastry.

"Please don't feed him that garbage, Mother."

"Garbage? Are you referring to the pastries you brought for my consumption?"

"You know what I mean."

Elysia was already on another track. "Mark my words, pumpkin, the female is always the deadlier of the species. What about this Suze? I remember from *221B Baker Street* that the person who discovers the body is always a prime suspect."

"I can't picture that," A.J. said. "She really doesn't seem like the type."

"But that's just the point. It's always the person you least suspect." She sipped her tea. "I'm worried about this child, Clara."

"Chloe."

"Right, Chloe. I wonder if I should talk to her."

"Why?"

"I'd hate to see her start using again."

A.J. opened her mouth but controlled herself. It was difficult for her to believe her mother could provide counseling to a troubled teen; her mother hadn't been sober enough during A.J.'s adolescence to provide much in the way of anything but comic relief—depending on your sense of humor. A pep talk from Elysia was liable to drive the kid back to drugs.

On the other hand, A.J. was surprised and impressed to find that her mother cared enough to want to talk to Chloe. From what Nancy Lewis had said, it sounded as if the young woman had been special to Diantha.

She compromised and changed the subject. "Why do you think Aunt Di changed her mind about leaving the studio to Lily?"

"Who says she did?"

"It seems to be common knowledge that she originally planned to leave the studio to Lily."

Elysia said dryly, "Common knowledge often boils down to rumor and speculation."

"So Aunt Di never talked to you about leaving the studio to Lily?"

Elysia sighed. "We never talked about the studio."

"But you were a shareholder."

"A mere technicality. I loaned Di part of the money she used to start the first studio. It wasn't a big deal. She could have paid me back, but she chose to give me shares instead." Fairness seemed to compel her to add, "The shares are, of course, worth ten times the original amount."

"So you were really never involved in any decisions regarding the studio?"

"Never."

A.J. thought this over, munching on her almond-iced pastry. "Do you know if she and Lily quarreled or if she had any reason not to trust Lily?"

Elysia was oddly silent. She said at last, "The thing is, pumpkin, they needn't have quarreled. Lily needn't have done anything. You know how your auntie was. If she believed that Lily had violated some sacred yoga principle, well, that might have been enough to get her excommunicated."

"Okay, but then why leave the studio to *me*?"

"Who knows. She was getting on, after all."

"What are you saying, Aunt Di was senile?"

Elysia made a face. "Of course not. But she was always a little . . . eccentric. It would be a mistake to place too much importance on one of her whims."

A.J. stared unseeingly out the window at her mother's immaculately tended rose garden. "Did she know about Andy and me?"

"That your relationship was having a few growing pains? I suppose I might have mentioned it."

"We weren't having growing pains, Mother. We divorced."

Elysia savored a bite of pastry without comment.

"If she had totally lost faith in Lily, I don't think she would have asked her to stay on and manage the studio."

Elysia sighed. "It's not as though Di planned to shuffle off this mortal coil anytime soon, pumpkin. The truth is, she might quite as easily have changed her will back again in a few months. That's something we'll never know."

One of many things they might never know, A.J. feared.

It was late afternoon when A.J. pulled into the drive at Deer Hollow. She braked sharply at the sight of the familiar Volvo parked in front of the house. Aunt Di's car.

For a moment she couldn't connect the dots. Then the obvious answer occurred: the police impound must have released the car.

She pulled forward slowly, parked, and got out. Sure enough there was a sticker on the windshield that indicated the car had been released from custody. She tried the door handle. It was locked. Hopefully whoever had dropped off the car hadn't left with the keys.

Monster trotted off to investigate some especially alluring bushes, and A.J. slowly walked up the stairs and let herself into the house. Sure enough Diantha's keys had been dropped through the letter slot. She knelt to pick them up, and studied them thoughtfully.

Heading into the bedroom, she dug through her suitcase. Luckily she had brought a comfortable pair of sweats, a T-shirt, and a pair of sneakers. Not because she had planned on working out, but because these were the things she liked to wear around the house when she didn't have to worry about the way she looked. Maybe she'd go down to the studio and finish checking around on her own. It had been too awkward to really explore that morning with staff and students observing her every move. While she was there perhaps she'd try a few warm-up stretches— just to see if it helped her back at all. And maybe it would be easier to go through Aunt Di's things if she started with her studio office. Baby steps.

Driving to the studio took about fifteen minutes. A.J. parked in the empty parking lot and considered the building uneasily. She wished now she had brought Monster. The place looked very big and very empty—and they were a long way from town.

But, according to the police, the studio had been unlocked when Diantha was killed, so odds were, A.J. was perfectly safe inside the secured building. *Unless Diantha's murderer was one of the staff and had a key. . . .*

She shook off her nervousness and got out of the car. How likely was it that the murderer was still lurking around the studio on the off chance that A.J. might show up on the spur of the moment? After all, what would the motive be for getting rid of A.J.?

A.J. walked up to the glass doors, taking in Suze's homemade sign. It took a couple of tries, but at last one of the keys worked.

As she stepped inside it occurred to her that there might be an alarm system. She waited, but nothing happened.

That was one of the first things she would do: install a state-of-the-art alarm system.

Locking the doors behind her, A.J. walked through the eerily silent lobby. As she passed the gift shop, she paused.

Well, why not? It was her gift shop after all. And there was no better incentive for getting in shape than the excuse it offered for going shopping. She stepped inside and was astonished at the selection of workout gear hanging off racks. There were tidy shelves of mats and bags and exercise balls, pillows, bolsters. . . . Good lord, there was a lot of *stuff* in here. All high-end merchandise. It seemed such a long way from that little studio on Seventh Street.

A.J. browsed and found a cute pair of black yoga pants and a cotton T-shirt with a vintage print of a giraffe. The giraffe symbolized stretching, and that was exactly what

A.J. intended to do—physically, mentally, and emotionally. Maybe even spiritually, depending on how much time she had.

She grinned at herself and selected a nice thick mat to cushion her back and a bolster for her neck. She was going to take this nice and easy, but she definitely needed to concentrate on getting back in shape.

She picked a CD titled *Hearts of Space—Slow Music for Yoga* from her aunt's extensive collection, unplugged Diantha's CD player, and carried it upstairs. She unlocked the first studio, plugged in the player, and sat down on her mat feeling a bit self-conscious.

But after all, how hard could it be to sit there and breathe properly?

Crossing her legs at the shins, she tucked each foot beneath the opposite knee and rested her palms on her knees. She drew in a deep breath through her nose. She could feel the hardwood floor through the cushion of the mat.

What was this starting position called again? *Sukhasana.* That was it. One of the easy poses. In fact, it was called Pose of Happiness.

A.J. didn't know about happiness, but it was simple enough, and good for strengthening the lower back and opening up the hips and groin area.

She focused on her breathing, focused on emptying her mind, on relaxing her muscles.

A floorboard squeaked behind her. She spun around, but there was nothing there. Just the normal sounds of an empty building.

She forced herself to take a couple of deep breaths.

Spine straight, push the seating bones into the floor. . . . She could almost hear her aunt's voice.

Ten slow, deep breaths. On the next inhale, she raised her arms, stretching above her head. It felt good to reach out. She could feel the stretch all the way to her fingertips. She exhaled and lowered her arms slowly.

She repeated the motion. Breathing in and stretching up, breathing out and bringing her arms down ten times.

The next exercise she recalled was one she had always enjoyed as a child: Dog and Cat. A.J. moved cautiously onto her hands and knees, hands in front of shoulders, legs hip-width apart. She inhaled and tipped her tailbone and pelvis up, like Monster wanting his hindquarters rubbed. She lifted her head up, feeling the stretch in her neck and jawline.

Exhaling, she reversed the spinal bend, arching her back like a cat.

Ten times A.J. moved from dog to cat position. These were gentle stretches, but she could feel the pull all along her back muscles and shoulders. Which probably indicated just how totally out of shape she was.

She'd never really studied yoga, although she'd always accompanied Aunt Di to the studio during her summer vacations. In those days, her young body had been flexible and toned; it had been easy and fun to show off in class where she had always been by far the youngest "student." Aunt Di had used her to demonstrate positions and exercises; A.J. had enjoyed the attention, although yoga had been no more meaningful than the jumping jacks in gym class.

Later, during the Hell Year of her parent's separation, the studio had provided sanctuary from her mother. She had attended sessions faithfully. The soothing music and necessity of focusing on each movement had helped to calm her, but in all honesty, she had pretty much missed whatever philosophical message her aunt had hoped she would absorb. In those days all she had wanted was to grow up and get away as soon as she possibly could.

A.J. caught a glimpse of her scowling expression in the wall of mirrors. Those were not good memories.

Concentrating on the stretches was relaxing. She moved swiftly but carefully through the rest of the beginning positions that she could recall: Mountain, Forward Bend, Proud Warrior, Triangle. She remembered more than she had expected, but she was a heck of a lot stiffer than she'd hoped. If she did decide to stay and run the studio, she would have to get into shape herself.

If she did decide to stay . . . ?

Now where had that thought come from? She wasn't seriously considering staying, was she? Moving to *Sopranos*-ville? Of course not. Aunt Di could not have seriously expected *that*.

A.J. finished up with Corpse Pose, lying back, feet slightly apart, arms at her sides, palms facing up. She closed her eyes, gently breathing in and out—slow, deep inhalations. She could imagine Aunt Di's quiet voice telling her to relax each part of her body: her feet, her calves, her thighs, her hips. . . .

Soften the muscles in your face, feel the skin release, soften the top of your head. . . .

That wouldn't be hard, A.J. told herself grimly. Apparently my entire head is going soft.

She sat up. Hopefully she hadn't done any damage to her back. She did feel more relaxed, her muscles pleasantly tired.

She rose, rolled up her mat, unplugged the CD player, and went upstairs to find the showers.

She found the locker room and showers without problem, stripped, and stepped under the spray of hot water for a few refreshing moments . . . until she remembered the shower scene from *Psycho*.

Okaaay. So much for the soothing spa stuff.

Turning the taps off, A.J. grabbed a towel out of the stack of clean ones waiting on shelves. She quickly towel dried her hair and changed back into her sweats and T-shirt, stuffing her new workout gear in her purse.

She was walking along the upper gallery when she heard a sound drift up from the ground floor. A.J. froze.

What was that? It was definitely not the sound of the building settling. There it was again. The slide of a file-cabinet drawer?

She drew back, running softly on the balls of her feet to the window at the end of the gallery. The giant picture window gazed out over the treetops and parking lot below. She spotted a red pickup truck parked next to her rental car.

Whoever was downstairs had to know she was in the building, right? So it couldn't be someone afraid of discovery. Most likely one of the staff was here to pick up something. There was no reason not to; she hadn't forbidden anyone access to the building. Still, there was something . . . furtive in that quiet slide of drawers.

Cautiously A.J. crept down the main stairs. As she neared the ground floor, she glanced at the front doors. The little red flag on the door indicated it was still locked. So whoever was here definitely had to be someone with keys, a staff member.

Reaching the bottom of the stairs, she stood listening. Another drawer slid shut with a bang, instantly followed by a muffled exclamation, as though whoever it was hadn't meant to let the drawer shut so hard.

Lily, A.J. thought. Lily going through file cabinets and maybe taking files she had no right to?

A.J. hesitated. She wasn't sure she wanted to confront Lily on her own. Not that she believed Lily had killed Aunt Di—but someone had. And someone had tried to mow down A.J. only a few hours after Lily had learned A.J. stood in the way of her ownership of Sacred Balance Studio.

Of course, Lily would have to be crazy to attack her after making her enmity so widely known. Then again, she'd have to have been crazy to kill Diantha—and if she had killed Diantha, she wasn't going to put up with A.J. as an obstacle for much longer.

A.J. reached for her cell phone. Either way she looked

at it, this thing with Lily was getting way out of hand. If Lily was back in the studio, going through files after A.J. had expressly said she wanted the studio closed until she could meet with everyone, well then, Lily was behaving inexcusably. And while A.J. knew the price of bad publicity, there was a limit to what she could put up with.

She pressed 0, then stopped.

Of course if the person in the office *wasn't* Lily, and A.J. called the cops on, say, Simon Crider, she was going to look foolish—and make another enemy of someone on her staff.

To make sure, A.J. tiptoed the rest of the way down the stairs, sneaked along the hall, and poked her head around the corner.

A light shone from Diantha's office.

Now that was *not* okay. It was one thing to come in to pick up something forgotten in one's own office, another to search Diantha's. Lily. Definitely.

Anger swept aside common sense, and A.J. stalked down the hall, pausing in the doorway to the office and announcing, "Just so you know, the cops are on their way."

Oops. Wrong again, she realized too late. Not Lily.

The man flipping through the files in the tall cabinet jerked upright and stared at her.

Big shoulders, a blond mop of curls and dark eyes wide with fright.

Michael Batz.

Twelve

⊷

After a stricken moment, Batz lunged toward the door.

Wanting to keep something between them, A.J. instinctively grabbed for Diantha's desk chair, rolling it into Batz's path. He crashed into the chair and sprawled headlong on the floor.

Apparently stunned, he lay there for a moment, shoulders heaving as though the wind had been knocked out of him.

Seconds passed and he made no move to rise; A.J. realized he wasn't struggling for breath, he was crying.

"Uh . . ." she said.

Batz raised a tear-stained face. "I was just looking for my training schedule," he said.

Okay, granted everyone here took physical fitness way seriously, but this seemed a little extreme.

Warily, she asked, "Why would you be looking for it in Diantha's files?"

"It wasn't in her desk."

Had she stepped into some kind of alternate reality?

"And why would it be in Aunt Di's desk?"

"That's where she kept it. My training schedule and my diet plan." He sat up and mopped his wet face. "Sorry, but you don't understand the stress I'm under."

"Well, no, I don't."

"Can you please explain to the police? I can't get arrested. It'll destroy my chances of making the team."

"The team? You mean the Olympic team?"

"Right." His tone implied there was only one team. "Di was helping me get in shape for the 2012 tryouts. It's my last shot. I didn't make the cut for this year, and if I don't make it in 2012, it's over for me."

A.J. tried to picture life being over at twenty-something. Apparently being an aspiring Olympian was as brutal as being a fashion model. "Di gave you a key to the studio?"

"Yeah." His eyes met hers and then slid away. "She was giving me private lessons, working with me one-on-one. It was really paying off."

Something about the way he said it didn't quite ring true. A.J. said noncommittally, "You didn't find the schedule?"

"No. Di called Friday afternoon to tell me she'd completed it for the next four months and to come by and get it whenever I was ready. I meant to stop by that day, but . . ." He shook his head.

A.J. asked slowly, "Did you search Aunt Di's home on Sunday?"

"Of course not!"

He seemed outraged at the idea, but again A.J. wasn't quite sure she believed him.

"Why didn't you call and ask for your training schedule?" she asked. "Wouldn't that have been a lot easier?"

Batz raked his curls back with the air of someone pulling himself together. "I didn't realize it would be a problem. It never was before. I *have* a key." He even sounded a little indignant.

"Speaking of which"—A.J. reached out her palm—"may I have that key? I'm having the locks changed anyway, just as a precaution."

He stared at her for a long moment. Then he pulled his keys out and worked one free of the ring.

"Will you explain this to the police? Please?" he asked as A.J. dropped the key in her bag.

She nodded. "All right."

"Thanks." He got up painfully and limped out. A.J. followed him, unlocking the front door and watching him cross the parking lot.

She bit her lip. He could have been telling the truth—or at least part of the truth—but it was fishy that he had left without finding his precious workout schedule and hadn't even asked her to keep an eye out for it.

Returning to the office, she picked up the fallen chair and sat down at the desk. Opening the top drawer she found the class schedules for the next few weeks. Even before Diantha's death Lily had carried the lion's share of classes. It surprised A.J. Diantha had loved teaching, loved being hands-on.

Denise Farber had the lightest load; her classes appeared to be packed, and it looked as if they could have added another session or two of Pilates. Simon was busy with the Beginner classes and Senior Yoga. Clearly they were overdue for hiring another instructor, and the studio seemed to be a thriving enterprise, so it couldn't have been financial concerns that prevented bringing someone new on board.

It would take A.J. time to get up to speed. And she very much doubted whether Lily was going to want to stay on. Even if Lily chose to stay, A.J. was pretty sure she wouldn't be able to work with her, although it was clear this was what Diantha had wanted, had intended.

If she was going to do this, she needed to take charge. She flipped through her aunt's Rolodex and began to make calls.

Simon and Denise both took the news that A.J. had decided to reopen the studio with guarded optimism. They agreed to meet with her on the day following Diantha's funeral.

There was no answer at Lily's home. Or, if Lily was there, she was not taking A.J.'s calls.

A.J. was opening a can of salmon for dinner when Andy called.

"How are you holding up?"

"I've had better weeks." In fact, she'd had better years, but why dwell on negatives?

"Are the police—?" He paused delicately, and A.J. said, "So far I remain at large."

"Do you think they have any other suspects?"

"It's not like I'm in their confidence."

"Have you talked to a lawyer?"

"Only Mr. Meagher. You'll be interested to know that I just inherited eighteen million dollars. But don't get your hopes up. I'm changing my will."

Andy made sputtering sounds. "Well, I would have thought you already did," he said at last.

Because he had?

"It wasn't exactly foremost on my mind. I'm going to have to go now," A.J. said. "My dinner is on the stove." And it was; she had set the can of salmon on the stovetop when she went to answer the phone.

"Wait a minute," Andy said. "When is the funeral?"

"Mine?"

"What the hell has gotten into you? Of course not yours! Diantha's." It took quite a bit to rattle Andy, but A.J. seemed to be scoring tonight.

"As soon as the authorities release the body for burial," she answered.

"And when are you coming back to town?"

"I haven't quite decided. In fact . . ." She hesitated.

"In fact?" prodded Andy.

"I was thinking of staying here for a while. Would you mind hanging on to Lula Mae?"

"Why in the world would you consider spending an extra hour in that place?"

"Because I have some things to sort through." She wasn't merely talking about Aunt Di's belongings, although she rather hoped Andy took it that way.

Andy, unfortunately, knew her far too well. "For God's sake, A.J. New Jersey? *Rural* New Jersey? Look, sweetheart, I know you're feeling a little . . . lost, but you need to come back to town and have your nervous breakdown in a civilized place."

"You haven't been here in eleven years. You have no idea what this place is like. You'd be surprised. It's kind of nice. Sort of artsy-craftsy. They have wineries and balloon rides and organic farms."

"It's the home of the Jersey Devil," Andy said. "It's mob country. Didn't you ever watch *The Sopranos*?"

"Aunt Di left me the studio. I think she really did mean for me to run it."

"You can't be serious."

"I haven't made my mind up, but I'm considering it."

"Does Ellie know?"

Now that was truly low: threatening to tell her mother.

"There's nothing to tell at this point. I'm just weighing my options."

Andy would have gone on arguing, but apparently his lord and master had arrived home. He promised—it was more like insisted—he would call A.J. back later, and hung up.

A.J. returned to the kitchen and had another whack at the salmon with the old-fashioned can opener. She had managed to detach half the top and bend it in half—just wide enough to scrape out the salmon—when she heard the sound of a car door slamming out front.

She muttered under her breath, banged the can back down, and walked out onto the porch. Her stomach knotted at the familiar sight of the police SUV and Detective Oberlin.

Monster waved his tail enthusiastically as Oberlin approached the stairs.

"Thought you'd want to know we found the vehicle involved in that attempted hit-and-run," he informed her. "It turns out the driver left the keys in the ignition while she ran into the market. A couple of local kids decided to play a prank."

"A *prank*?"

"They decided to take the Hummer for a spin."

"Who was the driver? The official driver, I mean."

"Alice Kennedy."

A.J. shook her head; the name meant nothing.

"She's the housekeeper for the Stevensons. Apparently the daughter, Jennifer Stevenson, and a couple of her pals thought it would be funny to take the Hummer for a spin. Kid stuff."

Walking up the steps, he headed toward the door, apparently bent on another one of his house calls.

"And did they think it would be funny to run over someone?" A.J. found herself leading the way down the front hallway.

"Jennifer's story is—" He broke off. She heard that funny scrabbling sound behind her again. She glanced around in time to see Monster picking himself off the floor and shaking his coat.

She gave the cop a suspicious look. Oberlin met it with an expression of total blankness.

"Jennifer's story is what?"

"Hmm? Oh, Jennifer's story is that the Hummer was harder to control than she'd expected. It's a lot of horsepower, that's for sure."

A.J. sighed. "I guess I'd prefer to think I was just in the

way rather than an actual target." She went to the counter and finished draining the can of salmon. Monster sat down and wagged his tail.

"I think you can rest easy on that score," Oberlin said. His steady gaze made A.J. uncomfortable. Not just his gaze. The confident arrogance with which he stood taking up more than his share of floor space, the scent of his aftershave, the warmth of his body a few feet from her own. It was really annoying.

She glanced sideways at him. "So . . . have you made any progress on finding out who killed my aunt?"

He didn't seem to hear her. "You feed your dog salmon?"

"My dog? This is *my* dinner."

Oberlin raised his eyebrows.

"I'm trying to eat healthier," she explained, although why she was explaining to him, she had no idea.

"With all the mercury in that salmon you could probably find work as a barometer."

A.J. bit her lip against an unwilling laugh. She covered by asking, "What do you know about Michael Batz?"

"Hometown hero. Runner and track star, Olympic hopeful. Why?" He watched her dump the can of salmon in a bowl. So did Monster. The dog shifted on his haunches and licked his chops noisily.

A.J. gave the dog a quelling look, which was totally ineffective. To the detective, she said, "Batz says Diantha was helping him with his training. That she was giving him private lessons, creating a special diet for him and special workout schedules."

"That sounds plausible. Your aunt mentored a number of local athletes."

"He has—had—a key to Sacred Balance." She hesitated. She had told Batz she would not say anything about his unauthorized visit to the studio, but it wasn't like she owed him her silence or loyalty. She wasn't sure she even believed his explanation. Did promises made to potentially dangerous intruders count?

Oberlin grunted. "On that subject, it wouldn't hurt to get the studio rekeyed."

"I plan on it." She glanced at him. As tall as she was, she had to look up to Oberlin. It was sort of disconcerting. She had stood eye-to-eye with Andy. "I found him searching my aunt's files today when I drove over to the studio."

"When was this?"

"This afternoon. I went over to look around and work out."

"By *yourself*? In an empty studio where your aunt was murdered a couple of days ago?" His expression was grim; A.J. could practically see him mentally totting up the numbers: she hadn't been afraid to go to the studio because *she* was the killer.

"I thought it would be safe with the studio locked up. I didn't realize everyone on staff—and a few other people—had keys."

"Those are the kinds of questions it helps to ask up front."

Man, he was annoying. "You're right. I should have. But even so, no one has a motive for hurting me. You just said my nearly getting run over was an accident."

Oberlin continued to stare at her in that narrow-eyed way. It was probably very effective with suspects—whether they were guilty or not.

At last, he said grudgingly, "From what we can tell, your aunt was killed when the studio was open—which appears to be most times she was on the premises. Which doesn't change the fact that going there by yourself wasn't the smartest move you've made."

Maybe for a variety of reasons.

A.J. was getting ready to argue her point, but he went on before she could speak. "So what happened with Batz?"

"He tried to run out the door when I surprised him. He, um, fell over a chair and we talked."

"He fell over a chair and you talked?"

"Right. He said he was looking for his workout schedule and his meal planner." At Oberlin's expression, she said, "I'm just telling you what he said. I'm not sure I believe him, either, but why should he lie? I mean, what else could have been of interest in Aunt Di's files? I looked. They're all customer files: emergency contact information, height, weight, medical problems, what the client's goal is."

"Goal?"

"Like if they want to lose weight. Or get their blood pressure down. A lot of people have a certain goal in mind when they begin a fitness program."

"So then what happened with Batz?"

"Nothing. He said was under a lot of stress and he really needed that workout schedule. I said I'd keep an eye out for it." A.J. fished a fork out of the drawer.

Silence.

"Well," A.J. said, "is that it? You just dropped by for a quick interrogation? You don't actually have anything to report?"

His mouth quirked, as though—against his will—he found something funny.

"You've got a smart little mouth," he observed at last.

"Why, thank you," A.J. said. "It goes with my smart little black dress."

He did laugh then. "I'll bet. Look, why don't we go grab a burger somewhere and I'll bring you up to date on the case?"

A.J. blinked. He wanted to have dinner with her? Okay, it was just a burger, and he was putting it on very casual terms, almost businesslike terms, but still . . .

Surely Elysia couldn't be right about—no. Elysia's hints notwithstanding, A.J. didn't sense any particular interest on Detective Oberlin's part; if anything, he was probably trying to lull her into a false sense of security so he could later trap her into some admission of guilt.

The smartest thing would be to politely decline.

She knelt down to set the plate of salmon in front of Monster. "Okay," she said.

Thirteen

They ate at Bill's Diner on the outskirts of town.

Walking through the front door was like stepping through a time tunnel. At Bill's it was forever the 1950s. A jukebox belted out Patsy Cline while a buxom waitress with the name tag "Flo" led them to their booth beneath a display of vintage lunch boxes. Come to think of it, maybe the lunch boxes weren't vintage; maybe they belonged to the staff. A.J. was willing to believe it.

"Do you think her name is really Flo?" she asked Oberlin after Flo handed out the menus, took their drink requests, and sashayed away.

Oberlin's brows drew together; it seemed to be his habitual expression around A.J. "Her name *is* Flo."

Andy would have caught the joke immediately, but what did it matter whether Detective Oberlin was on her wavelength or not? This was *not* a date. That had been made more than clear on the drive over, which Oberlin had spent talking exclusively on his car radio and cell phone.

"What's good here?" A.J. asked.

His menu was already closed and placed to the side. "Pretty much anything. I think tonight's special is the meatloaf."

She managed not to shudder. Glancing over the menu, she closed it and set it aside.

Flo returned to take their order. Oberlin requested the Brawny Burger, and A.J. had the same, requesting a chocolate milkshake for good measure. Flo bent over the table to pick up the menus, offering Oberlin a close-up and personal view of her plump bosom, but he didn't so much as bat an eyelash.

Aha, Watson, A.J. thought. Just as I suspected.

True, with the possible exception of his lack of interest in impromptu female anatomy lessons, Jake Oberlin was as different from Andy as two men could be. Of course, she didn't have a lot of dating experience, since she and Andy had been inseparable through college and had married shortly after.

Andy would have been chatting about this and that; they'd always had a lot to talk about, even before they were business partners. Jake Oberlin was the laconic kind. He didn't seem to have much to say, although breaking bread had been his idea.

One thing she had learned the hard way, gay guys didn't fit any particular type. Andy hadn't been aggressively masculine, true, but his new boyfriend was about as manly man as they came. Tall, dark, and inarticulate. Okay, maybe that wasn't fair; naturally Nick Grant hadn't had much to say to A.J. Presumably he and Andy had something to talk about over the breakfast table.

Besides, although Oberlin didn't wear a ring, that didn't necessarily mean he wasn't married. Not that she could ask that without giving the totally wrong impression.

She sought for a neutral topic and said, "So you're completely satisfied that Jennifer Stevenson and her friends were just joyriding?"

"Looks that way." His mouth twisted in something distantly related to a smile. "Yeah, I'm satisfied."

"I take it they weren't charged with reckless driving or anything?"

He gave her a level look. "Jennifer Stevenson is the daughter of this town's leading family. I could arrest her and you could press charges, but I don't think much would come of it, do you?"

And it probably wouldn't be very good for his career—or her popularity rating.

"The receptionist over at Sacred Balance was telling me that my aunt worked with a lot of teens."

"That's true. Jennifer's in college, though."

"Is teen crime a problem up here?"

"Not especially. A couple of kids have had some problems. Your aunt was good at getting through to them."

A.J. nodded, smiling reminiscently. "You could talk to Aunt Di about anything, and you knew she wouldn't judge. She'd give you her thoughts, and she'd been around, done a lot, but she didn't judge. And she never revealed a confidence or broke a promise. That means a lot when you're a kid."

"It means something to adults, too."

"Of course, that doesn't mean she didn't have *opinions*."

This time the smile actually touched his eyes. For a moment she saw what he must be like when he wasn't on duty.

She asked curiously, "Did you know my aunt?"

He shook his head. "I knew *of* her, of course. I'll say one thing for the lady: she riled a lot of people, but she had a strong sense of community. She made her decisions based on what she believed was best for this town and the people in it. A lot of business people try and justify their actions by claiming what's good for business is good for a community, but your aunt made her decisions whether the results were good for her financially or not."

A.J. was touched, despite herself. "Did you grow up around here?"

"No. I grew up in Maine. I moved down here a few years ago." His face seemed to close. In an obvious and abrupt change of subject, he said, "Did it occur to you that Batz might have broken into your aunt's house?"

"It went through my mind. He says no."

"You *asked* him?" For the second time that evening she seemed to have caught the detective entirely off guard.

"Well, sure. If he's so desperate to get his hands on that training schedule, it follows that he'd have checked the house."

"That's not my point—" Flo arrived, balancing an over-sized tray with their steaming plates. Oberlin waited for her to finish her juggling and jiggling routine, and as soon as she was out of earshot, said, "He had a key to the studio. Do you think it's possible he had a key to her house?"

A.J. flushed at the implication. "You think they had some kind of relationship?"

"They obviously had some kind of relationship; I'm just exploring the possibilities of what that might have been."

"I think it's obvious that it was instructor to student. She was old enough to be his mother."

His green eyes considered her thoughtfully. "Now that's an ageist remark."

"I'm glad your sensitivity training is paying off, but the fact remains that my aunt was devoted to the memory of Gus Erikkson."

He selected a French fry. "Hey, cops see a lot. We see enough to know that 'normal' is in the eye of the beholder. Your aunt was, what? Sixty-something? But she looked younger, and I'm willing to bet she felt younger. She was in good shape, she was attractive. There's no reason she couldn't have enjoyed a healthy sexual relationship with someone."

No reason at all, and even less reason for A.J. to feel defensive about it. In fact, she couldn't understand her own reaction.

"Something wrong?" Oberlin inquired.

"Hmm? No. Why?"

"You're looking at me like I just gave you a parking ticket."

He was right; she was scowling across at him. It occurred to A.J. that he was just doing his job. It also occurred to her that he really was pretty darned good-looking. Most definitely not her type, but she could objectively admire.

She covered by sliding her chocolate shake over and popping the straw into the creamy contents. She took a sip. Her eyes widened. It was probably one of the best chocolate shakes she'd ever tasted.

Oberlin asked, "What did you think about Lily Martin's reaction to the reading of the will?"

A.J. hastily swallowed a mouthful of chocolatey shake. "I think she was shocked and angry. She believed my aunt was leaving the studio to her, and she's not the only one. As far as I can tell, everyone believed Diantha was leaving the studio to Lily."

"Had your aunt ever discussed her plans for the studio?"

"No."

"What are your plans? Do you intend to keep the studio open and try to find someone else to run it for you?"

"I don't know." She sighed. "I know that's not what Diantha wanted. She wanted me and Lily to work together in harmony, but I just don't see that happening at this point. Not to mention the fact . . ."

His mouth did that quirky thing. He had a nice mouth, actually: the shape of his lips was unexpectedly sensitive. "Which fact was it that you weren't going to mention?"

She made a face. "Just that . . . while I admit I'm ready for a change in my life, this isn't exactly what I had in mind."

His gaze was a little too close for comfort.

A.J. said at random, "My aunt left Lily a half million

dollars, so clearly she could open her own studio if she wanted, but apparently she prefers to spend the money suing me for control of Sacred Balance."

The burger bun paused a fraction from his lips. "Half a million? That's interesting." He bit, chewed, swallowed. "Does she have a case?"

A.J. ignored the question. "You didn't know about the half million that went to Lily? Great. Can I ask whether you have any other suspects besides me?"

"We're looking at a number of possible scenarios." Meeting A.J.'s accusing gaze, he said, "Okay, I admit that my initial interest was in your aunt's main bequests. The investigation doesn't stop there, obviously."

"I'd hope not, since I'm innocent!"

"I'll be checking with Meagher for a complete copy of the will."

"Michael Batz inherited a hundred grand, but it's supposed to be used for training purposes. There was a special codicil to the will that we didn't hear. Mr. Meagher is supposed to go over it with Batz this week."

"I'll look into it," Oberlin said noncommittally.

"I guess he'd have to be fairly obsessed to make the Olympic team."

She was thinking out loud, but his glance was ironic.

"Can I get you folks anything else?" Flo stopped by their table. The question was clearly for Oberlin, but he continued to be oblivious about what was really on the menu.

He paid—apparently taking it for granted that he would—and they walked out to the moonlit parking lot.

"I don't remember this place at all," A.J. said as he unlocked the SUV passenger door. "How long has it been around?"

"Forever, I guess."

It was funny how much she didn't remember from her summers at Stillbrook. She had truly been in her own little world. But that was true of adolescents in general, wasn't it? They practically lived in a parallel universe where life and death issues consisted of stuff like acne breakouts and who got invited to the cool parties.

Oberlin came round and climbed into the SUV, starting the engine.

It had been a long day and A.J. found she had little energy for chitchat as they drove along the mostly deserted road on the way back to Deer Hollow.

The moon, absurdly large and golden, seemed to hang low, like a giant peach over long stretches of black water. Jagged trees, oak, hickory, maple, and beech, ringed the glittering river. Here and there the lights of a lone farmhouse shone through the wall of forest.

"Seems like a long way from anywhere, doesn't it?" she asked vaguely.

"It's a long way from Manhattan, anyway," agreed Oberlin.

"And Maine."

He shot her a quick glance. "Yes."

Another silence fell between them. Not exactly awkward but not comfortable. This time Oberlin broke it. "Back in the sixties there was a plan to dam the Delaware. The Army Corps of Engineers forced thousands of people out of their homes before the project was finally shelved. Something good came of it: the Delaware Water Gap National Recreation Area. It was a major victory for environmentalists around here. But you can still find abandoned and decaying houses in the parklands."

"Creepy."

"Yeah, it is. Occasionally we find squatters living in some falling-down house that ought to be listed in the National Register of Historic Homes."

"But you don't think someone like that murdered my aunt?"

"No." He added quietly, "And neither do you."

The porch light burned a cheery welcome as they pulled into the front drive of Deer Hollow. Along with the porch light, A.J. had left the lamp on in the front parlor; it created the illusion that someone waited for her. She wished it were true.

"You want me to check inside?" From Oberlin's brusque tone it was clear he was not making a pass.

"I'm sure it's okay. I live in New York. I'm not easily scared."

"Did you get the locks changed?"

"Yes, I did."

He nodded.

"Thanks for dinner—and the update."

He nodded again, more curtly this time. "Check through the house and give me a wave when you're done."

A.J. nodded, climbed out of the SUV, and picked her way through the muddy yard by the glare of the headlights. She walked onto the porch and unlocked the door.

The SUV waited, rumbling quietly in the darkness.

Monster rose from his sleeping space in the front hall, shook himself, license jingling, and padded over to greet her.

"Well, hello, good boy, were you waiting up for me?"

She made a quick and cursory check of the rooms, the dog trailing after as she flicked lights on and off, before trotting back to the front door.

Returning to the window, she waved to the SUV. Oberlin blinked the headlights, backed the car, and swung around in a wide arc. His headlights briefly illuminated the sheds, swing, bird house, and Buddha statue.

The SUV taillights vanished into the night.

A.J. knelt down. She had always considered herself a cat person, but she had to admit, as she rubbed Monster's silky ears, that she was getting fond of the old guy.

The dog panted happily into her face. He seemed a little perkier after today's outing. Maybe he was getting fond of her, too. What would happen to him when A.J. returned to Manhattan? She couldn't take him with her. A large dog like Monster would never be happy in a small Manhattan apartment.

She sighed. She'd have no trouble sleeping tonight. Apparently even trauma had its silver lining. Rising, she refastened the lock on the front door and did another quick tour of the house, this time double-checking the locks on the doors and windows.

Satisfied that all was secure, she headed for the bedroom, trailed by Monster, who promptly curled up in his favorite place by the fireplace and watched her with his big brown eyes as she undressed, slipped on her favorite flannel pjs with the martini glasses, and vanished into the bathroom.

Had she really gone to dinner without a scrap of makeup on her face? Wow. It was as if she were experiencing a reverse makeover. Maybe Elysia's fears that she would stop shaving under her arms weren't so far removed. Her eyebrows were certainly looking a bit wild. One good thing about this au naturel bit, she decided as she brushed her teeth, was that it made the before-bed routine a snap.

She grinned at her fresh-scrubbed complexion, patted her face with a towel, and snapped out the bathroom light.

The branches outside the bedroom window scratched against the window. The wind, A.J. thought, getting into bed. She switched on the bedside lamp, and paused.

Wind? What wind?

Monster suddenly leapt to his feet, hackles raised, growling at the window. A.J. jumped out of bed as something brushed against the side of the house.

Fangs barred, Monster began to bark.

Fourteen

Frozen in place, breathing fast, heart slugging away, A.J.'s eyes were pinned on the pull-down shade where her silhouette must appear like a shadow puppet to whoever stood out there watching. She reached over and snapped out the bedside lamp, plunging the room into darkness.

Monster continued to bark in that frenzied way. It was as unexpected as if a bearskin rug had come to life, and A.J. didn't for one minute doubt the dog's instincts.

A.J. fumbled for the phone, lifting the handset. She needed to see to dial the numbers. Feeling on the old-fashioned rotary dial, she counted back from the bottom: *, #, 0, 9. Got it. She ran her fingers forward. 1,1.

"Emergency services!" announced a male voice. He sounded unreasonably happy about it.

"Someone's trying to break into my house." She gulped.

"Can I have your name and location, ma'am?"

A.J. got out her name and location.

"Is the intruder in the house, ma'am? Are you able to get to a secure location?"

"I don't know. . . ." She dropped the phone, ran to the bedroom door, and banged it shut, locking it with unsteady hands. When she retrieved the phone, the 911 dispatcher was calling, "Ma'am? Ma'am?"

"I'm here," A.J. said. "I just locked the door. I can go into the bathroom and lock that door, too." But what if the person came through the window like someone in a horror movie? It wouldn't take more than a minute to break down the flimsy bathroom door. A.J. didn't like the idea of being cornered in that tiny space.

Monster continued to growl and snarl at the window. A.J. couldn't hear what was happening outside over the dog's racket.

"Stay on the line, ma'am. Help is on the way."

Yeah, whatever, A.J. thought. Meantime, I need a weapon. She dropped the phone again, ran to the bathroom, and grabbed her hair spray. On her way out she snatched up the poker from the bedroom fireplace.

She could hear the 911 dispatcher squawking for her on the other end of the line.

"I'll be right back," she yelled. Her instinct told her that it would be far better to keep the intruder out than try to defend herself once he was inside the house. She unlocked the bedroom door and poked her head into the hall.

Monster brushed past her through the open door, going down the hall like a shot. A.J. stole after him.

As she passed the kitchen she could see bushes moving through the windows. Had the wind picked up or was something making its way along the outside of the house? She hesitated, glancing around herself. The rooms were illuminated by moonlight spilling through the windows and making crouching shadows of the furniture. Slats of silver striped the wooden floor. She crept past the window.

Nails scrabbling on the wooden floor, the dog lunged toward the back porch, barking furiously.

And then—the sound of a siren floating in the distance.

A.J. could have cried with relief. So much for the quiet country life; this place made Manhattan look like *Mayberry R.F.D.*

Monster gave a final bark in the tone of "And let that be a lesson to you!" He looked to A.J. as though seeking approval.

"You were wonderful!" A.J. informed him.

Monster wagged his tail.

A.J. hurried to the front window and peeked out. The now-familiar SUV was parked in her front drive. Detective Oberlin stood on her porch, hand on his gun. She had never seen anything so beautiful in her life. There was definitely something to be said for a man with a gun.

She jumped as a heavy hand banged on the front door. Monster started barking again.

"It's okay," A.J. said. "He's a friend."

Which was certainly a new way to think of Detective Oberlin.

A.J. hurried to the front door and opened it. "He was outside my bedroom window."

"Close the door and lock it," Oberlin ordered.

She obeyed. Following his progress, she ran from window to window as he slowly worked his way around the perimeter of the house. Monster trotted after her, apparently thinking this was a new and entertaining game.

Then Oberlin moved out of view to investigate behind the sheds and outbuildings, and A.J. could no longer see him. She waited tautly by the door until the bell rang.

"It's me!" Oberlin's voice was muffled, but it was definitely him.

A.J. opened the door. She was still shaking; she hoped he couldn't tell.

He took in the hair spray and the poker without comment. Maybe he thought they were part of her nightly ritual.

"I never thought I'd say this, but I'm glad to see you," she greeted.

He raised his eyebrows.

She stepped aside, and as Oberlin entered the house, flipped on the hall light switch. How the heck did he still manage to look crisp and ready for action at this time of night? She was only too aware of how she looked: hair sticking on end, feet bare, and her body trembling within oversized flannel jammies decorated with martini glasses and cocktail shakers.

"Tell me what happened," he ordered.

"I was getting into bed when the dog started barking. I heard something brushing against the side of the house." She swallowed. "I know it doesn't sound like much."

"It sounds like plenty to me," Oberlin said.

For some reason, it was a relief to hear him say it. "Were you able to . . . tell anything?"

"There are footprints outside your bedroom window and some broken branches in the bushes. I'd say someone was looking for an easy way in. The good news is he wasn't too determined or he'd have broken a window and crawled inside."

"That is good news," A.J. said.

He grinned at her tone. "You have anywhere you can stay tonight? Maybe your mother's place?"

Let's see. A slumber party at Elysia's or the threat of being murdered in her bed?

"I think I'll be okay here tonight," A.J. said.

"**Rise** and shine!" Elysia crowed.

A.J. cracked one eye open and moaned. Elysia bent over her bed with an expression of unholy glee.

"Now, now," Elysia remonstrated. "The kettle's on the hob. You'll feel better after your morning cuppa."

She'd known it was a mistake to give her mother a key to the farmhouse. "What are you doing here?"

"I thought you'd like some help sorting through Di's things."

A.J. blinked up at the ceiling, thinking this over. She didn't mind the idea as much as she might have expected. In fact, it would be kind of a relief not to face the job ahead all on her own.

"Did you say there was coffee?" she asked feebly.

Two cups of coffee and a bowl of granola later, A.J. was feeling a little more like her old self. Having filled Elysia in on the events of the night before, she had to listen to a lecture on why she should be staying with her mother instead of on her own, followed by Elysia's theories as to why Lily was trying to kill A.J.

"Mother, she doesn't have a motive. Even if she did kill me, the studio wouldn't revert to her. It would go to you—or possibly Andy, if Mr. Meagher hasn't finished the new will yet."

Elysia's long dark hair was swept up into a teased ponytail that looked unreasonably saucy for a woman of her age. The ponytail bobbed earnestly as she said, "But perhaps she believes that I would have her manage the studio—or even sell it to her."

"I don't think she'd be content managing it. I'd have been happy to have her manage Sacred Balance if she could have handled the thought of me owning it." A.J. considered this. "Would you sell the studio to her?"

"I'm not sure. She does seem very qualified. But I should take a very dim view of her murdering you."

"Gee, thanks. But I mean, if I happened to die a natural death."

"This is an extremely morbid conversation," Elysia protested. "In any case, I don't suppose Lily could afford to buy the studio. It's worth a good deal more than half a mil."

"So she really doesn't have a motive."

"Revenge," Elysia said darkly.

"Revenge against whom? Me for inheriting? Or against Aunt Di?"

"Time will tell," Elysia prophesied.

Following breakfast, A.J. and Elysia retreated to Gus Eriksson's study and began the tedious and depressing task of sorting through Diantha's private papers.

In addition to the normal bank statements, bills, property tax and mortgage-related correspondence, there were numerous articles by Diantha on fitness and yoga, and a manuscript for a yoga book that appeared to be at the copy-edit stage. A.J. began to understand why Diantha had cut back her teaching schedule.

"There's nothing here relating to the studio itself," she observed to her mother. "Aunt Di must have kept that all at Sacred Balance."

"A lot of this is from Gus's day," Elysia said absently, shuffling through a stack of yellowed papers. "I don't think she threw anything away that had Gus's name on it."

That seemed too sentimental, too romantic to fit with A.J.'s picture of her aunt. She said, "Maybe she didn't know what to throw away. It's hard to know what you may need later."

"Very true."

A.J. glanced at her mother. No one had been less equipped to deal with the early death of a spouse than Elysia, but somehow she had coped. She had coped and stayed sober doing it. For the first time it occurred to A.J. that that had taken a certain amount of grit and determination.

She flipped through another stack of papers, spotting an envelope that appeared to have been mixed in with scripts for something called *Organic Living*.

Organic Living. Why did that ring a bell? She thought back to her trip the day before to Sacred Balance. Lily had been talking to Chloe about A.J. having pulled some spots. It appeared that Diantha had a weekly segment on a local radio show.

She pulled the single type-written sheet from the envelope.

Type-written? Who used a typewriter these days? She began to read.

"Hey, listen to this."

Elysia looked up absently. "Mmm?"

A.J. read, " 'Why don't you read this on your radio show? I dare you two.' He's spelled 'to' wrong. 'People like you put your principals'—he's spelled 'principle' wrong—"

"Pumpkin . . ." objected Elysia.

" '. . . before people. You don't care who's'—"

"He's spelled 'whose' wrong," Elysia guessed.

"Yep. '. . . life you ruin. My family has been earning our living off the land for generations and you are not even a American citizen. You are so concerned with trees and squirrels—'Speaking of squirrels, who *is* this guy?" A.J. glanced at the signature at the bottom of the note. "John Baumann. Do you know who that is?"

"There's a Baumann Dairy Farm," Elysia said vaguely. "I don't recall Di ever mentioning the fellow."

" 'You do not care who you hurt or the lives you destroy. I will do what I need to, to protect my family.' " A.J. studied the badly typed note. "This is a threat. I wonder if Detective Oberlin knows anything about John Baumann."

"Call him, pumpkin. I'm sure he's longing to hear from you."

A.J. ignored her mother's rather sly smile. She picked up the phone on the large paper-strewn desk and dialed the police station. After a brief wait, she was informed that Oberlin was unavailable.

She left a message that she had something to show him, and hung up.

"Nicely done." Elysia approved, as A.J. sat back in the desk chair. "I think the bit about having something to show him will prove highly effective."

A.J. mentally replayed the message she had left, and blushed.

"Oberlin knows perfectly well I don't mean *that*."

"Men live in hope," Elysia said airily. "Much like dogs."

The next few hours were spent in relatively harmonious productivity. They discovered nothing else that shed any light on Diantha's death—certainly nothing that could be considered a clue—but they made a fair amount of progress sorting and discarding Diantha's papers.

At one thirty Elysia mentioned that she had some shopping to do and would be on her way.

A.J. was surprised to realize she was a tiny bit sorry her mother was leaving. She supposed it was because she was so unused to being on her own that she welcomed any company at all. And Elysia had been surprisingly helpful all morning.

"I'll see you tomorrow then?" she asked.

"If you like," Elysia said casually. "I don't want to get in your hair."

"My hair?"

"Your way, pumpkin. I know you want to work through this on your own." She gestured vaguely to the stacks of files and papers.

"Well . . ."

But, never one to hang about, Elysia was already on her way out the door, the brisk click of her heels fading down the hallway.

Slightly bewildered, A.J. went to the kitchen to find something to eat. Deciding that granola for breakfast took care of all her healthy-eating points for the day, she settled on a glass of milk and two cherry Pop-Tarts, returning with her dish to Diantha's desk. She continued separating papers and files into small piles until at last she found a box of audiotapes.

The tapes were marked "Organic Living" and were labeled with dates. She picked up the one marked with the date of the week before Diantha's death and popped it in the stereo system in the entertainment center on the other side of the room.

"Welcome to *Organic Living*," Diantha said in that low, cultured voice that A.J. remembered so well. Her throat closed and she had to struggle for composure.

Diantha continued to speak, not sounding at all as though she were reading—sounding so close, so *immediate*. A.J. moved over to the blue velvet-covered sofa and put her head back, listening. She was only half aware when Monster climbed up on the sofa—avoiding her eyes—and curled up beside her.

Diantha's familiar voice filled the silent room as she argued that cow's milk was an inefficient food source and that dairy products were a health hazard.

No wonder she hadn't won any points with John Baumann.

"Dairy products contain no fiber or complex carbohydrates and are laden with saturated fat and cholesterol. Furthermore, milk can be contaminated with cow's blood and pus and sometimes has trace amounts of pesticides, hormones, and antibiotics."

A.J., who had just reached for her glass, choked on a mouthful of milk.

Diantha's educated voice ran smoothly on. "Dairy products can be linked to a number of health problems including allergies, constipation, obesity, heart disease, and cancer. Even the late Dr. Benjamin Spock spoke out against feeding cow's milk to children. He believed it could be associated with anemia, allergies, and insulin-dependent diabetes; a diet heavy with dairy products could set our children up for a future of obesity and heart disease, America's number one cause of death."

A.J.'s stomach roiled.

"And in adults dairy products may actually *cause* osteoporosis, not prevent it. Their high protein content actually leaches calcium from the body. Even some of our esteemed universities have done studies on this. For instance, a groundbreaking Harvard study of more than seventy-five thousand nurses suggests that drinking milk can actually cause osteoporosis. Others have found that milk causes phlegm to accumulate in the body, making people stuffed and congested. Milk also contributes to an unhealthy environment. I suggest you visit milksucks.com for further information."

"But I *like* milk," A.J. protested aloud. "How can I eat Cocoa Puffs without milk?"

Diantha closed by inviting the listeners to next week's show, "Death by Dairy," targeting local milk producers and exposing their farms to the public.

But that was the show that had never taken place because by then Diantha was dead. Silenced by someone like John Baumann? Someone who viewed Diantha as a threat to a way of life?

"Not convinced?" Diantha inquired coolly. "Listen in next week. I guarantee you'll never willingly drink milk from cows—contented or otherwise—again."

Diantha's voice faded in silence. Only the hiss of the unrecorded tape remained. A.J. put her toaster pastry down and carried her half-finished glass of milk into the kitchen.

She dumped the milk down the sink drain.

Fifteen

⤙⤚

A.J. was making soup—it was good weather for soup—and feeling virtuous.

She'd spent another informative hour listening to her aunt's radio shows, then in an impulsive burst of health-consciousness, made a quick trip into Stillbrook to purchase "real" groceries.

She had been paying for her portobello mushrooms and canned tomatoes when the sallow-faced woman at the counter said without preliminaries, "Do the police have any suspects?"

"I don't know," A.J. admitted. She didn't want to admit to being a suspect herself. She wondered if local opinion favored any particular villain.

"I didn't like your aunt," the woman continued, staring at A.J. gimlet-eyed. "I thought she had a bad habit of butting into things that weren't her business."

A.J. said shortly, "I appreciate your honesty."

"No, you don't." The woman gave a sharp laugh. "I didn't like your aunt, but she was a good woman. She didn't deserve to die like that. I hope they catch whoever did it and put him away for life."

What could A.J. say to that? She nodded curtly.

"I guess you're going to want me to stock all these weird things your aunt liked. Soy patties and tofu."

"I don't know," A.J. admitted. "I haven't made any plans yet."

The woman looked shocked. A.J. couldn't understand why, and was still puzzling over it as she sprinkled minced garlic and onion into the oil heating in the skillet on the old-fashioned range.

Were people expecting her to stay and run Sacred Balance? Did they *want* her to stay? She added the chopped mushrooms to the garlic and onions, and reconsidered. True, Sacred Balance employed only three instructors, but it was a thriving enterprise—in a rapidly growing township—and apparently an important social center. Once the Organic Living food lines and Organic Living clothing lines were up and running—if they ever were now—they would provide additional employment and revenue for the town and its citizens.

A.J. stirred in the tomatoes, lentils, and vegetable stock. This sudden burst of domesticity felt a little like playing house, but nonetheless she was pleased with herself. She needed a change in her life, and these were little steps toward a new future. She had even gone through a slapdash version of her yoga routine from the day before. Her back was feeling surprisingly better, and she had decided to put off seeing a chiropractor until she returned to Manhattan. She was going to eat better, and she was going to try to be more physically active.

Stirring the soup, which was now releasing a mouth-watering aroma into the air, she felt surprisingly optimistic. The phone rang, she picked up, and it was Oberlin.

"I got a message here you have something you want me to see?"

Elysia's naughty comment flashed into her brain, and for a moment A.J. couldn't think of a sensible reply.

"Oh . . ."

Maybe Detective Oberlin had more imagination than she suspected, because there was a funny pause, and then he said uncomfortably, "That is . . ." He cleared his throat. "You found something in your aunt's papers, is that correct?"

"That's correct," A.J. said with relief. She quickly explained about the letter from John Baumann.

Oberlin had her read the letter over the phone.

"What do you think?" A.J. demanded as soon as she finished.

He said neutrally, "Interesting."

"Interesting? He threatened her."

"Yes."

"He threatened her, and a week later, before the 'Death by Dairy' show could air, she was dead."

"I realize that."

"Are you going to arrest him?"

Oberlin said, "I'm going to talk to him. I don't know at this point that we have enough to arrest him. His threat isn't specific, and he dared your aunt to read the letter on her show. I don't think he would do that if he considered the letter to be a death threat." He added, "Unless he's really dumb."

"Maybe he *is* really dumb."

"Okay," Oberlin said in the voice of one who didn't have the energy for this. "If you don't mind, I'll stop by this evening and pick up the letter. We'll get it analyzed. In the meantime, I'll have a word with John Baumann."

"Thank you."

He hesitated. "I'll . . . see you tonight."

"See you then," A.J. said, and hung up.

She picked up the receiver, listened briefly, and then dialed her mother's number.

"Hello, pumpkin," Elysia greeted her languidly.

"How'd you know it was me?"

"A mother always senses when her child needs her."

"Caller ID," guessed A.J.

"That helps," Elysia agreed.

"I was wondering," A.J. said casually, turning down the heat on her soup, "if you'd want to go with me to visit the Baumann Dairy."

Elysia gave a little squeal of pleasure. "What a *brilliant* idea! But what will our cover be?"

"Our cover?"

"We can't simply barge in there asking if Baumann committed murder most foul. We need a cover story."

"We can say that we found the letter and we . . . I don't know. Wanted to understand what Baumann meant."

"We can't tell the *truth*." Elysia sounded shocked. "That would spoil everything. You give it some thought, pumpkin, while I come and fetch you."

She hung up before A.J. could formulate a reply.

About fifteen minutes later Elysia's blue and white Land Rover tore into the front yard at Deer Hollow and skidded to a stop. Apparently Elysia thought they were already in some kind of police pursuit.

A.J. locked the front door, crossed the barren yard, and climbed into the Land Rover. Elysia caught her eye.

"What?" she asked innocently.

"You know, most mothers would try to dissuade their children from poking around in a murder case."

Elysia laughed a jolly little laugh and put the clutch in. "I learned long ago there was no point trying to dissuade you once you made up your mind, pumpkin. Besides, I think you'll be a great deal of help to me in my investigations."

"*Your* investigations?"

"After all, I am the qualified sleuth of the family."

"You were on a TV show, Mother. You weren't really a policewoman."

Elysia gave a little disapproving sniff and concentrated on her driving—which was probably just as well.

The Baumann Dairy was a small farm tucked away on the other side of the valley. To A.J.'s eye it looked like the farms in every children's book: big red barn, cows and sheep in the green, green pastures; pigs and dogs and children and ducks running freely about the shady front yard.

Elysia parked beside a white fence. "Showtime," she murmured as the gaggle of children, dogs, and ducks headed their way.

Elysia and A.J. got out of the Land Rover. A.J. wrinkled her nose at the strong smell of alfalfa and cattle. Apparently there were side effects to the pastoral life. A tall middle-aged woman with lank blonde hair and a worried, ruddy face came toward them, a baby hanging off each arm.

"Can I help you?"

Elysia extended a hand in the same way the royal family did in one of their "walk abouts."

"I'm Elysia Alexander. This is my daughter A.J. We saw your sign a few miles down the road and thought we would stop in."

"Esther Baumann." The woman shifted the toddler on the right, and shook hands. "You're very welcome. Would you like to come inside?"

A.J. couldn't help a surprised look her mother's way. Elysia gave her one of those I-told-you-so expressions.

They followed Esther into the ramshackle old farmhouse. The smell of homemade bread greeted them, which was an improvement over the great outdoors. The house was comfortably shabby, the furniture battered and the drapes and carpet well worn. Esther deposited the babies in a big old-fashioned playpen, dumped some Cheerios in with them, and led the way through to the huge sunny kitchen.

A radio was playing an old Beatles song.

Inviting them to sit at the scratched and dented table, Esther poured milk into tall glasses and cut wide slabs of cheese and homemade bread at the old-fashioned bread-board. She placed the cheese and bread in front of them, seeming quiet and preoccupied as Elysia chattered easily about the farm, asking a dozen innocuous questions.

"How old must a cow be before it gives milk?"

Esther blinked pale blue, long-lashed eyes. They reminded A.J. of a doll's eyes. "Cows are like people. They have to give birth before they can start producing milk."

"Isn't that interesting?" Elysia asked rhetorically of A.J.

A.J. murmured something noncommittal. She was thinking of Aunt's Diantha's "Death by Dairy" segment as she passed on the milk and cheese, and reached for a slice of warm bread. Apparently reading her without trouble, Elysia threw her a reproving look and drank down half a glass of milk. Fair enough; Elysia had quaffed more dangerous brews than dairy in her day.

"Alexander?" Esther said slowly. Her red-rimmed eyes studied them. She turned to A.J.

"You're that girl, aren't you? *Her* niece."

A.J. swallowed a dry piece of bread crumb. No doubt Elysia wanted her to make up some elaborate spur of the moment story about being pursued by spies or neo-Nazis or agents for the Department of Agriculture, but A.J. felt honesty would serve her best with this tired, harassed woman. "I'm Diantha Mason's niece. Is that who you mean?"

"The police have taken John in for questioning. They think . . ." Esther's voice wobbled. She glanced quickly toward the doorway, and the sounds of children in the next room, and controlled herself. "Johnny wouldn't hurt a fly; you've got to believe me."

"We do, my dear," Elysia assured her. She sounded perfectly sincere, which was the advantage of having trained as an actress, or a sex kitten, or possibly both.

A.J. said, "He sent my aunt a letter—"

"I *told* him not to mail that letter. I *told* him how it would look!" She shook her head. "He never meant it the way it sounded. You have to know Johnny. You have to realize how desperate we are."

"Well," A.J. said reasonably, "what exactly did he mean then?"

Esther said earnestly, "She—your aunt—didn't understand how things are for us. Not just us, for all the farmers. This is a family business. We don't . . . we've been struggling since John took over the farm. Johnny's daddy struggled. Farming is a hard life, and it's getting harder. We work from sun up to sun down. We don't get days off. We don't get holidays or weekends. We don't get big government subsidies. It's everything we can do to keep from getting bought out by some corporation."

"I understand," A.J. said. "But—"

"You *don't* understand," Esther said. "We do things the old-fashioned way here. We don't force our cows to calve every year, and we don't go for any genetic manipulation. We don't stuff them full of high-energy feeds. Our cows are clean and disease free."

"And it is *well* worth it," Elysia said. "This cheese is absolutely *fabulous*."

A.J. wouldn't have blamed Esther Baumann if she'd reached over and clunked Elysia over the head with her rolling pin, but instead the woman gave a weary little smile.

"Thanks. The thing is . . . we've talked about trying some other things. We've had good luck with bee farming, but John promised his daddy he would never give up the Baumann Dairy Farm. It's been in his family for seven generations. It's not easy to quit that."

Esther had a point. Unfortunately, as far as A.J. could see, everything the woman said merely reinforced the idea that John Baumann did have a motive for shutting Diantha up permanently.

When they finished their cheese and bread, Esther took them for a quick tour of the farm. A.J. was touched by the simple life these people seemed to live. Vegetables grew in a small garden in the back, clothes hung drying on the line, the numerous kids scampered about doing chores between their home-school lessons.

This wasn't a simple matter of finding a new job or starting a new career path; this was a way of life, and it was under siege.

Elysia must have been equally affected. She bought several pounds of cheese as well as two quarts of ice cold buttermilk and cream in old-fashioned glass bottles. They were loading this cholesterol catastrophe into the back of the Land Rover when a police car pulled into the yard.

A large man in overalls got out of the car and waved a tired hand to the driver, who promptly turned the car around and disappeared down the dirt road.

"John!" cried Esther Baumann, and she ran across the yard to him.

A.J. felt a lump in her throat as she watched them hug. They clung to each other like lovers reunited in the last reel of a particularly grueling war movie.

"Apparently the plods don't think they have enough to hold him," Elysia remarked. A.J. glanced at her. But anything she might have said had to wait as Esther led her husband over to the car.

Baumann was not just tall; he was big—even bigger than Detective Oberlin. But where Oberlin was all lean muscle, Baumann was meaty bulk. His hair was sandy and thin, his eyes were the velvety brown of those Jersey Maid cows on the TV commercials; and, like Esther, he looked too old to be the parent of that passel of little kids running in the yard.

He offered a big callused paw to A.J. "I guess I owe you an apology. Essie tells me you found that letter I wrote your aunt."

He had a surprisingly gentle grip. A.J. said, "I think I understand a little better why you might have felt . . . Aunt Di wasn't being fair to you and the other dairy farmers."

"I won't speak ill of the dead. Your aunt did a lot of good things for this valley. Nobody could argue with that. But she saw things one way. Her way. She thought she knew best. I just want you to know I never meant her any harm. I wish I hadn't of written that letter. I never thought how it would sound." His eyes moved to Elysia, and he added, "I'm sorry she's gone. That's the truth. She was like . . ."

"An institution," Esther put in.

"I suppose that describes my sister as well as anything," Elysia said. Something in her tone caught A.J.'s attention. She glanced at her mother and realized that she was genuinely moved.

They said their good-byes then and got into the Land Rover. As the red barn and silos of the farm grew tiny in their side mirrors, A.J. realized that for the first time in a very long time she had not once thought of her failed marriage, her career, or Andy.

She glanced at her mother's profile. Elysia was scowling at the road ahead.

A.J. heard herself say, "That was a nice gesture, buying all that cheese and milk. You're not really going to eat all that are you?"

"I thought we'd divvy the spoils at your place."

"Clearly you haven't been tuning into *Organic Living*."

"I loved my sister, but she could really be a bore sometimes." She glanced at A.J. The elegant brows arched. "What's the Cheshire grin for?"

A.J. realized that she was smiling. "I don't know. I . . . had a good time today. Thank you for coming with me."

Elysia made a noncommittal noise, but her ivory cheeks seemed a little pink. Perhaps it was the sunset flushing the fading sky and golden fields behind them.

Still smiling, A.J. felt in her purse for her cell phone and checked for messages. To her surprise, for the first time in days, she actually had one. The number was local and unfamiliar. She played it back.

She listened. Then listened again. She flipped the phone shut.

"Oh my God," she said quietly.

Elysia nearly swerved off the road. "What? What is it? Whatever's wrong, pumpkin?"

"I think Detective Oberlin just asked me to dinner."

Sixteen

◦₰

"Dinner?" Elysia said it in the same tone she might have said, *"Satanic sacrifice?!"*

"I think so." A.J. fished in her purse again, pulled out the phone, and played back the message, placing the phone against her mother's ear. "What's that sound like?"

Elysia's eyes briefly met her own. "It sounds like a dinner invitation. Made at gunpoint."

"He doesn't sound very happy about it, does he?"

"He sounds out of practice." She was silent. "Hmm. Most interesting."

"Interesting" was hardly the word for it.

"Do you think he's trying to trap me?"

"Well, he is male." Elysia gnawed her lip; somehow no matter how much talking and pouting and nibbling and sipping she did, her lipstick never seemed to fade. A.J. wondered what the secret was. "And he does know you're married."

"I'm *not* married."

Elysia made an impatient sound as though divorce were

a mere technicality. "Are you thinking of going out with him?"

"I don't know."

The invitation would have been flattering—in an alarming way—if she didn't suspect Oberlin's ulterior motives.

"It's an excellent opportunity to pump him for information," Elysia remarked. "You just have to keep your head. He's an attractive brute. Not your style, but still . . ."

A.J. considered her romantic "style." Talk about what not to wear. She tuned back in as Elysia said, "Perhaps you can discover whether we can safely scratch Mr. Baumann off our list of suspects."

"If the police let him go, he must have an alibi."

"Alibis can be broken," Elysia said knowledgably. She launched into a story about a guest appearance she had once made on *The Professionals*, which led her into a naughty reminiscence about the show's leads. A.J. went back to weighing whether she should accept Detective Oberlin's dinner invitation.

"I think I'm going to go out with him," she said abruptly.

"Pumpkin, Martin Shaw is married. You do seem to have a wee bit of a—"

"I'm not talking about Martin Shaw. Who the heck is Martin Shaw and how did he get into this conversation? I'm talking about Detective Oberlin. I'm going to accept his dinner invitation."

"I don't know about that, pumpkin."

"I thought you believed he was susceptible to my feminine wiles." A.J. found her cell phone and checked the phone number Detective Oberlin had left. She began to dial.

"Possibly. But you mustn't be susceptible to *his*."

"His feminine wiles?"

"Be-*have*!" Elysia said, sounding too much like Austin Powers for comfort.

"Anyway, I'm immune to men. I just want to pick his brain."

"That's the way it starts," Elysia said breezily. "One moment you're thinking king and country, but then, before you know it, you're doing the horizontal—"

"I don't want to hear it!" A.J. shook her head as though to knock away that famous earwig from the Laurence Harvey episode of the *Night Gallery* from crawling into her brain.

In the end she was unable to reach Detective Oberlin and had to leave a message on his cell phone. As seven o'clock rolled round, A.J. tried to tell herself that her acceptance had been as casual as she had now convinced herself the invitation had been—and if Oberlin hadn't received her message in time . . . no problem.

Maybe even relief.

In fact, the more she thought about it—and unfortunately she was thinking about it a lot—Oberlin had probably intended the invitation in the same spirit as the dinner invite the evening before. He probably worked so much overtime he didn't take meal breaks, and this was likely his way of killing two birds with one stone. And that being the case, it was really silly to worry about what the heck she was going to wear tonight.

All the same A.J. spent a good twenty minutes pawing through her suitcase's frugal contents before settling on an all-purpose DKNY gray jacquard skirt and a cute pink tank.

It really was ridiculous when she had given up on men, and besides if Oberlin let Baumann go, he must be trying to trap her into a confession of her aunt's murder. So what was she doing stressing out over this non-date? She should cancel. Instead she was perspiring her makeup off as fast as she was applying it. And her hair! She looked like a frightened porcupine, which, frankly, wasn't too far from how she felt.

This was where a bit of that yoga serenity would have come in useful. A.J. splashed cold water on her face, took a couple of deep breaths, and restarted applying her makeup.

Finally, powdered, mascaraed, and lipsticked, she dumped Monster's dog food in his bowl and went into the parlor to wait for Detective Oberlin.

Two minutes after seven, she was checking her cell phone to see if he'd left a message canceling when she heard a car roll into the front yard.

She went to the window.

Oberlin was getting out of a sports car instead of the usual police SUV.

She gulped. He wore Dr. Martens boots, a snug pair of jeans that were clearly not Levi's, and what looked like a suede jacket. Attempts had been made to control his unruly dark hair. From the momentary scowl on his face he appeared to have just received word that the governor had turned down his appeal. Then the scowl disappeared and he approached the front steps with the expressionless face of a cop who had no idea what might lie on the other side of the door.

A.J. ducked away from the window, heart pounding.

Dear God. It really was a date.

Monster shot past the parlor door, woofing a guarded greeting. A.J. grabbed her coat and ran to head him off.

"Hey, there!" she said too brightly, hanging on to Monster's collar with one hand and the door with the other. "I wasn't sure if you got my message."

"Yeah, I got it." He studied her from her punk haircut to the pointy tip of her kitten heels. He wasn't exactly smiling, but he looked less severe than he had when he got out of the car. Maybe this was the closest he got to actual friendliness. Maybe this explained why he wasn't married.

Nah, he probably *was* gay, and this was all part of a plan

to lull her into that false sense of security. For some reason that thought really calmed A.J. down. She clung to it.

Not a *real* date. Just . . . part of his job. Or maybe he felt sorry for her sitting here without a TV and eating cans of salmon all by herself in the dark.

"Good night, Monster. Don't wait up," A.J. said, closing the door on the dog.

Oberlin laughed. It was a quiet laugh, but it relaxed her a little.

"What do you feel like?" he asked as A.J. buckled up and he started the engine.

"Huh?"

"What do you feel like eating tonight? Italian? Steaks? Chinese?"

Duh! What did she think he meant? "Italian sounds good." Andy disliked Italian food, so during their marriage she'd rarely had the opportunity to indulge her unnatural love for pasta—and post-Andy she just hadn't been hungry.

"There's a new Italian place in town. We could try it out."

"Okay."

Silence.

"My name is Jake, by the way."

"Oh? Okay."

Silence.

Oh God. It was going to be *that* kind of an evening. A.J. wracked her brains for something intelligent to say. All that came to her was to ask why he was taking her out for dinner. Wasn't that a conflict of interest or something, since she was his main suspect?

Jake nodded toward the radio/CD console. "Do you want to find something to listen to?"

"Sure!" She fiddled with the radio, pausing when she heard the distinctive tones of Rufus Wainwright's "Cigarettes and Chocolate Milk."

Did Jake perk up at the sound of Rufus? Andy adored

Rufus. And that should have been a clue right there, shouldn't it? A grown man "adoring" anything but his lovely wife and potential children was really not a good sign.

She glanced Jake's way. "I love his voice. That sort of drowsy, silky way he sings."

His eyes briefly left the road. "Who?"

She nodded toward the radio. "Rufus Wainwright."

"Never heard of him."

"He's the one who sang 'What Are You Doing New Year's Eve?' on that old Gap commercial."

"I don't watch a lot of TV."

Of course not. He was probably too busy using the lathe in his woodshop to build a gun cabinet. She wondered if he was armed right this minute. She wondered if he'd shoot her if she became too annoying over dinner.

The restaurant was small and dark. In the gloom she could just make out wall stencils of balconies and fountains and bougainvillea. There were profusions of plastic flowers hanging from baskets, candles in wax-covered bottles, and red and white checked tableclothes. Dean Martin crooned romantic nonsense on the piped in music.

They were seated right away, handed menus, and left to their own devices. Jake glanced at his, apparently made an instant decision, and set the menu aside. A.J. quickly selected something at random and followed suit.

"So. Catch any bad guys today?"

He eyed her thoughtfully. "No. The bad guys caught all the breaks today."

She wondered how the interview with John Baumann had gone and if there was any possible way of asking him about it.

There was another of those silences, this one mercifully broken by the waitress who took their drink order.

"Wine?" Jake asked.

A.J. assented. Andy would have asked all kinds of

pertinent questions about the wine; Andy was a wine connoisseur. Jake just asked for a recommendation, checked to see that A.J. was okay with it, and that was that.

A.J. told herself that she really, *really* needed to stop comparing every other man to Andy—and, uncannily, Jake chose that moment to ask how long she had been divorced.

"Didn't you find that out when you got hold of my bank and business records?"

He met her gaze levelly. "Sure. I'm making conversation."

She blinked, then laughed. "We've been officially divorced four months."

"Not a long time."

She lifted a shoulder. "I guess not." He was making her uncomfortable. That unwavering stare—was it part of his cop training?

The waitress arrived with their wine. Jake tasted and approved in that brisk, businesslike way he seemed to do everything. The waitress filled their glasses, took their meal orders, and departed once more.

"What about you?" A.J. inquired—and found she really was curious. "You've never been married?

"Nope."

"Do you live with your mom or something?"

He laughed. He had a nice laugh. "No. Although I'm guessing my mom is easier to live with than yours."

"Elysia's okay." She realized he had changed the subject. "So how is it you never married?"

"It's not easy being married to a cop. Even a small-town cop." Once again he changed the subject. "What happened with your marriage?"

"Oh, the usual," A.J. said. "My husband decided he was gay and ran off with an FBI agent."

Jake swallowed his wine wrong and had to lower his glass quickly. A.J. watched him cough and splutter with faintly malicious amusement.

"You're . . . kidding," he said hoarsely, at last. His green eyes were watery. Boy, he had long eyelashes.

A.J. was astonished to hear herself chuckle. Even a week ago she wouldn't have believed she could ever see the irony, much less the humor, in her situation.

"Straight up, as my mother would say. He—Andy, my ex—was buying a cake for my birthday, and as he was leaving the bakery he was hit by a car. It turned out that the car was an FBI vehicle in pursuit of some counterfeiters. Anyway, the agent who was driving apparently felt bad about mowing Andy down, and he showed up at the hospital to see how he was."

"And what? Your ex sustained some kind of brain damage in the accident?"

A.J. laughed again, although it didn't come quite as easily this time. "I thought so at first. Apparently not. Apparently we'd been living a lie for ten years."

The grave sympathy in those keen eyes was too much to take. She was relieved when the waitress arrived with their dinners.

The food turned out to be delicious, and a couple of glasses of wine eased A.J. over the conversational lulls. She found that talking to Jake was much easier than she'd expected. She couldn't imagine ever being actually comfortable with him, but she felt certain she was going to enjoy this one date.

Over dessert and coffee she relaxed enough to ask, "So isn't this dinner some kind of ethical breach? I'm your main suspect, aren't I?"

Jake's expression was odd. "No. You're no longer a suspect. If you were, we wouldn't be having dinner."

"When did that change?"

He seemed to hesitate. "We confirmed your alibi for Friday night."

"What alibi? I didn't have an alibi. I was home in bed."

"You were home, that's true. You weren't sleeping,

though, because your neighbor heard you fixing dinner around ten thirty and then later watching TV until about six in the morning."

A.J. blinked. "I didn't realize the TV was that loud."

"Yeah, well." She couldn't understand the apologetic look he cast her. "According to your neighbor you have a lot of sleepless nights."

Six months worth. Ever since her husband had told her he wanted a divorce. She was silent. "Actually, I was sleeping. I have a habit of falling asleep on the couch watching TV." It was a fairly recent, postdivorce habit, and she was not thrilled that the neighbors and now the cops were aware of it. It seemed so . . . pathetic.

"We've confirmed your mother's alibi as well," he added.

"You cannot seriously have thought . . ."

"Hey," he said calmly, "unfortunately I see the worst side of people in my line of work. I've learned not to take anything for granted."

"That's a pretty cynical way to live."

He didn't respond.

"So . . . do you have a suspect now?"

He flicked her a look and didn't answer that either. Instead, he said, "I really didn't want to bring this up at dinner, but we're releasing your aunt's body for burial."

A.J. couldn't immediately think of a response, her emotions instantly in turmoil.

Jake said slowly, "The . . . autopsy revealed something strange."

A.J. gathered her wits, looked inquiringly at him.

"Your aunt wasn't strangled. Someone—a not very knowledgeable someone—apparently tried to stage it to look like she died of asphyxiation, but the fact is, she died of anaphylactic shock."

"I-I'm not following."

"The yoga tie around her neck, the swelling of her

throat, the apparent asphyxiation initially threw us off. Your aunt was injected with bee venom."

A.J. felt the blood draining from her face. "Aunt Di was deathly allergic to bee stings."

Jake nodded. "We now believe the yoga tie was placed around her neck after she was already dead."

"Oh my God. But . . . why?"

"Either someone hoped to hide the real cause of death or someone hoped to implicate the owner of the yoga tie. Unless the owner of the yoga tie is the killer."

"That would have to be a very stupid killer."

"Yeah. Someone didn't do his homework, that's for sure."

"Who owns the yoga tie? Do you know?"

Jake shook his head. "How many people knew about your aunt's allergies to bees?"

"It wasn't a secret. Aunt Di didn't make a production of it, but she always had the EpiPen with her. She was outdoors a lot, so she did occasionally have to use it."

A.J. felt numb. Good-bye to the theory of a roving maniac killer. Someone really and truly had plotted to kill Aunt Di—and then cold-bloodedly carried out that plan. As little as she wanted to believe it, she could think of only one person who fit this particular murderous profile.

"If this is true, then I can't for the life of me understand why you've let John Baumann go," she said, her voice trembling despite her effort to keep it steady. "He had the motive, and he certainly had the means. They're farming bees right there in the pasture!"

Jake stiffened. "What the hell do you know about the Baumann's bee farming?" There was not a vestige of friendliness in his face now.

"We drove out there today."

"Who?"

"My mother and I. We thought . . ." Speaking of thinking,

she realized it would probably be smarter not to complete that sentence.

"You thought what?"

"We—I—we—"

"Just spit it out," Jake advised. "You thought what?"

"Well, I found that letter from him to Aunt Di, and you didn't seem to take it that seriously, so I thought . . ." She faltered into silence at his expression.

"God almighty," Jake said. "Did you watch an episode of *Scooby-Doo* and decide anyone could be a detective? What the hell do you think you're doing tromping around in my homicide case?"

She tried not to get mad at the Scooby-Doo crack. She had suspected he might view her well-meant interest as trespassing. "I just wanted to—"

"Let's get something straight. Interfering in a police investigation is a crime. If I catch you poking your nose into this again, I'll haul your cute little ass right down to the jail. Got it? I do not need or want the help of an amateur sleuth."

Jake Oberlin was chewing her out in public as though she were a dumb and disobedient subordinate. A.J. was so angry and embarrassed she was shaking—and trying hard not to show it. It didn't help that she knew in her heart that he was right. She had no business sticking her nose in his investigation. It wasn't even like her, really.

"Have I made myself clear?" he demanded into her furious silence.

"Crystal."

"Good." He nodded curtly to their unfinished desserts. "Finished?"

"Oh, we're finished," A.J. returned.

Seventeen

✦

"**Even** the gorgeous royal chariots wear out; and indeed this body too wears out. But the teaching of goodness does not age; and so Goodness makes that known to the good ones."

The owlish priest in his saffron robes paused in his reading of the Buddhist text. The silence was filled in by a woodpecker high in the tree overhead, and one of the young women at Diantha's graveside—Jennifer Stevenson, A.J. guessed—giggled nervously.

Of course this was not really Diantha's grave. Diantha's ashes were in the simple urn that was to be handed over to A.J. at the end of the funeral ceremony. Instead, the headstone on Gus Eriksson's grave was being exchanged for a lovely hand-carved stone that had both their names and the inscription: *They that love beyond the world cannot be separated by it.*

White flowers and white candles were arranged around the gravesite, and the contrast between these and the autumn colors of the trees and woodland was striking.

A framed picture of Diantha and Gus rested on a small table with a basin and a pitcher of water.

The priest inclined his head to a grim-faced Lily, who nodded to the circle of students from the Yoga for Young Adults class. A.J.'s eyes rested momentarily on Chloe William's pale, hollow-eyed face.

It appeared as though every person in Stillbrook was attending the late afternoon funeral in the old cemetery. Mr. Meagher stood next to Elysia; Michael Batz was there with a slim red-haired woman; the Baumanns and their flock of children were present as were all the instructors from the studio. Most of these people were strangers to A.J. Her mother and her old school chum Nancy Lewis had filled her in on names and faces as necessary.

Feeling someone's gaze, she glanced around and caught sight of Jake Oberlin. He looked heart-stoppingly handsome in a dark blazer—and tie. The tie had a strange effect on her; she got the impression Oberlin rarely went in for neckwear.

Their eyes held. He nodded curtly. They hadn't spoken since the unpleasant ending of their first and only date two nights previously. She didn't want to think about the long silent drive back to Deer Hollow after they'd left the restaurant. Not that it had been a lot more silent than the drive out, but the mood had definitely been different. When they finally reached the farm, Oberlin had requested John Baumann's letter, waiting on the porch while A.J. went to get it. He had taken it with brusque thanks, and that had been that.

Which suited A.J. fine, she told herself, offering an equally tight nod in return.

At Lily's nod, the students—all young women dressed in virginal white—fumbled to open the triangle-shaped white cardstock boxes they held.

Lily began to give her eulogy. "Diantha Mason was my good friend and colleague, but more than that, she was my teacher. . . ."

As Lily read, painted lady and monarch butterflies began to emerge from the boxes and flutter away, swooping and flitting through the yellow and scarlet leaves of the surrounding trees.

Chloe Williams began to cry. Jennifer Stevens had to shake her box to get the butterfly out of it.

It occurred to A.J. that that young lady owed her for the dry-cleaning bill of her coat. Frankly, Jennifer seemed a little old for pulling pranks—although A.J. had an uncomfortable memory of one or two college escapades—including a game of quarters that was now legendary with her former roommates.

She stiffened as someone took her hand. Turning, she caught her breath. Andy, looking unusually somber in his favorite Hugo Boss suit, leaned over and kissed her cheek.

"Sorry I'm late," he said softly.

A.J. opened her mouth but couldn't think of anything to say. She looked past him to see if Nick Grant was in tow, but he was nowhere to be seen. That was one bright spot. She wasn't sure she was prepared to deal with Andy, let alone his boyfriend.

Lily suddenly broke down in the middle of her eulogy.

It seemed to A.J. from the sympathetic murmurs of the crowd that most of the people here seemed to genuinely grieve with her, although Diantha's stance on certain political and social issues had not made her universally beloved.

Lily stepped away from the graveside, shooing the young students before her with her usual diplomacy, and Stella Borin took her place.

"Oh crikey," muttered Elysia on A.J.'s other side.

Stella, garbed in what appeared to be a white bedspread, raised her hands and said, "The Goddess wishes all here to remember Diantha Naomi Mason, born of man and woman. The wheel has turned, and our sister has gone on to Summerland and now awaits rebirth. I ask you to join hands for a moment and let us meditate together on our own past lives and our approaching death."

Andy squeezed her hand very lightly; A.J. knew instantly what he was thinking. Andy found all of this silly and a little tasteless, but she tuned out that thought. Diantha's funeral was not so much about what her aunt had believed as it was a chance for the people who loved her to say good-bye in their own way, and A.J. thought that was rather a lovely thing—although Stella was sort of pushing it with that particular meditation request.

A.J. prayed Elysia would manage to make it through the entire ceremony without some outrageous comment.

Her attention was momentarily diverted by the sight of an extraordinarily beautiful woman in a wheelchair parked in front of the row of seats. According to A.J.'s old friend Nancy Lewis, this was Pamela Stevenson, Jennifer's mother. When A.J. had asked what ailed the immaculately groomed and frozenly lovely woman, Nancy explained that Pamela suffered from horrible arthritis that crippled her at a very young age.

It was interesting and sad, A.J. thought, studying Pamela now. The Stevensons were probably one of the wealthiest and certainly most socially prominent families in the county, but neither of these things had been able to shield Pamela from disabling pain and illness. A.J. glanced at Jennifer's stony face and felt a stab of sympathy. She knew firsthand the difficulty of having a disabled parent. True her mother's disability had been self-induced, but it had been a terrible strain on her family, nonetheless.

Pamela's eyes were trained on Jennifer. Jennifer's own gaze rested for a moment on the still-sobbing Chloe. Then she leaned over and whispered something to Nancy Lewis's daughter, Charlayne. Charlayne bit back a laugh and then looked guiltily in her mother's direction. Nancy Lewis smiled wryly at Pamela Stevenson, whose face grew even tighter.

Nancy had commented earlier that Diantha had always hoped Jennifer would prove stronger than circumstances; that sentiment confirmed A.J.'s own feelings. What would have happened to her had she not had Aunt Di to depend on during those bleak years her mother was drinking and her father working himself into an early grave?

She blinked back tears and then realized that Stella had finished communing with the Goddess on Diantha's part, and it was time for A.J. to speak.

She let go of Andy's hand, crossing round to the table with Diantha's picture. She opened the book of poems she had selected from Diantha's collection, and turned to the page she had marked. Quietly, she read, "Do not stand at my grave and weep. I am not there, I do not sleep."

She glanced up, catching and skirting Andy's sympathetic gaze, finding Jake Oberlin's serious green eyes in the crowd. She swallowed hard, looking away. Even now, inappropriately, that man had an unfortunate and distracting effect on her.

"When you wake in the morning hush, I am the swift, uplifting rush . . ."

At least it was a relief to know he was no longer trying to prove she was a murderess.

She looked back at the text. ". . . of quiet birds in circling flight. I am the soft starlight at night. . . ."

"**Why** don't you drive back to the house with Andrew," Elysia suggested after the service, as they stood accepting final condolences.

"Because I don't—"

"She has all kinds of things to get ready before people start arriving," Elysia told Andy, who stood patiently to the side. "Would you be a love—?"

"Of course," Andy said. "Come on, A.J."

A.J. opened her mouth to decline his services and her

mother's suggestions in no uncertain terms, but she caught sight of Jake Oberlin moving toward them through the crowd.

"Fine. Whatever," she said ungraciously, and allowed Andy to take her arm, steering her through the grass and leaves away from the gravesite. Her heels kept sinking into the soft ground, like crampons. She felt a little like she had been scaling cliffs. She felt tired and remote, tightly clasping her aunt's ashes in the titanium urn. It was such a sad occasion, and yet every moment seemed to teeter on hysterical farce—as though she had somehow wandered into a Woody Allen movie.

"Are you okay?" Andy asked once they were in the car and he was skillfully negotiating his way out of the cramped parking space.

"Numb."

"I never told you how sorry I was . . ."

"It's okay," A.J. said. "I know you didn't like her. The feeling was mutual."

He was silent.

"How's . . ." She struggled with herself briefly. "Nick?"

Andy brightened. "Good. Out of town as usual."

Was he excusing Nick's absence? Did he honestly think she'd have wanted Nick there today? She asked automatically, "Does he travel a lot?"

"Yeah. It's . . . I'm getting used to it, I guess. In fact, he was up this way just a couple of weeks ago."

Andy didn't like living alone; he wouldn't be happy with Nick being gone a lot, she recognized with a little flare of satisfaction—and was immediately disgusted with herself.

"How's business?"

The business they had formerly shared. They had split their clients along with their CDs, books, and artwork. That had been A.J.'s decision. Andy couldn't understand why they shouldn't continue as business partners.

"Good." He hesitated. "A.J., you have to come home pretty soon. Your clients are calling me. They don't understand what's going on. Neither do I, to tell you the truth."

There was a worried frown between his wide blue eyes.

"Well, that makes it unanimous," A.J. said wearily. She pointed at the curve in the road ahead. "Turn left up here."

When they reached the house the catering van was already out front. A.J.'d had neither the energy nor inclination to prepare food for the crowd that was liable to show up at Deer Hollow following the funeral. She had hired a local company to provide food. It had been a wise move, as several cars were already parked in the front yard and people she did not know were walking toward her front porch carrying potted plants.

"It's going to be a long day," Andy remarked, turning off the engine. He glanced at her. "What do you need me to do?"

She was suddenly and unexpectedly grateful for his presence. "Watch my back," she said, and he grinned at what had once been a familiar joke between them.

A few minutes later she watched Andy slipping automatically into the role of host: offering people food and drink and being generally charming, which was something he was very good at. The only person who did not seem impressed by Andy was Monster, who took one look at him and growled, actually showing his teeth.

"Monster!" exclaimed A.J., startled.

Monster gave her a guilty look and nervously wagged his tail, then turned a disapproving eye back on Andy.

"Di must have told him about me," Andy tried to joke. Having been badly bitten as a child, he was fearful of dogs, especially large dogs.

A.J. had no choice; she dragged Monster—who sat determinedly on his haunches—into the bedroom and shut the door on him.

The next hours passed in a blur of people stopping by

with flowers or food or off-beat gifts and offering their condolences on her aunt's passing. It seemed as if everyone in the county had shown up. It was possible, though hard to believe, that one of these people had killed Diantha.

A.J. snagged a crab puff off a passing tray. She was starting to feel light-headed. She hadn't slept the night before and had been unable to eat anything that morning. From a low-blood-sugary distance she watched Elysia deftly handling the caterers and the reporter and photographer from the local paper.

She wondered if Lily would stop by. She was prepared to be cordial if Lily made the effort.

"That him?" Stella Borin asked, appearing—gnome-like—out of nowhere.

"That who?" A.J. asked uncertainly.

Stella's expression was surprisingly intense. She held the long trail of her white bedspread—er, dress—in a way that reminded A.J. of how people wearing giant animal costumes hitched their tails out of the way. She nodded toward Andy. "Is that the ex?"

"Yes."

Stella nodded grimly.

"What's the story between you and my mother?" A.J. asked suddenly.

To her surprise Stella giggled hoarsely. "I'll leave that to Elysia to explain."

"Is it a secret?"

"Noo. She's the one with the problem, though."

Stella moved off and A.J. listened to person after person sharing some little recollection of Diantha: some made her laugh and some brought tears to her eyes, but it was good to hear these things. At some point Andy pressed a gin and tonic into her hand, so she was slightly . . . fortified . . . by the time Jake Oberlin showed up.

She noticed him the moment he appeared in the

crowded room—which was irritating. More irritating was the fact that he immediately caught her staring at him. He edged his way through the press of people, and A.J. tossed off the last of her gin and tonic.

She straightened, spine erect, shoulders back, as he reached her.

"I just wanted to pay my respects," Jake said, as if there could be any doubt as to why he stopped by.

"Thank you."

He hesitated. "You did a nice job of reading that poem."

"It was one of Aunt Di's favorites."

She met his gaze and he asked brusquely, "How are you?"

She opened her mouth to shoot back an equally curt "Fine. And you?" That would be the beginning of the end of this conversation. But it occurred to her that she did not really want the conversation to end. "Tired," she admitted. "Sad."

Something changed in his face. He opened his mouth, then glanced at Andy, who stood a few feet away making a pair of Sacred Balance yummy mummies giggle.

As though feeling their regard, Andy looked up. This should be interesting, A.J. thought, as he met her eyes. He detached himself from the disappointed women and made his way over to A.J.'s side.

A.J. introduced the two men. Andy offered his most engaging grin and shook hands with Jake.

Maybe she'd have to revisit the notion of Jake's sexuality—either that or Andy was not his type. Jake was at his most crisp, his handshake perfunctory.

Turning back to A.J., he said, "Anyway . . . I'll be in touch."

"I never doubted it," replied the gin and tonic.

He gave her an odd look, nodded even more briefly to Andy, and withdrew.

"Do you think he got the wrong idea?" Andy said

doubtfully as they watched the wide pair of shoulders moving through the crush of people in Diantha's parlor.

"About what?" A.J. asked.

But Elysia swept up and drew Andy away before he could answer.

After a time, the crowd thinned until at last it was down to a handful of people sitting around reminiscing about Diantha.

"Did Lily ever show up?" A.J. asked.

The others looked uncomfortable. Suze MacDougal, who rose to take the tray of sandwiches Elysia carried, said, "She said she didn't feel welcome."

"She's certainly welcome to pay her respects. I'm not the one who—" A.J. stopped herself from finishing.

"Who's Lily?" Andy asked.

"A thorn by any other name," said Stella Borin, who had also been on the receiving end of Andy's gin and tonics.

This reminded A.J. of things she would sooner forget. She shot her mother a narrow look, but Elysia was sipping tea and looking unreasonably sangfroid. "Something amiss, pumpkin?" she inquired.

A.J. tried to fill Andy in on who and what Lily was, trying to be objective and neutral—aware of Suze and Simon Crider's lingering presence. Unfortunately Elysia and Stella kept interrupting with their own unflattering views of Lily and her recent behavior.

Before her explanation went very far, Simon rose abruptly and said his good-byes. He told A.J. he would be at the Sacred Balance staff meeting the next day.

With the exception of Lily, all the Sacred Balance employees had put in an appearance at Deer Hollow. Of course that was out of respect for Diantha, not any show of loyalty to A.J. She understood that and resolved, as she walked Simon to the door, to be on her best behavior the following day.

When she returned to the parlor she heard Stella saying,

"I think Slapsy would be more cooperative in familiar sur-roundings."

"Wouldn't that be a wooden box six feet under?" sug-gested Elysia, and Stella glared at her. Mr. Meagher, reach-ing for a turkey croissant, made tut-tutting noises.

"Did I miss something?" A.J. asked. Andy wore a very peculiar expression. He seemed at a loss for words, which was not like him. "Who's Slapsy?"

"Slapsy Malone," Suze told her. "Mrs. Borin's spirit guide. Mrs. Borin suggested we hold a séance. She said that maybe Diantha could tell us who . . . who her killer was." A.J. understood what people meant when they said someone's eyes looked like saucers; Suze's blue eyes were enormous.

"Uh . . ." A.J. said.

"My thought exactly," Andy murmured.

Stella's eyes gleamed with eagerness—or maybe it was plain old fanaticism. "I know what you're thinking—"

Elysia cut in, "I doubt it, old thing. You wouldn't still be sitting here."

Stella ignored her. "I've been witness to some amazing events. And Di was most receptive to all things pertaining to the spirit. She always kept an open mind and an open heart. I feel certain she'll try and contact us if we open the door."

"Oh wow," breathed Suze.

"Jesus, Mary, and Joseph," muttered Mr. Meagher.

Elysia drawled, "Don't get your hopes up, ducks. We'll be lucky to find my sister at home."

"What do you say, A.J.?" Stella asked. "It's up to you."

"Why is it up to me?" protested A.J.

"Possibly something to do with your share of stocks," Elysia said vaguely. "Look, pumpkin, if you want to try and ring your aunt on the celestial plane, the rest of us will be happy to tag along. Say the word."

"We should at least *try*," Suze said enthusiastically.

Why? wondered A.J. She stared at the ring of watching faces. Frankly, she wasn't sure what she believed anymore. If her husband was gay, why couldn't her dead aunt speak to her from beyond the grave? If nothing else, it might be interesting to watch the people closest to Diantha interacting together. It was a pity she couldn't think of a way to get Lily to pop in.

"All right," she said. "Let's have a séance."

Eighteen

❧

A.J. had not especially noticed Chloe Williams at the house, but when they all arrived at Stella's farm a few minutes after eight, the girl was there, looking like a teenaged ghost in knock-off designer jeans and an oversized yellow sweater that emphasized the sallow pallor of her skin.

"Is anyone looking after that child?" Elysia murmured disapprovingly, watching Chloe shyly tuck herself in the corner of the giant plaid couch.

A.J. shrugged. Her own attention was captured by the extraordinary hodgepodge of Stella's home. She had never seen so many different patterns or colors in one room: black and yellow checks, blue and pink stripes, green and red flowered chintzes. The only theme seemed to be cats—live ones and pretend ones. Cat-shaped throw pillows littered the sofas and chairs, and there were framed cross-stitches of cats hanging on the walls along with decorative cat motif plates. Cat-shaped candles sat on the fireplace mantle beside cat-shaped vases and cat statues, and there were at least five full-sized and very much alive cats taking up most of the available seating.

Stella quickly ushered them into her dining room, where they all found seats around the dark oval table. A.J. positioned herself between Elysia and Andy. She didn't want those two sitting together, knowing from past experience how they egged each other on. This way she could always kick the ankle of whichever one showed signs of getting out of line.

Mr. Meagher and Chloe sat across from them. Suze took the empty seat at one end of the table. Then Stella turned the lights down low and took her seat at the other end. She had changed out of her bedraggled bedspread dress into something black and shiny and equally shapeless. Obviously the spirits were not into handing out fashion advice, A.J. thought.

"Before we start," Stella said in that toneless, sexless voice of hers, "I want to explain something. You've probably all seen séances in movies or TV shows. You're probably picturing floating musical instruments and jumping tables and green fuzzy holographs." Her eyes rested on Chloe's white, strained face. "Or maybe you're expecting something frightening and horrible to happen. I've sat in on or directed séances for over twenty years, and nothing like that has ever happened. The séances I've been part of have been uplifting and healing experiences. All that I'm asking tonight is that each of you keep an open mind." She stared directly at Elysia when she made that request.

Elysia yawned elaborately, and A.J. gave her a warning look. Elysia's answering smile did not reassure her.

"Now it's very important that we approach our séance with a unity of purpose. Are we agreed that we wish to contact Diantha to ask her if she can identify her killer?"

No one spoke. No one moved a muscle. No one seemed to even blink.

Stella seemed to read agreement in this absolute stillness.

"Good. We must all focus on this. If everyone would place their hands on the table . . ."

They obeyed. A.J. found herself staring, fascinated, at Andy's left hand. He was wearing what appeared to be a wedding band. A new wedding band.

That was her last conscious thought for some minutes. The next thing she realized was that everyone was singing "Danny Boy." Mr. Meagher was particularly enthusiastic on the high notes. It sounded like last call at an Irish pub, she thought. She could have used a Guinness about then.

The song ended. Stella said, "Now close your eyes."

A.J. closed her eyes. She heard Elysia heave a long-suffering sigh.

Silence.

The table seemed to shake. Or did it? It was so slight, A.J. couldn't be positive.

Stella said gruffly, in what sounded like a bad imitation of James Cagney, "Okay, youse guys. What's up?"

Suze breathed, "Oh, wow! She's already in a trance. That's the voice of Slapsy Malone, her spirit guide!"

"He must be rooming with Bugs Bunny," Andy murmured.

A.J. raised her lashes to give him a quelling look, but Andy just laughed at her with his eyes.

"Saints preserve us," muttered Mr. Meagher. He patted Chloe's trembling hand. "It's all in fun, lass."

Chloe nodded hastily and made a ghastly attempt at a smile.

"Someone has to ask a question," Suze hissed, as though Slapsy couldn't hear across the length of the table. "Someone should act as the control."

"That sounds like a job for you, pumpkin," Elysia remarked to A.J.

"Why me?"

"You're Di's . . . heir. Heiress. Not just financially. Spiritually. No?"

A.J. absorbed this silently. Yes. It seemed that perhaps Aunt Di had something of the sort in mind when she left Sacred Balance to A.J. instead of Lily.

She stared at Stella, whose grey head now bobbed gently on her pillowy chest as though she'd nodded off.

A.J. cleared her throat. "Uh, Mr. Malone?"

Stella's head lifted. "Slapsy'll do, toots. Didn't never stand on ceremony. What can I do you for?"

"We were hoping to, um, speak to my aunt." She glared at Andy, who was obviously struggling not to burst out laughing. "My aunt Diantha."

"Oh yeah? Newly crossed is she?"

"Uh, yeah. Yes, I mean."

"Yeah? So what's she look like?"

"Uh . . ."

"It's difficult to say," Elysia drawled. "Barefoot, something loose in breathable cotton, and a harp, I imagine—she was always fond of folk music."

Andy buried his face in his folded arms. His shoulders shook. Chloe, on the other hand, looked ready to faint.

"I like a dame what can crack wise," Slapsy via Stella remarked. "I'll ask around. See what's what."

Stella's head fell forward again. It bobbed gently on her chest as she breathed in and out in long sonorous gusts.

"Is that it? Is the séance over then?" Mr. Meagher demanded. "Are we not going to speak to Diantha?"

"Oh, don't *you* start," Elysia protested.

Mr. Meagher blushed.

"I think he's checking around," Suze said. "That's what he said. He's probably checking in the spirit world to see if she's nearby."

"Oh. My. *God.*" Elysia shook her head. "Bradley," she said to Mr. Meagher, "that child should be home in bed." She nodded to Chloe.

"I'm okay," Chloe said quickly. "I want to stay. I want to talk to Di!"

There was a funny little silence. Andy stopped laughing and sat up.

Mr. Meagher said uncomfortably, "Now, lass, it is getting late, and I did promise your ma. . . ."

"I want to stay!"

The shrill voice seemed to disturb Stella's trance. Her shoulders twitched, pain flickered across her blunt features. She lifted her head. Her pale eyes stared blindly around the circle.

"A.J. . . . danger . . ." Stella gasped the words out painfully. "Great . . . danger."

A.J. sat frozen. No one said a word; all gazes were riveted on Stella.

"Chloe . . . take . . . care. . . ."

"Di . . . ?" wavered Chloe.

Elysia sucked in a sharp breath. "I've had quite enough for one evening," she snapped.

Suze reached across, clutching at Elysia's arm as she rose. "You can't wake her out of a trance! It's super dangerous. At least, I think it is. It always is in the movies."

Elysia shook her hand off and went to the wall light switch. Mellow light from the copper hanging lamp flooded the table to reveal the circle of stricken faces. Stella moaned and slumped forward.

"Oh no!" Suze jumped up and ran around to Stella, but the older woman was pushing herself up, mumbling, "What happened? Were we successful?"

Chloe was sobbing. Mr. Meagher looked helplessly around, and Elysia joined him, coaxing the girl to her feet.

"Here now, pet. That's enough of that. Let's get you home and to bed."

Observing her, A.J. felt something weirdly like jealousy. All that maternal concern for a girl Elysia had never even heard of before this week.

"Were we successful? Did Di come through?" Stella was asking, looking from one to the other of them.

"Something came through," Elysia said tartly. "Loud and clear." With Mr. Meagher's help she got Chloe into the next room, where they bundled the trembling girl into her coat.

"Gosh, that was totally *amazing*," Suze was telling Stella. Stella smiled feebly. One of her many cats leaped lightly on the table, and she picked it up, cuddling it against her.

"You seem shocked," she said to A.J.

Elysia poked her head back in. "Andy, you're staying with A.J. tonight?"

"I—" Andy looked uncertainly at A.J. He looked pale, she thought, although perhaps it was just the faded light.

She opened her mouth to reject any such arrangement, but she realized she didn't want to have this discussion in front of her neighbors. She also realized that the last thing she wanted was to be alone tonight. If it weren't for Monster, she'd have been inviting herself over to Starlight Farm for a sleepover.

She nodded shortly.

She could tell that Stella wanted to talk to her, but A.J. felt too strange and confused by the events of the séance. Trailed by Andy, she followed her mother and Meagher as they helped Chloe outside and into Mr. Meagher's car. Elysia climbed in as well.

Andy said, "Is it really okay if I stay at the farm, A.J.? I can get a room at a motel in town, if you'd prefer that. I'm too tired to try and drive back tonight."

"It's okay. It's a big house," A.J. said.

"I remember."

Yes, that was right. They had spent a weekend at Deer Hollow not long after they married. It had not been a wildly successful weekend. Until then it had never crossed A.J.'s mind that the two people she loved most in the world would not love each other equally as much.

He unlocked her car door and then went around to the

driver's side and started the engine. Neither spoke as they pulled out of Stella's yard and sped down the unlit highway.

A.J. shivered and Andy leaned forward, switching the heat on full blast.

"That kid's on the verge of a nervous breakdown," he said.

A.J. murmured agreement. The skeletal trees that appeared in the spotlight of their headlights looked stark and tortured.

"I wouldn't let a kid of mine—" He broke off.

She stared at his profile.

After a very long moment he said hesitantly, "Are you okay? You went white when she . . . pretended she was Diantha."

A.J. said slowly, "Did you see her eyes?"

"Whose eyes?"

"Stella's. When she was . . . supposed to be channeling Aunt Di. Her eyes were pale blue!"

"So?"

"Her eyes are *brown*."

"No way," said Andy. "That had to be some trick. Fake lenses or something."

"I know. I do know. It just . . . freaked me out."

Andy was silent. They were turning into the drive to Deer Hollow before he said, "That was kind of weird. The stuff about 'grave danger' and 'taking care.' What do you think it meant?"

"That there's a murderer running loose."

He glanced her way. "Do they have any suspects beyond you?"

"I'm not a suspect anymore."

"You're not?" His surprise was evident.

"Detective Oberlin was able to verify that I was home during the hours that Aunt Di was killed."

After a thoughtful silence, Andy said, "Well, that's good news anyway. So who's this Chloe kid?"

"One of Aunt Di's protégés, as far as I can gather. She's had a rough time. Her dad committed suicide and she developed an OxyContin addiction. I think she's having trouble coping with Aunt Di's death."

She thought of that lost and childish *I want to talk to Di* and was ashamed of her earlier spark of jealousy.

"Maybe she killed your aunt."

A.J. stiffened. She tried to read his face in the eerie glow of the dashboard. "Why would you say such a thing? She's just a kid."

Even as she spoke the words, she knew they were ridiculous. As appalling as it was to consider, teen violence was nothing new; it just got more airplay these days. She thought of her own turbulent adolescence. She had been a quiet kid, a "good" kid, but without the stabilizing influence of Diantha, who could say how she might have acted out her resentment of her mother's illness—and her father's preoccupation with the same?

But Andy seemed to understand her shock. He shrugged. "I don't know. She seems like a nice enough kid. A little fragile. It just occurred to me that that 'Chloe . . . take care' bit could just as easily mean 'Watch out for Chloe.'"

A.J. opened her mouth and then closed it. There really didn't seem much to say after that. The night lurking beyond the headlights of the car seemed pitch-black and crowded with ominous, unseen figures.

Monster showed serious disappointment in A.J.'s decision to bring Andy home. He wasn't actually growling—once A.J. scolded him—but he did keep muttering under his breath in canine fashion as he settled on A.J.'s feet in the kitchen, where she and Andy sat at the table eating leftover sandwiches and drinking cocoa.

Actually, only Andy was drinking cocoa. A.J. hadn't

been able to enjoy a glass of milk since listening to Aunt Di's radio program. She drank chamomile tea and talked about Diantha's will and her own nebulous decision to, perhaps, stay just for a time in Stillbrook.

"Just till I get things in order here."

"You can't stay here," Andy argued. "What about your job? Your apartment?"

Monster gave another of those sleepy groans—which he did every time Andy spoke, as though the sound of Andy's voice were unbearable to him.

"I'm burnt out," A.J. told him. "That's the truth. You can have my clients. They all like you better anyway. I'm ready for a change."

"But—"

"And the truth is, I don't have to work. I'm . . . well . . . rich."

Andy stared at her as though he'd never heard the word before.

"And I have Aunt Di's empire to run, if I want. Somebody has to run it. And apparently she intended for it to be me."

"That sounds about right. It wouldn't occur to her that maybe you had your own plans for the future. And if it did occur to her, she'd assume she knew better."

A.J. wasn't surprised at Andy's hostility, but she was surprised that he voiced it now. Andy cared about appearances, and slagging someone five minutes after her funeral was definitely bad form.

She said neutrally, "And as for my apartment, I kind of like seeing the stars at night and walking in the woods. I even sort of like chasing the deer out of my garden."

"It won't last," he said. "You're a city mouse, not a country mouse. What about your chiropractor? What about Lula Mae? She's not going to put up with that four-footed thug snoring on your feet."

"I'll find a new chiropractor. And . . . I don't know what to do about Lula Mae. She's your daughter, too."

Andy's smile was half-hearted at best. "What about me?" he asked.

"What about you?"

"I'll never see you again."

"I'm not moving to Poland! And you don't see me now." She stared at him with a mix of anger and bewilderment. "Why would you even say that to me after everything that's happened?"

"Because I miss you!"

Monster growled at Andy's raised voice, and A.J. stroked him with her stockinged foot. "It's all right, boy," she said, although she was having to work not to get angry herself. Andy was staring at his plate, his mouth held in firm check against emotion—emotion that A.J. found utterly baffling.

"Look, you left me, remember? You're the one who ended everything."

He looked up. "Why did *everything* have to end? Why couldn't we have stayed friends?"

Now A.J. really *was* angry. "Um, because friends don't cheat on friends? Friends don't leave their friends for *other* friends—"

"Don't . . . don't negate what we had."

"Everything we had together was a lie."

He was shaking his head. "I loved you, A.J. I *still* love you. It's . . . different from . . . what I feel for Nick. But it's real."

This was the conversation she had not wanted to have—and she sure as hell hadn't wanted to have it now. But she couldn't seem to stop herself from responding. "You were pretending to be someone else the entire time. How real could it have been?"

"Look, I wanted to be that someone else. I really did. I tried. All my life I tried. I never wanted to hurt anyone. Especially you. I never wanted to be . . . on the outside." He swallowed hard. "I mean, it's crazy, A.J. People hate you for being gay, but then they blame you for trying to build a normal life."

"Only if you fail."

She regretted it the moment she said it. He went as white as paper.

"I didn't mean that," she said, and she realized it was true. The pleasure had gone out of hurting him. They had built a successful business together; they'd had a wonderful ten years of laughter and companionship and shared passions. True, the one great passion had escaped them.

"Andy," she said. She put her hand over his motionless one.

He raised his lashes and stared at her with those so-blue eyes. "You're my best friend in the world. I miss you so much. . . ." He leaned across the table and kissed her. His mouth was gentle and familiar.

A.J. kissed him back. She knew his taste, his scent, the softness of his lips—it was all familiar to her. It was what she had been missing, what she had been longing for. . . .

And it no longer mattered to her.

She drew back, raking a hand through her hair. "I miss you, too," she admitted.

Andy had a very funny look on his face. He started to smile. "There's someone else, isn't there?"

"Talk about ego. No. I'm just over you. There is no one else." When he continued to grin, she said exasperatedly, "I am capable of letting go and moving on, you know."

"I know."

"I'm capable of forgiveness."

"I know you are. You're a wonderful, forgiving person."

"I'm not going to loan you a million dollars even if we are still friends."

"That's okay. I only need half a million."

She laughed reluctantly.

"Is it that cop?"

"Is what who?" she asked reluctantly.

"Are you interested in that cop? The one who stopped by today. The one who doesn't like me."

"No. I am not interested in Detective Oberlin. Not if he was the last man on earth."

"That's what I thought," said Andy.

Nineteen

❧

Feeling uncomfortably like it was her first day at a new school, A.J. parked Diantha's Volvo in the Sacred Balance Studio lot and counted cars. Four cars, not counting her own. She recognized Suze's blue Beetle, which meant that the remaining vehicles belonged to Simon, Denise Faber, and Lily. It had to be a good sign that Lily had shown up for the meeting, right?

So why did she have that sinking feeling in her stomach?

Breathe deep, A.J. instructed herself. She huffed in and out a couple of times, grabbed the box of pastries from Tea Tea! Hee!, and slipped out of the car.

The glass doors were unlocked, the lobby empty when she walked in. Walking upstairs to the third level, she could hear voices down the hall from the conference room. She followed them to the large sunny room. Her staff was seated around the conference table; they fell silent as she appeared in the doorway.

"Good morning!" she said.

They returned her greeting with significantly less

enthusiasm—with the exception of Suze. Suze, bless her heart, had a genuine smile of welcome on her face. It almost made up for Lily's dour expression. The number one instructor slouched in the chair at the head of the table looking like an insolent elf in her usual black Capri pants and cut-off top.

"I brought pastries." A.J. set the box on the table.

"Oh, yum!" Suze said, reaching immediately for the box. "There's coffee on the counter."

"Caffeine and sugar, the breakfast of champions," quipped a tall, thin blonde woman who had to be Denise, the Pilates instructor.

Lily snorted.

A.J. told herself to stay cool. Naturally the instructors were going to view her skeptically. She was going to have to prove herself. Being Diantha's niece was not enough of a qualification—she'd have felt the same way in their place.

She glanced at Simon. He gave her a cordial nod and selected one of the plain doughnuts. See? Divide and conquer.

A.J. poured herself a cup of coffee, doctored it with raw sugar and soy milk, and seated herself midway down the table next to Denise. Suze smiled encouragingly at her—a couple of colored doughnut sprinkles stuck to her lips.

"I guess we may as well get down to it."

Lily murmured something, which A.J. ignored.

"I know the question first and foremost on everyone's mind is what will happen with Sacred Balance. According to the terms of my aunt's will, the studio now belongs to me."

"Just you?" Denise asked.

A.J. nodded. She glanced at Lily. The other woman's face was tight.

"It was my aunt's sincere wish—that's exactly how she phrased it—that Lily would continue on as lead instructor and a . . . mentor to me." She almost choked on that last bit, but honesty compelled her. "And because that was my aunt's wish, it's my wish as well."

No one spoke. Lily glared at her.

A.J. said to Lily, "I know this is difficult for you. I know you believed that the studio would be yours one day. I'm asking you to stay on and . . . help run things."

"Help *you* run things?"

"I've decided to stay, at least for the time being, and follow my aunt's wishes." A.J. hoped that was a diplomatic way of putting it.

"Do you have any training in yoga?" Lily asked.

"No—"

"Do you have any teaching experience at all?"

"No."

"Do you have any experience in running a business, large or small?"

"I've worked as a freelance—"

"Freelance isn't running a company, is it?"

"Look, Lily," A.J. said, her patience running thin, "this was Diantha's wish. I think you'll agree that Diantha was experienced in yoga, teaching, and running a business—and she was certainly the person best qualified to know what her own wishes were. This is her decision, and I'm trying to honor it the best I can."

"This is ludicrous," Lily said to the others. "She can't do this without your cooperation."

"Lily," Simon said uncomfortably, "there doesn't seem to be any question about what Di wanted."

"Well, I'm willing to give it a shot," Suze said.

"Who the hell asked you?" Lily retorted. "You're just the receptionist."

Ugly color flooded Suze's face. She bit her lip and wiped hastily at the sprinkles.

What a lovely yoga spirit, thought A.J. But she didn't say it aloud. It was better to let Lily handle her own PR.

"If it makes it any easier, I don't plan on changing

anything right away. I'm going to spend a few weeks talking to you all, talking to our clients, getting a feel for the studio—and getting myself up to speed."

"You think you can get yourself 'up to speed' in a few weeks? We've trained for *years*."

A.J. hung on to her temper with difficulty. "I realize that. I wasn't proposing taking over your courses in a few weeks. But I thought it might be fun if I took on a couple of new . . . lighter classes. Yoga for Children. Yoga for Dogs."

"Doga?" Simon said doubtfully.

"I've been doing some reading; Doga is very popular in the media right now."

"Yoga for Singles?" Suze suggested.

"Perfect," Lily said sarcastically. "Exactly what I'd expect."

"It's not a bad idea," Denise said slowly. She looked at Lily and qualified hastily, "I don't mean Yoga for Singles, just that I'd like to add more Pilates courses. We get a lot of requests."

"I think that's a great idea," A.J. said.

"I've been thinking maybe we could offer something geared to enforcement," Simon said, getting into the spirit. "Yoga for Cops maybe?"

A.J. pictured Jake Oberlin's tall, lean form in a cute pair of prAna warm-up pants—and suddenly felt a little warm. "Sure, great idea!" It was the first thing that popped into her head. "Over the next few weeks, it would be really helpful if you all jotted down any notes on ideas you have for the studio. Whatever you think of, whether it's new classes or, well, anything."

"We need another instructor," Denise said. She met A.J.'s gaze and added, "Even if you take on the lighter stuff, we'll need another full-time, experienced instructor. We've needed one for months."

"Okay." She glanced at Lily. The lead instructor's face was scornful. "Can we maybe give it a trial run, Lily?"

Lily's mouth was a straight line. She stared down the table. The rest of the staff waited.

"Fine," she said. "A trial run. And don't say I didn't warn you."

After posting a sign-up sheet for the proposed new classes, A.J. dug Chloe Williams' personal info out of her files and called the girl's mother to see how Chloe was doing. Worried about the possible effects of last night's séance on the girl's fragile psyche, she wasn't totally shocked to hear that Chloe had not attended school that day.

"Do you think it would be all right if I stopped by and visited with her?" A.J. asked tentatively.

Mrs. Williams, who hadn't mentioned anything about the séance, seemed oddly indifferent to A.J.'s request to stop by. "If you want to," she said vaguely. "I guess that's better than her sitting and staring at the TV all day."

It was only too easy to form a picture of a tuned-out and disinterested parent, but maybe that wasn't fair, A.J. told herself. After all, Mrs. Williams had lost her husband only a few months before; she was probably dealing with a fair share of her own issues, and A.J. knew firsthand how secretive and defensive an alienated teen could be. Luckily, for most of her life A.J. had had her aunt and father to act as a buffer between herself and a self-absorbed Elysia. Chloe no longer had a shock absorber—assuming she'd ever had one.

Getting directions to the Williams' house, she called Deer Hollow to see if Andy was up yet. They had talked late into the night, and Andy had reluctantly agreed to at least hear out A.J.'s proposal on taking over her client list.

Andy answered on the first ring. A.J. explained her mission of mercy and said she would be back after lunch.

"Okay, but will you do me a favor and bring me back some fast food. I don't care what, just . . . something."

"You never eat fast food. Why don't you just fix something?"

"Like what? A bowl of Cocoa Puffs? Compared to your larder, McDonald's qualifies as health food."

"Hey, I have been eating *a lot* more healthily lately."

"Yeah, well I'm hoping for something that falls in between Gardenburgers and Ding Dongs."

"Okay, okay," A.J. agreed. "I'll bring you something back."

She poked her head into Denise's office before she left. Simon and Lily were both in there. They instinctively cut off their conversation, but only Lily looked unfriendly.

"I'll see you tomorrow," A.J. said. She offered what she hoped was a confident smile. "I'm really looking forward to working with all of you."

Denise returned the smile with a practiced one of her own. Simon said, "We all want what's best for Sacred Balance." Lily said nothing, her face stony.

A.J. sighed inwardly and went out to her car.

The Williamses lived in a tidy little house on a quiet street in one of the newer developments in Stillbrook. A.J. parked under the spreading trees, nonplussed to see Elysia's familiar blue and white Land Rover on the other side of the street. She got out of her car and walked slowly up to the front door.

Chloe herself answered the doorbell, looking as peaked and melancholy as she had the night before.

"Hi, Chloe. Your mom said it would be all right if I stopped by to visit with you for a little while."

Chloe studied A.J. and then shrugged. Turning, she led the way through chilly but immaculate rooms to what was apparently a family room—although it was hard to picture a family actually relaxing in that magazine perfection.

A very fat beagle lay under the coffee table. Elysia sat

on the pristine sofa eating microwave popcorn and drinking a diet soda.

"Two minds with but a single thought," she said by way of greeting.

"Sounds like a shortage of good ideas," A.J. returned. She wasn't exactly annoyed to find her mother there, but she hoped Elysia was not planning on "grilling" Chloe a la *221B Baker Street*. The kid already looked one step from locking herself in the bathroom with a razor blade.

"Would you like a Diet Coke?" Chloe inquired dutifully.

"Oh, that's o—"

"Yes, she would," Elysia broke in. "Thank you, pet."

Chloe vanished down the hallway, and Elysia said in a low voice, "Let me do the talking, pumpkin. I think I've managed to establish a rapport with the poor tyke."

"Tyke? She's got to be seventeen or eighteen, right? And either way, the last thing she needs is to be interrogated."

"That's where you're wrong. That child is *desperate* to talk to someone." She straightened up as Chloe reappeared apparition-like with a glass of soda and a small bowl of popcorn, which she handed to A.J.

A.J. sat down across from Elysia, giving her mother a warning look, which Elysia ignored.

"Now, pet." Elysia patted the sofa next to her, and to A.J.'s astonishment Chloe sat down next to the older woman. "You were telling me about Steve."

"Steve?" It popped out before A.J. knew it.

"Steve Cussler, captain of the basketball team and the cutest boy at Reading College," Elysia informed her. "Steve has asked Chloe to the Midwinter Ball."

Chloe nodded. "But I don't see how I can go," she said, glancing from Elysia to A.J., "even if I *could* afford my own dress. . . . Steve used to go with Jennifer."

"And Jennifer and Chloe are best friends," Elysia said in response to A.J.'s perplexed expression.

"We used to be," Chloe said. She swallowed hard. "She's in college now. I got held back a semester because I missed so many classes when I . . . got sick."

"Well, that'll change next spring when you're in college, too," A.J. pointed out.

Chloe shook her head. "We don't even speak to each other since . . . since Steve asked me out."

"Oh."

"It turns out that Steve dumped Jennifer," Elysia said to A.J. "After he caught Jennifer with his best friend Stu behind the gymnasium."

"Ah. I'm sure the bard has something to say on that subject," said A.J.

" 'You pays your money and you takes your choice,' " quoted Elysia.

"Now, I *know* the Bard never said that."

"Possibly not." Elysia absently tucked one long lank strand of Chloe's hair behind the girl's ear; A.J. bit back a sardonic smile. She didn't know how much of a backbone Chloe possessed, but she'd need stainless steel vertebrae to withstand Elysia's . . . "maternal instinct."

As Chloe's eyes filled with tears, Elysia patted her hand absently. "Funds have been rather scarce since Chloe's dad died," she said. "Di was arranging with Nicole Manning, who, from what I gather, is someone very popular on the telly these days, to borrow a dress for Chloe from wardrobe."

"She's the star of *The Family Business*." Chloe wiped her eyes.

"I know Nicole," A.J. said in surprise. She had been sitting there wondering what the heck any of this had to do with Diantha's murder, wondering whether Elysia really was there out of simple concern for this girl, when Chloe's words sank in. "I did some PR for her a couple of years ago, right before she landed the *Family Business* gig."

"Well, isn't that lovely," Elysia cooed. "Perhaps A.J. could speak to Nicole about the dress."

A.J. shot her mother a warning look, but Chloe was already gazing at her hopefully. Then the hope died. "But even so . . . what about Jennifer?"

"What about her?" Elysia said. "Jennifer can easily afford her own dress. Her family has pots of money."

"But . . . I mean . . ."

"There, there, poppet. Jennifer will have to work these things out for herself. You have to do what's right for you."

"That's what Di always said." Chloe burst into tears.

"Now, now." Astonished, A.J. watched Elysia pull the girl into her arms. "You just let it all out."

Chloe did just that. Muffled against Elysia's bony shoulder she sobbed out how much she missed Diantha, how Diantha was so much more than a fitness instructor, how she was like a friend and a mother and a sister and no one really cared about Chloe anyway, and she was so ugly—Chloe, not Diantha, who was so beautiful—and why would anyone have killed her, and why did everyone have to die, and she missed Di so much, and maybe Steve didn't really want to go to the Midwinter Ball with her anyway. . . .

And on and on and on.

A.J. watched in disbelief as Elysia sat calmly through the torrent of tears and talk, patting the girl's thin shoulder and murmuring soothing things.

Finally Chloe regained control of herself.

"Why would anyone want to kill someone as wonderful as Di?" she asked plaintively, for the third time.

Elysia shook her head sadly. "I can't imagine. I've tried to figure it out many times."

Her mother was going over the top, in A.J.'s opinion, but Chloe seemed to be looking inward and didn't appear to have heard the answer.

"Maybe Lorraine," she said.

"Lorraine?" A.J. and Elysia chorused. They each looked at the other.

"Lorraine Batz," Chloe said. She looked at A.J. and then Elysia. "Because of Michael. Michael and Diantha, I mean. Because they were having an affair."

Twenty

✦

"I don't believe it," Elysia said.

They were sitting at a table outside a Starbucks; they had the small patio to themselves, as, judging from the low-hanging clouds, rain was imminent.

A.J. stirred her chai latte absently. "He had a key to the studio. I never quite understood that."

"She wouldn't meet him in the studio," Elysia protested. "She wouldn't meet him at all. He was half her age."

"And married."

"And married," Elysia agreed. She brooded over her black coffee.

"Remember Detective Oberlin saying that the police had locked up after searching Aunt Di's house? But the guy who knocked me down didn't break in."

"You think Michael Batz had a key to Deer Hollow as well as the studio?" Elysia asked, her eyes narrowing. "You think he was searching for something—anything—that might reveal his affair with Di?"

"It's possible. I sure as heck wouldn't want evidence

found that I'd been having an affair with someone, if something suspicious happened to that someone."

Elysia shook her head repudiating this. "I know Di. She wouldn't have had an affair with a man half her age—especially a married man!"

"She must have been lonely. All those years without Gus. And . . . neither of us were around much."

"She didn't have an affair with that man."

"Why does the idea bother you so much?" A.J. asked curiously.

"It doesn't bother me *so much*; it bothers me the amount one would *expect* it to bother me." Elysia drank some coffee. "I suppose this does strengthen his motive."

"How? I can see it might give his wife a motive."

"Very likely Di wanted to break it off, and he didn't."

"Maybe," A.J. said doubtfully. "He seems pretty self-absorbed, though. I get the impression the only thing on his mind is getting to the Olympics. I can't see him committing a crime of passion. And I can't see Aunt Di threatening to go to his wife."

Elysia snorted at the idea. "Hardly. His motive remains financial. He had to know Di was bequeathing him money for training; perhaps he thought it was more money than it is."

A.J. tried to think back to the afternoon when the will had been read. Batz had not been surprised at the legacy, only the codicil. She wondered if she could convince Mr. Meagher to reveal what was in the codicil. Probably not. But what if Elysia were to do the asking?

She said, "Do you think Detective Oberlin knows Aunt Di was having an affair with Batz?"

"There's no proof that she was."

"According to Chloe it was pretty much common knowledge."

Elysia said shortly, "Then I imagine Detective Oberlin knows about it." She sighed and stubbed her cigarette out in the lid of her coffee cup. "How are things going with Andrew?"

"We talked last night."

"And?"

"I guess I feel a little better about things," A.J. said unwillingly. "I know in my heart that he was almost in as much pain over our divorce as I was."

"Of course he was!" Elysia patted A.J.'s hand. "You just give it some time, pumpkin. You two will work it out."

A.J. opened her mouth, but Elysia was already on her feet.

"I must dash." Her eyes glinted. "Why don't you speak to Detective Oberlin about Michael Batz? Pick his brain. And I'll have a word with Bradley."

"Mr. Meagher?"

"That's right. I want to know more about that codicil," Elysia said.

A.J. watched her go, slim and long-legged in her tight jeans and stilettos, and she realized she was smiling. Elysia was never going to be cast as the lead in *I Remember Mama*, that was for sure.

She was finishing her tea when she noticed the hair salon across the street. *Impulse* read the pink and black window script. A.J. touched her cropped head self-consciously. Her hair was beginning to grow out, giving her a tufted shaggy look. She was starting out on a new phase in her life; it was time for a new haircut. Something a little more subtle than the last new-phase cut she'd treated herself to with her own trusty scissors.

Tossing her cup in the trash, she rose and ran across the street. The salon was slow on a weekday afternoon and A.J. had no problem getting an immediate appointment. She sat down in the chair, reassuring herself that the gum-chewing stylist could hardly do more damage than A.J. already had—even if she did sport a green mohawk and look about Chloe's age.

The stylist examined A.J.'s hair, touched the ends

lightly, blew a giant pink gum bubble, and popped it. "I don't know if I can match that cut," she said regretfully.

Lost in her own thoughts, hypnotized by the snip, snip, snip of glinting scissors, A.J. was oblivious to "Edna's" chatter until a name registered.

"Lorraine Batz?" she said, raising her eyes to Edna's face. "She's a client of yours?"

"Mmm-hmm . . ." Edna squinted at a tuft of A.J.'s hair pulled taut between her fingers, and gave another judicious snip. "She and Michael both."

"He's got beautiful hair," A.J. said, momentarily distracted. "Like one of those Renaissance angels."

"Thanks."

A.J. tried again. "I guess it can't be easy being married to an Olympic hopeful."

Edna snorted, apparently concurring.

A.J. racked her brain for something to say that would stimulate the conversation. "Is Lorraine a runner as well?"

"Well, yeah, but not in Michael's class."

"Did they grow up around here?"

"Yep."

"Do they have any children?" Now *that* was lame, A.J. reflected.

But to her surprise Edna paused in her pruning to meet A.J.'s mirrored eyes. "Not *yet*."

Trying to interpret that particular inflection, A.J. ventured, "Not while Michael's in training?"

"Not until Michael's made the Olympic team."

"What if he doesn't make the team?"

"Girlfriend, do not *even* go there," said Edna.

Detective Oberlin was not available when A.J. phoned the police station. Or, if he was available, he was not taking A.J.'s calls. She remembered his scathing comments about amateur sleuthing and decided it had been a bad idea to try to talk to him about Michael Batz anyway.

She wondered if Elysia had been successful in getting Mr. Meagher to reveal the contents of the codicil to Diantha's will, but Elysia was not picking up her phone either.

For a few moments A.J. sat in her car drumming her fingernails on the steering wheel, trying to decide what to do next.

She didn't wanted to place undo importance on what she had learned from Edna, but it did seem that Michael Batz had a complicated personal life. Had things become so complicated he had resorted to murder? Of course they had only Chloe's word that Aunt Di had been romantically linked with Michael Batz. It was possible that Chloe was mistaken. True, she had seemed to take it for granted that they knew about the affair—as though she believed it was common knowledge—but no one else had so much as hinted at such a thing.

Then again . . . a hundred-thousand-dollar bequest seemed like more than just a show of faith in someone's Olympic potential.

Lily would know, A.J. reflected. But she couldn't imagine herself asking Lily. And she couldn't imagine Lily confiding in her.

A.J. conceded defeat and started the car.

When she arrived home she found Andy in the kitchen cooking herb-roasted chicken, one of her very favorite meals.

She stopped dead in the doorway. "Oh my gosh. I totally forgot I was supposed to bring you something to eat. I decided to get my hair cut."

Andy grinned. "In that case, I forgive you." He cocked his head. "And I approve of the new cut."

He was being *so* nice; it made her a little uncomfortable. She felt better after their talk last night, but it wasn't that easy to let go of all her anger and bitterness. She wasn't sure if she was truly ready to be friends with Andy. She wasn't sure she would ever be. A.J. sat down at the table. "Where's Monster?"

"I put him out when I got back from the market. I think he's in the back harassing some innocent squirrels."

She bit back a smile at his expression.

"So how did the sleuthing go?" Andy inquired into the silence that fell between them. He opened the oven door.

"I wasn't sleuthing," A.J. said defensively. "I was on a mission of mercy."

Andy looked amused, and before long A.J. was filling him in on everything Chloe had said, her spike of discomfort forgotten.

"I can see Di having an affair," he said when she had finished. "Thirty-something years is a lot of loneliness."

"He was less than half her age. What would they have had to talk about?"

Andy cocked a knowing eyebrow, and A.J. felt her face heat up—which was ludicrous. It wasn't like she didn't appreciate the idea of hot sex—although appreciating the *idea* was about as close as she'd ever come to it.

"He's *married*," she said shortly, and to that, Andy had no answer.

"What about this kid, Chloe?" he suggested after a moment or two. "She sounds pretty unstable."

"I think she's just your normal, run-of-the-mill, mixed-up eighteen-year-old."

"With a serious drug addiction."

"Which Diantha helped her beat."

Andy asked, "What if the kid started using again?"

"There's absolutely no reason to think—"

"I'm just saying—theoretically—what if the kid started using and Di found out?"

"She'd have tried to help her." A.J. could feel her temper rising. Andy had never liked Aunt Di.

"What if she didn't want to be helped?"

"Well, of course she'd want to be helped!"

"Not necessarily, A.J. She's seeing this hunky guy, and she's already upset about not going to college with her pals. She wouldn't necessarily enjoy being bounced back to rehab, and that's what helping her would amount to, right?"

A.J. said reluctantly, "I'm sure Aunt Di would have tried to find another way."

"You think so?" Andy's lip curled. "Your aunt was the type who'd burn you at the stake for your own good."

A.J. stared at him. Hindsight being twenty-twenty, she now glimpsed at least part of the reason for the antipathy between Diantha and Andy.

It was hard to stay peeved at a man who cooked you cheddar and bacon mashed potatoes. By the time Andy served the cheesecake he had picked up at Tea Tea! Hee!, A.J. had moved past her earlier constraint, and they bickered amiably over the merits of their favored suspects. Andy clung to the belief that Chloe's fragile demeanor concealed the heart of a murderess, while A.J. insisted that Michael Batz was the most logical contender.

So by the time they finished the dishes and settled down to business, A.J. was feeling more relaxed than she had for some time. They spent the rest of the evening hammering out the details of a letter to A.J.'s clients that managed to be both reassuring and vague about the future, and directing them—at least temporarily—to Andrew.

"Are you sure you want to do this?" Andy asked when they had finally agreed on the wording.

"No. But I'm going through with it."

He studied her unhappily. Whatever he might have said was interrupted by the phone ringing in the hall. A.J., who was lying on the floor in the hope of giving her aching spine some respite, turned her head cautiously toward the clock on the mantle. Eight o'clock.

"Can you get that?"

Andy nodded and rose, giving wide birth to Monster, who lifted his head from his paws to glare at him inimically as he passed by.

Andy returned a moment later. "Do you get a lot of hang-up calls?"

"What do you mean?"

"Whoever was on the other end didn't want to talk to me."

"It was probably just a wrong number."

"Could be. He—or she—hung up when I said hello."

"Something to remember when you're teaching your own classes: start out with the more complicated poses. As the class progresses, your students' bodies and minds tire." Lily studied the small group of aspiring yoga teachers before her. "Okay. Let's run through our *Asanas*."

Let's run through our Asanas?

A.J., seated in the rear of the class, thought that sentence alone summed up everything she disliked about Lily's attitude and teaching style. Admittedly, she was biased, both by her antipathy toward the other woman and her own youthful introduction to Aunt Di's more spiritual and loving approach to yoga. This Teacher Training class was comprised of aspiring instructors, not novices; so perhaps that's why Lily's approach was so . . . aggressive.

Perhaps.

As disloyal as it felt, A.J. had to question Aunt Di's judgment in wanting her and Lily to work together. Watching the other woman in action, A.J. grew more and more convinced they were never going to be a team.

It could happen.

Sure. And maybe one day A.J. would learn to love soy

patties as much as bacon burgers, but it wouldn't be any-time soon.

"Larry, are you sure you want to be here this morning?" Lily asked a tall, skinny young man. The young man turned a painful plum color and nodded humbly.

A.J. had to bite back her objection. She knew it was al-ready irritating Lily that she was simply observing and not taking part in the class. Lily wanted A.J. on the mat; she wanted to be able to demonstrate—both to A.J. and every-one else—that A.J. knew nothing about yoga or teaching. A.J. would be the first person to admit that she had a lot to learn, but she knew instinctively Lily would not be the right person to teach her. She was not sure, observing the lead instructor in action, that Lily was the right person to teach anyone.

Surely Aunt Di had been too shrewd about people to miss the fact that A.J. and Lily were like chalk and cheese—to risk a dairy reference. Had she believed that their differ-ences were complementary and that grief would bring them together? Or was this teaming yet another example of the stubbornness that had led Aunt Di to design a building that was contrary to most rules of architecture?

"Nice job, Andrea. That's right. Invite the pose into the body. Larry, take a look at Andrea. . . ."

Rather than creating a safe learning environment, Lily seemed to be deliberately fostering a competitive atmos-phere. Her focus was entirely on technique rather than spirit, and instead of inspiring and challenging her stu-dents, she criticized.

As A.J. watched Lily walk through the rows of students, she could almost see the tension rippling in her wake as she barked out orders, fixing postures, belittling some students, and pointedly praising others. She watched the stu-dents, muscles quivering, faces tense as they struggled to hold poses—many of them clearly being pushed beyond their limits.

It was like . . . Extreme Yoga.

"Suze, maybe you need to rethink the teaching thing," Lily said to the receptionist in that sweetly sarcastic tone.

A.J. felt a rush of anger as she watched poor Suze flush and then go pale. For a moment the girl looked as if she were going to burst into tears, but she managed to control herself.

"Sorry," Suze muttered.

Lily shook her head as though she simply didn't have the strength to continue dealing with idiots. A couple of other students snickered.

So much for finding a sacred balance. A.J. rose from her mat, rolled it up, and headed for the doors. She had seen enough for one morning.

The problem was, what could she do about it? Given the terms of Diantha's will, she wasn't exactly sure—and neither was Mr. Meagher—that she could fire Lily. Aunt Di couldn't have been clearer about her desire for the two women to work together.

A.J. trusted Aunt Di; it was difficult to accept that such a wise and wonderful woman could simply have been . . . wrong. That she could have been mistaken in her assessment of both Lily and A.J.

A.J. proceeded downstairs to the offices.

Simon Crider looked up from his desk and nodded politely as she passed his door.

A.J. smiled in return. Simon was the sort of man A.J. could picture her aunt turning to—not someone like Michael Batz. Aunt Di had made such odd choices during the past year; it was hard for A.J. to accept some of those decisions. And as she considered her reluctance, it occurred to her for the first time that maybe there was a smidgeon of truth in a comment Elysia had made. At the time it had seemed unfair, but maybe she *did* have trouble accepting imperfection—weakness—in the people she loved.

Disquieted, A.J. entered Aunt Di's office—her own office now—and sat down, idly shuffling through phone messages. She was surprised to see that Nicole Manning had called.

Her cell phone rang. She opened the desk drawer, pulled her purse out, and found her cell.

She didn't recognize the number and considered letting it go to message, but then she remembered the hang-up call the evening before.

There was just an outside chance. . . .

She picked up.

"A.J.?"

Her heart gave a little leap at the familiar deep tones of Jake Oberlin.

"Oh. Hello," she said in a voice that didn't sound quite like her own.

"Listen," he said in a hurried tone that sounded nothing like his usual one, "I just got a call over the radio. Your aunt's farmhouse is on fire. You better get out there right away."

"Fire?" she shrieked, jumping to her feet.

"The fire department is on the scene. I'll meet you there. Watch your driving—"

The phone dropped from A.J.'s nerveless fingers. She grabbed her purse and ran out of the office, oblivious to the crowd of chatting and laughing clients making their way from the top floors as classes ended.

Pushing through the glass doors, she sprinted to her car. Monster, she thought with sickness pooling in her stomach. Oh, Monster.

Her next thought was even more frightening: *Andy*.

Twenty-one

❧

Fire trucks were parked in the front yard of Deer Hollow Farm, and streams of water were shooting into the sky, hitting the trees and raining down on the smoking roof. A.J. pulled up next to a police SUV and fell out of the car on shaky legs. Trucks rumbled, exhaust and smoke billowed around her, and male voices called back and forth as she made her way to the front. The fire appeared to have been contained, but most of the front porch was gone, reduced to a charred skeletal framework.

She looked around, searching for Andy . . . for Monster. She couldn't see them anywhere. Stella Borin stood talking to someone who appeared to be the fire chief. A.J. pushed through the milling firefighters.

"My hus—friend," A.J. gasped, reaching Stella and the fire chief. "Is he all right?"

"Nobody was inside the house," the man in the yellow slicker replied. "You've got some smoke and fire damage in the front parlor, and the hallway's a loss, but the porch took the worst of it."

"My dog," A.J. interrupted. "Did he get out?" She had left Monster penned in her bedroom just to make sure he didn't nip Andy when she wasn't around to control him.

"Oh no!" cried Stella as the fire chief shook his head reluctantly.

"I didn't see any—"

Barking interrupted him, and they all turned to see. Jake, thoroughly exasperated, came around the corner of the house, dragging Monster on his leash. The dog was frantically trying to hump the cop's leg, barking crazily all the while. The firemen began to laugh.

"My *hero*!" hooted the fire chief, and Jake's face, if possible, grew even darker.

"I think this belongs to you," he told A.J. as she ran forward. He handed over the leash.

She nearly threw her arms around him, but that crack of the fire chief's held her back.

"Where did you find him?' she asked instead, kneeling down to hug the panting dog. Monster slimed her with his tongue and gazed adoringly up at Jake.

"He was running loose in the pasture. I remembered seeing a leash on your back porch, so I grabbed it and then I grabbed him." Jake's green eyes studied her face. "You okay?"

"I think so. I haven't seen the damage yet. And . . . Andy seems to be missing."

"Andy?" His voice changed. "Oh. Right. The ex. He's still staying with you?"

"Only while we hammer a few things out." She wasn't sure why it seemed important to explain, but Jake was listening attentively, so she added, "He's going to be taking over my clients and projects while I try to get the studio back up and running."

"So . . . the partnership is back on?" It was asked neutrally, but something in the question made A.J.'s heart beat a little faster.

"Only the business partnership. And even that's . . . probably temporary."

His gaze sharpened, but their attention was distracted by the crunch of tires on gravel. Andy's car pulled up and Andy got out.

"Oh, thank God," A.J. breathed.

Andy pushed through the crowd, his face bewildered. Monster growled softly as he reached them.

"What the hell happened?" Andy could hardly seem to tear his gaze from the porch.

"Where have you been?" A.J. cried.

"I drove into town to pick up some things for dinner." He stared past her to Jake. "How did the fire start?"

"We don't know yet." Jake excused himself and went over to talk to the fire chief.

"You just went to the market yesterday," A.J. said.

"I was going to make lasagna for dinner."

A.J. said, sounding uncomfortably accusatory, "You don't like lasagna!"

"You do!"

"Why are you yelling at me?"

"Why are you yelling at *me*?"

They both fell silent. A.J. stared at Andy, unwillingly recognizing what lay at the root of her anger. She said, struggling for calm, "Jake found Monster running loose in the pasture."

Andy looked down at Monster as though expecting an explanation. As none was forthcoming, he said to A.J., "That's a good thing, right? You're glad the dog's okay?"

"I left him shut in my bedroom so he wouldn't bother you."

Andy looked confused. "I let him out before I left. I didn't think I should leave him shut in all day."

"But you're afraid of him."

"I'm not *afraid* of him," Andy said indignantly. "He's

not Cujo." He stared at her. "If I hadn't let him out he'd probably be dead from smoke inhalation."

"I know."

"Well . . ." Andy stared at her. His eyes went wide. "You don't think *I* had something to do with the fire?"

"I . . ." She swallowed hard. She had told Andy she was planning to change her will, and that was true, but she hadn't signed the new will yet. Hadn't seen the urgency. But eighteen million dollars was one heck of a motive. True she would never have suspected Andy of being capable of murder, but then she had never known he was capable of sleeping with another man. She had to accept the fact that she really didn't know Andy.

On the other hand, it was hard to picture Andy being cold-blooded enough to murder her aunt—because if this was about money, she also had to consider that he might have killed Aunt Di so that A.J. could inherit so that he could then kill A.J.—but too soft-hearted to let her dog die. Especially when he didn't particularly like the dog in question.

"A.J.!" Andy looked stricken. "You can't think . . ."

"No, of course not," she exclaimed. She wasn't sure whether that was true, but she had to say it for both their sakes.

Stella joined them, her face grim. "A.J., there's a chance this might be arson."

Was that a news flash from the spirit world, because if so, Slapsy Malone seemed to be asleep on the job.

"I was just telling the chief that UPS nearly mis-delivered a parcel to me this morning. It was addressed to Diantha, so I caught the driver and gave him directions over here. Now they think that package might have contained some kind of incendiary device."

"This proves we're getting very close," Elysia said darkly, pouring A.J. another cup of tea.

"Close to what?" A.J. asked. Half of her attention was on the murmur of Andy's voice from the other room, where he was talking to Nick on the phone. They had driven to Elysia's after being allowed to pick up a few clothes and necessities from the farm. Deer Hollow was now officially a crime scene. The suspected crime: arson.

"To solving the murder, naturally. The killer clearly feels that you're becoming a threat to his safety."

"Mother, no one could seriously think my sleuthing skills are a threat. Besides, the parcel was addressed to Aunt Di, so if there was some kind of incendiary device inside, it was aimed at her."

"No, no!" Elysia waved an impatient hand. "They addressed the package to Di to avoid confusing the delivery people. The killer sent the bomb—"

"It wasn't a bomb!"

Elysia waved this away, too, and reached for a lavender legal pad on the coffee table. "I've been jotting down a few notes on the case. . . ."

Andy appeared in the doorway. He seemed to have trouble meeting A.J.'s eyes.

"That was Nick," he said unnecessarily.

Elysia picked up a purple pen and scribbled something on the pad. Then she chewed on the end of the pen, staring into space.

"He wants to know when I'm coming home," Andy said.

"There's no reason for you to stay," A.J. answered. "We've settled what we needed to, right?" She ignored Elysia's ferocious scowl. "You can start back this evening or . . . now."

"I feel bad leaving you in the lurch."

What are you doing??? Elysia communicated with her eyes. A.J. avoided her gaze.

"Everything's fine," A.J. assured him. "Everything's under control here."

Elysia looked ceilingward as though seeking divine intervention.

"Are you sure, A.J.? If you need me to stay . . ."

"I'm sure."

The minute Andy left the doorway Elysia threw down her pen and pad, rattling the teacups. "Crikey, pumpkin. The man is begging you to give him a reason to stay, and what do you do? You practically shove him out the door."

"He wants to go home. His boyfriend wants him home. *I* want him to go home."

"I don't follow your strategy."

"It's not a strategy, Mother. Andy and I are divorced."

"That is a mere technicality."

"It's not a technicality; it's reality. Our marriage is over." She listened to the words, and for the first time they brought no pain. A.J. gave a little relieved sigh. "I'm ready to move on."

Elysia moaned. "Please tell me it's not that big, dumb ox . . . that fascist copper."

"It isn't anyone," A.J. said, her cheeks hot. "And he's not a big, dumb ox. Although he probably is a fascist."

Elysia ignored this weak attempt at humor. "He's not your style, Anna. Believe me. I know men. He would not be good for you. He's not in your league."

Anna. Wow, her mother really was rattled.

"Mother, I have no idea what you're talking about. My league? Was Andy in my league? Because he was apparently playing for the other team." She reached for the legal pad her mother had tossed aside, and studied it.

Elysia had jotted down several notes next to four names:

JOHN BAUMANN—Made threats against Di, blamed her for his failing business, bee farmer—motive and means. Does he have an alibi?

"I thought you believed John Baumann wasn't capable of murder?"

Elysia said coolly, "Personally, I don't. But we have to look at this objectively. We have to look at this with the cold, clear logic of the professional."

The professional *what*? A.J. wondered, but she kept that thought to herself.

Elysia added, "After all, someone killed Di, and as that someone is still at large, we have to assume that he or she is someone who doesn't appear capable of murder."

A.J. read the next name.

ESTHER BAUMANN—Would do anything to help her husband, has as much to lose. Does she have an alibi?

"You must realize," she pointed out, "if either John or Esther showed up at the studio, Aunt Di would have been on her guard. From everything the police can tell, she wasn't. And it's hard to picture people as big as the Baumanns successfully sneaking up on her."

"Your aunt could have been meditating," Elysia returned instantly. "No one had greater focus than Diantha. A bomb could have gone off next to her and I doubt it would have disturbed her concentration."

A.J. read farther down the page.

MICHAEL BATZ—Stood to inherit sizable legacy, was caught searching Di's files—could he have been the intruder at Deer Hollow? Was he having an affair with Di?

A.J. glanced at Elysia. "Were you able to find out from Mr. Meagher what was in the codicil?"

Elysia's scarlet mouth twisted into a wry little moue. "Not yet."

A.J. bit back a grin. "I wouldn't have thought the old guy was capable of denying you anything."

"Me, too." Elysia's smile was hard to decipher. "And he's not that old."

A.J. nodded solemnly. "Batz could have been the intruder that day. If Aunt Di gave him a key to the studio, she might have given him a key to the house. And remember Jake— Detective Oberlin commenting on the size of the footprints? Michael has unusually small hands and feet for a man."

A spark of interest lit Elysia's eyes.

A.J. moved to the next name on the list.

LILY MARTIN—Believed she would inherit Sacred Balance Studio. Had a recent falling out with Di? No alibi. Dresses badly.

"Dresses badly?" A.J. read aloud.

"It was just a thought." Elysia said vaguely. " 'Clothes maketh the man,' as the bard says."

"How do you know she doesn't have an alibi?"

"Bradley told me." Elysia was smug. "He says she was questioned extensively by your pet policeman. She has a veritable mania about that studio."

"I won't argue that with you. Still . . ."

Still there were people with better motives. If they really were looking at this thing with the cold, clear logic of the professional, Andy should be on this list, A.J. reflected. Andy had eighteen million dollars worth of motive, although he probably didn't have access to bee venom; in fact, it was doubtful Andy would remember about Diantha's allergies. Still, she wondered if Jake—who probably did view everyone and everything with the cold, clear logic of the professional—had verified whether Andy had an alibi for the morning of Diantha's murder. Probably. She had a suspicion that Jake was a stickler for details.

Plus he didn't seem to like Andy much.

And even if she couldn't picture Andy killing anyone— and it *was* pretty darn hard to picture—what about Nick,

Andy's new partner? Hadn't Andy said something about Mr. G-Man being in the area around the time of Diantha's murder? She tried to think what exactly he'd said; she'd been distracted at the time.

It was all too easy to picture Nick as the embodiment of evil—everything from home wrecker to homicidal maniac—but it was pretty far-fetched.

Considering Andy's murderous possibilities reminded her of Andy's own suspicions.

"You're missing a name," she said.

"Who's that?"

"Chloe Williams."

Elysia made a sound that previous generations would have classified as "pshaw."

A.J. said firmly, "She could have snuck up on Aunt Di without her noticing. And she seems pretty fragile emotionally. What if Aunt Di found out that she was using again? Chloe might have panicked. . . ."

"You don't procure and inject someone with bee venom in a panic," Elysia pointed out.

A.J. acknowledged the truth of that.

"Nor do I believe the child is using again."

A.J. lifted a dismissing shoulder. She scrutinized the legal pad. "If today's fire was arson . . ."

"If?"

"If," she repeated firmly, "then what was the motive? Was the perpetrator hoping to destroy some incriminating evidence—of an affair, perhaps?"

"Michael Batz," Elysia said with satisfaction.

A.J. nodded. "If they *were* having an affair, he'd know about Aunt Di's allergies. And he could certainly sneak up on her without arousing her suspicions."

"But how do we get proof?"

A.J. blinked at her mother's determined expression. "Uh, we don't. That would be for the police."

Elysia waved this off impatiently. She said eagerly,

"And his wife. We mustn't forget his wife. She has quite a solid motive—doubly solid when you figure her husband's financial future hinges on his success as a competing Olympian."

Monster, who was sprawled out in front of the fireplace, suddenly opened his eyes and rolled onto his tummy. He thumped his tail heavily.

A.J. felt her heart speed up. Jake, she thought.

The doorbell rang.

Twenty-two

❦

"**There's** not much doubt it was arson," Jake said grimly.

He looked more than a little out of place on Elysia's brocade couch, absently balancing a china teacup in one big hand.

A.J. swallowed hard. It was one thing to view the possibility from an academic standpoint, but to face the fact that someone had actually committed arson against her? More than a little scary. "How was it done?" she asked tersely.

"A couple of Molotov cocktails lobbed at your front door. About as primitive a method as there is."

"So there was no incendiary device in the package that UPS delivered?"

"No."

Elysia said, "Was the package recovered?"

"What was left of it." He glanced at A.J. "Apparently your ex-husband brought it into the house and leaned it against the wall next to the door, so it went up with the door and the porch. You weren't expecting any UPS deliveries?"

"No. Anyway, it was addressed to Aunt Di."

But he knew that. Was he still suspicious of her? It probably went with the territory. Cops weren't the most trusting people in the world. Trusting people could get you killed in Jake's line of work.

"You should be able to get a tracking number from UPS and contact whoever sent the parcel."

She nodded absently.

"Mrs. Borin described the package as a large, flat brown box." He watched to see if this rang a bell.

"Wasn't anything left of the contents?"

"Material of some kind. It was pretty charred."

Andy entered the room, carrying his suitcase.

Elysia uncurled, swift as a cat. "Andrew, pet, there's really no need to leave. Why don't you wait for morning?" She directed an imperative look toward A.J., who pretended not to see it.

A.J. said, "I'll walk you out, Andy."

In silence they walked out to his car, and Andy unlocked the trunk, dropping his suitcase inside.

Slamming shut the trunk, he turned to A.J. "So are you breaking it to Lula Mae or am I?"

She managed a smile. "I'll break it to her. As soon as there's something to break. Nothing's really for sure yet."

He smiled faintly. "That's what I like about you. Once you make up your mind . . ."

She opened her mouth to retaliate, and then let it go. She no longer needed to hurt him. "Take care of yourself, Andy."

"You know if you need anything . . ."

She smiled. "Thanks, but it's under control." As under control as living in the shadow of a murder investigation could be.

They hugged, suddenly awkward again after the near-companionable truce of the past couple of days.

After he got into the car and drove away, A.J. walked

slowly back into Elysia's house. She could hear Elysia's voice from the front room.

"You're not married, Inspector?"

And Jake's low, contained, "No, ma'am."

"Divorced?"

"No." .

"Widowed?"

"No."

"Engaged?"

"I'm flattered by your interest, Mrs. Alexander, but I'm pretty much married to my job."

A.J. walked through the doorway, and Elysia, who had opened her mouth, promptly closed it. "There you are, pumpkin," she cooed.

"How is the investigation into my aunt's murder going?" A.J. asked, sitting in the chair next to the sofa. He shifted so that he faced her more directly. He glanced down at the fragile teacup in his hand as though he wasn't sure how it had gotten there.

"The investigation is ongoing."

"Is that copper lingo for stalled?" Elysia inquired sweetly.

His eyes narrowed. "No, ma'am. It means we're following leads, sifting evidence, and narrowing our field of suspects."

A.J. said, "Speaking of suspects, had you heard a rumor that my aunt was romantically involved with Michael Batz?"

"I'd heard that, yes."

"Is it true?"

He studied her for a moment. "It appears to be."

"Does he have an alibi?"

An expression of weariness crossed his face. "A.J., I can't discuss the particulars of this case with you."

"You can't give me a simple yes or no?"

"He has an alibi," Jake said curtly. "He was training at

the high school track. According to four different witnesses, he was never out of their sight."

"What about Mrs. Batz?" Elysia asked.

Jake shook his head. "Ladies, I cannot discuss the case,
except to tell you that we believe we are closing in on a
suspect."

Elysia and A.J. exchanged a look. Was he saying that to
shut them up or could it be true?

"Do try one of these chocolate biscuits, Inspector,"
Elysia murmured—in the same tone the spider would have
asked the fly to have a seat. She offered a plate of cookies.

Jake declined the cookies, drained his teacup in a gulp,
and rose, saying he had to be on his way.

Elysia shot A.J. a glinting look, and A.J. rose, too, although her motive was not the same as Elysia's.

"I'll see you out," she said.

Jake nodded and A.J. accompanied him out to his SUV.

Into his silence she said, "I'm sorry if we're pushing too
hard. You have to realize—"

"I do realize," he said quietly. "Look, I want this solved
nearly as bad as you do." He unlocked his door and then
hesitated. "Are you and Belleson getting back together?"

A.J.'s head jerked up. She couldn't read his expression.
"Uh, no," she said. "He's still gay as far as I can tell."

A reluctant smile tugged at Jake's mouth. He said,
"Would you like to go out again one night?"

Apparently her Snoop Sister status had been forgiven.

"Um, yeah," A.J. said off-handedly.

Jake nodded. "I'll give you a call," he said, and swung
himself inside the SUV, slamming the door after.

"There are tiny yellow feathers on your chin," Elysia
observed when A.J. returned.

A.J. brushed at her chin, then caught the canary-eating-
cat reference. She threw herself down in one of the fat
chintz chairs and chuckled.

Elsyia shook her head.

A.J. straightened up. "Mother, please try to understand. Even if Andy realized he made a mistake—which doesn't seem very likely—we couldn't start over. I couldn't forgive him, and even if I could, I just don't feel the same way about him."

Elysia bit her lip. "But you were so *good* together."

"Maybe. But it's over and I have to move on. *You* have to move on, too."

Elysia's face grew mutinous. "I love Andrew."

"You can still love him. Just don't ask me to."

For a long moment Elysia said nothing, then she sighed and relaxed. "Oh well. After all, I made one or two mistakes in the relationship department before I found my true love, your father. Did I ever tell you about the French count . . . ?"

Elysia was a good cook, she actually seemed to enjoy fussing over meals. A.J. amusedly watched her whipping up chicken cordon bleu for their supper that evening.

As her mother poured herself a glass of mineral water, A.J. asked curiously, "Do you have a sponsor?"

Elysia looked puzzled.

"In AA, I mean."

Elysia chuckled. "Not anymore. No, pumpkin, I *am* a sponsor."

A.J. tried to think of Elysia as a sponsor. At one time it would have been impossible. Now . . . she watched Elysia dive to turn the television sound up on one of those true-crime shows. Actually, it was still impossible.

"Do you know," Elysia said with a funny smile, turning from the TV, "that's the first time you've ever asked about AA."

"Well, I didn't want to pry."

"It's not prying, pumpkin. You can ask me anything you like."

A.J. tried to think if there was anything she wanted to know. Nothing came immediately to mind.

After dinner, Elysia headed off for her AA meeting, and A.J. headed back to the studio, where she'd left her laptop. She logged onto the UPS site and tried to find information on the package that had been delivered to Deer Hollow. But without a tracking number or the name of who had sent the package, she hit a dead end.

It probably didn't matter. The parcel had most likely contained workout clothing or yoga-related gear like mats or ties. Diantha had personally sampled everything used at the studio.

Shuffling through her messages, A.J. noticed again the message from Nicole Manning. An uneasy suspicion slithered through her mind.

There was no return number. The message simply said that Nicole would call back later. The other messages meant little to A.J. The local paper was requesting an interview—which was something she could use later on to promote the studio. Right now she felt the less publicity, the better.

A.J. glanced at her wristwatch. Simon's Yoga for Cops class was starting that evening.

She went upstairs to check it out. There were three female officers—looking a little self-conscious—sitting on mats. Simon, chatting pleasantly about the goals of the class, nodded cordially to A.J.

A.J. listened for a few minutes, wondering if Simon had hit on a surefire way to meet women, before moving next door to the Seniors class.

Surprisingly, the studio had nearly twenty students, and things seemed to be going very well as Denise patiently took her group through their moves. A.J. watched for a few moments as they did warm-ups for body and breath, and decided she liked Denise's laid-back teaching style.

Diantha had been the same age as many of these students,

but a lifetime of fitness and her mental attitude had made her seem a generation younger.

Once the class started struggling to perform sun salutations, A.J. figured she'd seen enough and headed back downstairs.

"Good news," Suze said cheerily. "We've got a full house this evening."

"That *is* good news." A.J. had worried that a lot of students would stay away, at least until Diantha's murder was solved. That didn't seem to be the case. She checked the roster for Doga and was astonished to see that ten dogs and their humans had already signed up.

Maybe she could bring Monster along for a class. Yoga just might help him deal with that obvious sexual frustration.

Yeah. Sure. Or maybe she could use the class to help find Monster a date.

She returned to her office, surprised to realize that it really did feel like her office now, and began to sort through the pile of mail that Suze must have thrown on her desk while she was upstairs.

The fountain in the corner splashed soothingly over the shiny stones in its basin. The clock on the wall quietly ticktocked. She could hear the murmur of voices from down the hall. A feeling very like contentment suffused her.

A large, flat manila envelope from Middlebury Medical Associates addressed to Diantha caught her eye. She tore open the envelope and slid out a letter and what appeared to be some kind of medical test report. Curious, she glanced over the letter. The name Michael Batz stood out. Her brows drew together as she began to read.

She finished reading. Then started back at the top. No mistake. These were Michael Batz's test results from the Middlebury Labs. Apparently Diantha had been testing his blood for health indications to help her best pick a diet suited to his needs. Not so surprising, since Diantha had been working closely with Michael on every aspect of his training. Her interest in organic living had been complemented by the fact that she was a certified dietician.

The part A.J. was having trouble with was the asterisk at the bottom of the page. A notation in the margin confirmed specific information Diantha had requested from the lab: Michael Batz had tested positive for tetrahydrogestrinone (THG).

A.J. rose and went to the medical dictionary on Diantha's shelf. She flipped to the index and then found the entry. She read and then re-read the first sentence:

A designer drug often referred to as THG or "the clear," tetrahydrogestrinone is an anabolic steroid banned by the Food and Drug Administration in 2003. Anabolic androgenic steroids belong to that class of natural and synthetic hormones that stimulate cell growth and division, in particular those relating to muscle and bone, resulting in the enhancement of athletic performance.

A.J. closed the medical dictionary.

Michale Batz, the Olympic wannabe, was using illegal steroids.

Twenty-three

～

A.J. fumbled for the card Jake had given her with his cell phone number. Stomach churning with icy nausea, she dialed his number. Her hands were shaking so badly she nearly dropped the phone.

When Jake's voice mail came on she could have screamed. She waited impatiently for the message to end.

"Jake, it's A.J. I'm at the studio. I was going through some mail for Aunt Di and I found a medical report on Michael Batz." She quickly let him know her findings, ending unsteadily, "Aren't anabolic steroids *injected*? *By syringe?* Whoever killed Aunt Di also used a syringe—and I think Batz would be desperate to keep his illegal drug use quiet. . . ."

At a noise outside the doorway, she looked up and jerked in a sharp breath. Michael Batz filled the door frame, gazing at her with an expression of horror. As their eyes locked, he grabbed for the phone. A.J. jumped back, dropping the paperwork she held.

Batz slammed the receiver down and then lifted it back off the hook.

"Wait a minute," A.J. said quickly, backing away from him. "What good will that do? Think about it. The building is filled with people. Jake—Detective Oberlin—is going to hear that message. You're just making it worse for yourself."

She was babbling as she tried to put some distance between them.

Batz shoved the door closed, and turned to face her. He stood motionless, chest heaving, eyes never leaving her face.

A.J. opened her mouth to scream, but hesitated. She was liable to trigger the very violence she feared. Maybe if she just kept talking . . .

"I know you didn't mean to hurt her. . . ." Did she know any such thing? Administering bee venom pretty much excluded the possibility of heat of the moment.

"I didn't kill her!" Michael cried. "I know how it looks, but you've got to believe me. I'm not a killer. Di was helping me achieve my dream. I never would have hurt her."

"Okay. I do believe you."

"No, you don't!"

"Okay. I don't," A.J. said bravely. "We both know if Aunt Di had reported those test results you'd have been kicked out of the trials. You'd never have made the Olympic team."

His eyes seemed to start from his face. "She wouldn't have turned me in!"

"Then why—" A.J. gestured helplessly to the papers on the floor.

"She didn't believe me when I told her I'd quit. You know how she was: she was like a pit bull. She was going to get the proof and then force me to stop. But I knew that, I understood that. I *was* going to stop. I just needed . . . an edge. Di promised she'd find me another way."

A.J.'s cell phone began to chirp.

They both stared at her purse as though it contained a bomb.

"Please," Batz said shakily, and A.J.'s eyes flew back to his face. "This is my last chance. You can't tell anyone. If I lose this shot, I may as well be dead."

Nothing he had said so far reassured A.J. In fact, everything he had said seemed to reiterate that he had the strongest possible motive for having committed murder. Which meant her job was to reassure *him*. Or at least keep him talking.

"It can't be that bad." She tried to sound soothing.

"What the hell do you know about it?"

Well . . . he had a point.

"It was you at Deer Hollow, wasn't it? You broke into the house and then knocked me down when I arrived."

"I didn't break in. Di gave me a key." He swallowed hard. "And I wasn't trying to hurt you. I just had to get those test results back before anyone else saw them. I knew how it would look. I knew no one would understand."

"And that's what you were looking for in the office the other day?"

Another nod.

"And when you couldn't find the test results here, you tried the house again. You tried to break in because I'd changed the locks by then."

He said miserably, "I didn't think you were home. I saw you having dinner with Detective Oberlin in town—"

A.J.'s phone, which had gone silent, began to ring again.

"Promise me you won't tell anyone," he begged.

"I promise."

"I don't believe you!" His eyes moved desperately around the room. Was he looking for something he could use as a weapon?

The door opened behind Batz, bumping into him.

"I didn't realize you weren't alone," Lily said shortly. She started to close the door.

"Wait!" A.J. shrieked.

Batz grabbed the edge of the door, throwing it open, and pushing Lily out of the way as he ran down the hallway.

"What is your *problem*, Michael?" yelled Lily. She turned back to A.J. "Has everyone in this place gone crazy?"

"Stop him!" A.J. cried.

"Stop him yourself." Lily's eyes fell on the papers on the floor. She stiffened and then knelt, starting to gather them up. Her eyes narrowed, reading the front page.

Legs shaking, A.J. sat down, fumbling for the phone.

Suze burst into the office, knocking Lily off balance.

"Would you watch it?" Lily snarled on her hands and knees, gathering the papers again.

Suze gasped, "A.J., the cops are here!"

A.J. stared at the phone. "That was fast."

"What do you mean the cops are here?" Lily exclaimed, getting to her feet. "What is going on?"

"I think Michael Batz might have killed Aunt Di," A.J. said. She was still rattled from her close call.

"Oh, this is going to be *great* for business!" Lily said. She turned to leave, still holding the medical report.

A.J. reached for the papers Lily held, and Lily stopped in her tracks.

For a long moment Lily stared at her. Suze gazed back and forth uneasily. Finally Lily shrugged, tossed the papers on A.J.'s desk, and walked out.

"What do I tell the cops?" Suze breathed. "A.J., what's going on?"

A.J. rose. "It's okay. I'll talk to them."

She stepped out of her office to find two police officers making their way down the hallway toward her office.

"Ms. Alexander?" The foremost officer was taller with slick black hair and a pencil-thin black mustache. "Are you okay, ma'am? We just got a call from Detective Oberlin saying you might be in trouble."

One thing about Jake, he wasn't someone who wasted a lot of time second-guessing himself, A.J. reflected. Not that she was complaining. "I'm okay," she told them. "I believe Michael Batz—the man who just walked out of here—might have been responsible for my aunt's death."

A.J. became uncomfortably aware that she had an audience, the hall crowded with seniors and her staff.

"Mike Batz?" The officer sounded shocked, and A.J. remembered what Jake had said about Batz being a hometown hero. "Did he make a statement to that effect?"

"No. He denied it."

"But he attacked you?"

She thought it over. Closing the office door was not exactly an attack. "Well, no. But . . ."

"But he threatened you?"

"Yes. Sort of. Not exactly." She realized she had slid out onto some very thin ice.

The other officer said, "Ma'am, did Batz verbally or physically threaten you?"

"Not specifically," she admitted. "We had a sort of confrontation. He wouldn't let me out of my office."

"We need to pick him up," the second officer said to the first one.

The first one said unwillingly, "Maybe, but what's a 'sort of confrontation'?"

The glass doors to the studio shoved open and Jake strode past the front desk making straight for A.J.'s office. She spotted him with relief. "Jake!"

"You okay?" he asked, his hard face seeming to relax a fraction.

"I'm fine. Thanks for sending the cavalry so fast."

"Where's Batz?" Jake demanded of the uniformed officers.

The two officers exchanged a look as though each suspected the other might have him in custody.

The first one said, "There's some question about—"

The second one started, "We were just going to—"

"I should hope to hell!" Jake said, disgusted. "Go bring him in."

The two uniformed officers departed hastily out the glass doors. Jake steered A.J. into her office and closed the door firmly on the crowd gathered in the hall.

"What happened?" His voice was still level, but he exuded a cool, dangerous competency that she found incredibly attractive. "I heard you gasp and then drop the phone."

She explained everything that had occurred between herself and Batz. Jake heard her out in silence.

"He has an alibi," he said at last, when she had wound to a stop. "He was at the track in view of witnesses."

"He must not think it will hold up."

Jake said, "I know you've had a shock, but let's look at this logically. His panic seems to revolve around his test results getting out. He didn't admit to killing your aunt. In fact, he repeatedly denied it."

"It doesn't matter," A.J. insisted. "Everything points to him. He has three motives: the money my aunt left him, their adulterous affair, and the fact that he's using illegal drugs that would get him disqualified from the Olympic trials. What more do you need?"

"Means, opportunity, physical evidence linking him to the crime. All we have is a motive."

"*Three* motives."

"I don't care if it's a baker's dozen. Motive isn't enough."

"He admitted to breaking into Deer Hollow to try and find the test results."

"He didn't break in if he had a key."

"But he tried again after I changed the locks!"

"If you want to press charges, we can get him for illegal entry and trespassing."

She stared at him. "I can't believe you're defending him!"

"I'm not defending him. If you'll notice, we're going to haul him in for questioning. I'm just saying, this doesn't necessarily prove anything." He looked at the medical report on A.J.'s desk. "I'll have to take this."

"Fine," said A.J. "But if it wasn't Batz, who was it?"

"That's the point of an investigation," Jake said with irritating patience. "To try to find that out."

"What about his wife?"

"Lorraine?" Jake got a funny look on his face. "We're checking into Lorraine's movements." His face softened. "Look, I know this is rough on you. You want immediate answers, but it takes time to build a case. We don't want to make a mistake and end up letting someone guilty walk."

She nodded wearily. All at once she was tired beyond belief, the surge of adrenaline draining away and leaving her feeling vulnerable and weak—a feeling she hated. She put her hand briefly over her eyes.

"Are you okay?" Jake asked with unexpected gentleness.

She lowered her hand. "Yes."

"Are you done here? Why don't we go get a drink?"

Three seconds before she'd been too tired to stand up; suddenly she had energy enough to carry her into next week.

A.J. followed Jake to a nearby pub called the Cock and Bull. Inside it was dark and cozy in a secluded-leather-booth kind of way. They settled at a table in the back. Jake greeted several of the patrons as they passed crowded tables; A.J. felt curious gazes on her.

"Hi, Jake!" said a perky little blonde waitress who arrived at their booth half a minute after they sat down.

"Hey, Deede," Jake returned.

"How come we never see you anymore?"

"I'm around," he said easily.

"Not often enough!"

A.J. rolled her eyes. Deede and Jake exchanged a few more pleasantries, then Deede finally took their drink orders and walked away, wiggling her cute little behind.

It looked as though A.J.'s earlier doubts had been completely unfounded; Jake appeared to be a perfectly healthy, precertified, red-blooded, heterosexual male. Which she was happy about—on behalf of womankind everywhere. A.J. resumed trying to come up with a way to question Jake about the case without antagonizing him, when, to her exasperation, Deede sauntered back with their drinks.

"Give me a call sometime," she said, placing A.J.'s drink in front of her without so much as the slightest glance.

Jake smiled that wickedly attractive smile. "I just might do that," he said easily.

A.J. sipped her drink and told herself she really didn't give a damn whether Jake dated every chick in town, she had no intention of getting seriously involved with anyone for a very long time.

When Deede finally departed for real, she said, "Just out of curiosity, what was Michael Batz wearing while he was training at the track the morning Aunt Di was murdered?"

"I'm not following you."

"It was a chilly morning, right? Was he wearing baggy sweats and maybe a hooded sweatshirt? These witnesses who saw him working out, did they talk to him? Did they see him up close? Or did they just see him running around the track from a distance?"

"No one spoke to him, but he's well-known there."

"If his wife is about the same height . . . She's a runner, too, you know. From a distance . . ."

To her surprise he actually seemed to briefly entertain her theory. "That would be a hell of a chance. They couldn't guarantee that no one would speak to him that morning."

"Whoever killed Aunt Di took a hell of a chance attacking her in the studio. That place is like a civic center. People come and go all the time."

Jake's cell phone rang. "Excuse me."

He slid out of the booth and walked away. A.J. waited, sipping her drink.

Returning to the booth, Jake said, "I apologize, but I've got to go. They've brought Batz in for questioning."

She nodded. Jake threw some bills—too many, in A.J.'s opinion—on the table, and they walked out together.

Jake waited while A.J. dug out her keys.

"Are you free for dinner one night this week?" he asked as she unlocked her car door.

Her heart did a little flutter as though it had dozed right through that self-lecture about not wanting to get involved for a very long time. She said, "I'll have to check with Monster. He may have plans."

"Okay, let me know what he says." He offered that crooked grin.

A.J. was wondering why she had to be such a smart-ass, because now she would have to call *him* back and try to set up which evening—and in the middle of these confused thoughts, Jake reached over, tilted her face up to his, and kissed her.

A warm pressure against her mouth, and her lips parted just the tiniest bit. He tasted warm, too, and kind of smoky-sweet from the bourbon he had drunk. Different from Andy. Very different. Nor was it a tentative kiss; it was an expert kiss: brief but to the point.

He raised his head. She felt his breath on her face, blinked into eyes gazing curiously into her own. A.J.'s heart pounded as hard as if it were her first kiss. Her lips actually seemed to tingle.

"That's nice," Jake said, letting her go. "Can Monster be bribed?"

"Uh . . . sorry?"

"I've got Wednesday night off. Do you think the mutt might give you the evening off in exchange for a couple of knuckle bones?"

"I think so," A.J. said.

Where *have you been?"*

"Please tell me you're not waiting up for me," she said, startled to find Elysia pacing the floor after she soundlessly let herself into her mother's house a short while after she had parted from Jake.

Monster watched them interestedly from the rug in front of the fireplace.

"We need to discuss the case," Elysia said—which was not really an answer.

"Whoa. *We* don't have a case." A.J. really didn't have the energy for this. She just wanted to go to bed and think about the feel of Jake's mouth on hers and what that meant. "And even if we did have a case, couldn't it wait till the morning?"

Elysia, wearing a pale pink penoir set more suited to the heroine of a romance novel than a former *221B Baker Street* sleuth, stopped pacing, her gown frothing around her ankles. "Something came up at tonight's AA meeting."

"What?"

"I found out who the yoga tie belonged to."

"Yoga tie? I'm not . . ." She remembered then: the green tie that had been used to try and make it look like Diantha had been strangled. "Who?"

Elysia bit her lip. "I can't tell you. I can't break the anonymity of the meeting."

"What are you talking about? You're not a doctor. You're not a priest. You were at AA."

"Everything said at the meetings is confidential. I can't break that confidence."

"So it's okay to let someone get away with murder?"

"Of course not."

A.J. stared at her mother. "Do you think this person is Aunt Di's killer?"

"No. Absolutely not."

"But he knows who the killer is?"

"She." Elysia's gaze met A.J.'s "I don't know. It's possible."

"It's Chloe, isn't it?"

Elysia seemed to struggle inwardly.

"I know it is. You convinced her to go to AA with you." A.J. tried to put this new piece of information in context with what she now knew about Michael Batz. Was Batz seeking treatment for his drug use? Was THG addictive? A.J. didn't think so, but she didn't know. But if Chloe and Batz attended the same AA group perhaps Chloe had discovered something incriminating about Batz—and if the green yoga tie was his, surely that clinched it? "If she thinks she knows who killed Aunt Di, she needs to come forward."

"I don't know that she really knows anything—beyond who the tie belongs to."

"How can she be sure it's the same tie?"

Elysia said awkwardly, "Because this person's tie is missing and it sounds exactly like the one that was used on Di."

"Does she have any theory as to how the tie ended up knotted around Aunt Di's throat?" A.J.'s voice shook.

"Of course not," Elysia said again.

"If she suspects someone, that person may also suspect that Chloe knows enough to incriminate him."

Elysia didn't say anything.

"What possible reason could she have for withholding this information?"

"She's frightened," Elysia said reluctantly.

"She ought to be frightened! She's withholding information in a murder case. Not only could she get herself arrested, she could get herself killed."

Elysia flinched. "I'll try again to convince her to go to the authorities."

"Doesn't she understand—?" A.J. stopped, the truth dawning slowly. "The tie belongs to Chloe, doesn't?"

Elysia nodded.

Twenty-four

❦

"**Nicole** Manning on line one," Suze said over the intercom.

"Thanks, Suze." A.J. picked up the handset. "Hello, Nicole. This is A.J. Alexander, Diantha's niece."

"Oh my *God*," Nicole exclaimed in a breathy Marilyn Monroe voice. "Oh my God, J.B., I couldn't believe the news! To think she's *gone*! And to think I missed the funeral. I mean, I *so* wanted to be there for her. If I'd only known!"

"Thank you," A.J. said mechanically. She all at once remembered why she hadn't been sorry when Nicole decided she needed to move her account to a large and prestigious PR firm.

"I'm serious, you know? Di was more than my teacher. She was my spiritual mentor. I *totally* owe my success to her. When I was first trying out for the role of Bambi Marciano in *Family Business*, Di was the one who helped me find my focus. My center."

Nicole continued to talk—mostly about Nicole.

"It's so sweet of you to have called," A.J. cooed when she could finally get a word in. It was obvious Nicole didn't remember her from Adam, which was fine. She didn't have time or energy to share an International Coffee Moment with Nicole.

"Well, the thing *is*," Nicole said quickly, "Di had asked me for a little *favor*, and I just wanted to make sure—that is—" She gave a light, artificial laugh. "I was wondering if my package had arrived safely."

"What package?" A.J. asked with a sinking feeling.

"Well, as I'm sure you know, Laurie Avon—who is just *fabulous*—designs all the gowns on the show, and Di had this *treasure* of an idea that I could loan one of Laurie's gowns to Di for one of her little students. Some poor kiddie who needed a dress for a prom or something."

"Oh . . . wow" was all that A.J. could manage.

"Sooo. . . ." Nicole gave a nervous little laugh. "I just wanted to make sure the gown arrived safely."

"Uh, I can check for you. Would you happen to have a tracking number on that," A.J. asked.

When she concluded her phone conversation with Nicole, she dropped her face in her hands. She had the most awful feeling that the package destroyed in the fire at Deer Hollow was Nicole Manning's seventeen-thousand-dollar Laurie Avon original.

Taking a deep breath, she signed into her laptop and surfed over to the UPS site. With the tracking number Nicole had supplied, she was able to verify that, yep, by some ghastly coincidence, UPS had delivered the designer gown the very afternoon someone had decided to firebomb A.J.'s residence.

Which created two problems: how to explain to Nicole that the gown she had borrowed on behalf of Diantha had gone up in smoke, and how to come up with a suitable replacement garment for Chloe? On the bright side, if Chloe was in jail, she wouldn't need a designer ball gown.

"Mail call!" Suze chirped, depositing a stack of letters, magazines, and a parcel on A.J.'s desk.

"You are *way* too cheerful this morning," A.J. informed her.

Suze giggled. "Hey, it's a wonderful day in the neighborhood! Did you see the roster for your class tonight? You've got twenty people—and their pooches—signed up for Doga."

"You're kidding," A.J. said weakly. *"Twenty?"*

"Two-oh."

A.J. swallowed hard. "I think I need to go home and practice my moves on Monster."

Suze giggled another one of those happy giggles and disappeared.

A.J. examined the parcel. Special delivery from Andy. She dug her letter opener out and cut the tape. There was a note inside. Curiously, she opened it.

> *Thank you for ten wonderful years. Thank you for your love and trust and faith. I'm sorry I let you down. I know it's too soon for you to forgive—and I don't want you to forget. I want to stay part of your life if you'll let me. You'll always be part of mine. Love you.*

> *Andy*

Tears pricked her eyes. She pulled aside the tissue, absently thinking that it was so like Andy to carefully wrap everything in soft tissue—A.J. would have settled for Ziploc bags.

Inside the box was her favorite beaded cashmere sweater, the pearls Andy had given her for their wedding—and which she had thrown in his face before she'd walked out of their apartment for the final time—her favorite body lotion, a box of Godiva chocolates, and Bear, the small stuffed teddy she'd had since she was ten.

She sighed and wiped her eyes with the back of her hand. Well, there were worse ways to end than friends.

She gathered up everything and put it back in the box, and quickly sorted through the rest of the mail and her phone messages, lingering for a moment over Nicole's number.

That was one piece of bad news she could wait to deliver. Of all the terrible luck . . .

It *had* been bad luck, right, that the dress had been delivered on the same day as the fire?

Except . . . what was the motive for that fire?

It couldn't have been a serious attempt on her life. She hadn't even been home. Was it a simple case of vandalism? But why target Deer Hollow Farm? The house wasn't on the main drag, and as far as A.J. knew there had been no previous incidents of vandalism or harassment.

Could anyone have known the dress was being delivered that day? And even if someone had known, why in the world would someone want to blow up an evening gown?

Elysia was out when A.J. arrived at Starlight Farm. That was a relief. A.J. wasn't up to another discussion of how they were going to trap Michael Batz into a confession of murder. By the time they had gone to bed the night before, Elysia had been asking about the feasibility of wiretaps and surveillance cameras. If A.J. told her about Nicole Manning and the destroyed designer gown, the conversation would naturally move to Chloe, and that was practically guaranteed to lead to an argument. She couldn't risk it. Over the past two weeks she and Elysia had approached something very like friendship. She didn't want to endanger that.

Taking out the Doga video tape she'd had FedExed a few days earlier, she headed for her mother's exercise room, popped it in the DVD/VCR player, and sat down on the floor to watch. She needed to learn all she could, and she didn't want to educate herself in front of the people who technically worked for her. For the time being she needed to train in private.

If you could call this training, she thought, watching the woman on the video.

"Monster, I hope you're taking notes," A.J. told the dog sleeping under her feet.

Diantha had hoped that Lily and A.J. would work together, but A.J. knew with each passing day that she and Lily were never going to be partners. She kept hoping that Lily would reach the same conclusion and leave Sacred Balance. Unfortunately Lily seemed to be using the same strategy on A.J.

Watching the video twice through, A.J. reassured herself that if she kept a positive attitude and a playful spirit it couldn't be that hard, right?

She decided to treat herself to a long, pampering soak. She was finding hot baths and her yoga exercises were paying off in reduced back pain.

Elysia's bathroom had all the amenities of a spa, including a sunken whirlpool bath. Soon A.J. was soaking in wonderful lavender and peppermint bath salts, scented candles burning on the ledge next to her while she flipped through a stack of magazines she had brought from the studio. Her aunt had subscribed to everything from *Yoga Journal* to *Natural Curatives*.

It was interesting stuff, but nothing that was going to replace *Allure* or *Cosmopolitan* as far as A.J. was concerned. She skimmed an article on nasal irrigation, wrinkling her nose in disgust, moved on to another piece on meditation, found herself unable to focus, and picked up the latest copy of *Natural Curatives*. Trying not to get the pages soggy, A.J. browsed, pausing over an article about bee venom and arthritis.

She remembered Aunt Di once saying that there was

nothing in the world that couldn't be put to some productive use. Bees obviously had their uses—her mouth watered thinking of homemade biscuits slathered in real butter and fresh honey—but who would have thought bee venom could ease the suffering of people crippled with arthritis?

Apparently the anti-inflammatory properties of bee venom were used to treat all kinds of diseases, including multiple sclerosis, tendonitis, and fibromyalgia. The patients interviewed for the article had used live honey bees to sting themselves numerous times to bring relief from their assorted ailments. Unfortunately it sounded like clinical case studies had been few and far between.

A.J. tossed the magazine aside and pulled the drain plug.

Dressing in jeans and a T-shirt, she went downstairs and started supper. She had no idea what Elysia's plans were for the evening, but since A.J. needed to eat light and early, she figured she might as well cook for two.

Turning on the television for background noise—Elysia seemed to have a TV in every room of the house—she explored Elysia's immaculate kitchen. Although she couldn't remember her mother cooking in all the years A.J. had been growing up, Elysia now seemed to own every culinary toy known to man or TV chef, as well as an impressive library of cookbooks. And Elysia was a pretty good cook, A.J. had to admit. Maybe cooking had afforded Elysia a kind of therapy. Or maybe it was simply a hobby. A.J. was beginning to realize that she didn't know her mother nearly as well as she had imagined.

The local news came on with the usual morbid focus on death and small-scale disaster. She listened with half an ear as she read through a vegetarian cookbook, which must surely have been a gift from Aunt Di. Elysia was definitely of the carnivore class.

The buxom and gloating TV anchor woman animatedly gave the latest on a teen shooting in the next county.

A.J. tuned out the bad news as she found a recipe for vegetable stir-fry that sounded pretty good. As she chopped zucchini and carrots, she realized that she too sort of enjoyed cooking, and that she did feel better when she ate healthy. Not that she was ready to renounce her passion for products labeled "Kraft" and "Nabisco," but she was willing to cut back a little. In fact, she was actually developing a taste for crisp fresh vegetables and fruit.

Maybe when the repairs were complete at Deer Hollow she would invite Jake over for dinner one evening.

A.J. glanced at the television. The news anchor had been replaced by an on-location reporter who was even more buxom and animated. A.J. sighed inwardly. The world seemed to be an increasingly violent place. Even out here in the sticks no one seemed safe from senseless violence.

She moved around the kitchen, stepping over Monster, who must have been a rug in his previous incarnation. She could tell he still missed Diantha—well, why not? She did, too. She stooped, giving him a quick hug.

"Are you going to be my yoga buddy tonight?"

Monster wagged his tail.

Elysia was still not home by the time A.J. finished preparing supper. She checked her cell phone and found a message from her mother saying she would be dining with Bradley Meagher.

Now that sounded promising, A.J. thought, serving herself stir-fry. Perhaps they would at last find out what was in that mysterious codicil to Diantha's will—although it might be moot at this point. A.J. had a strong suspicion that the codicil stipulated that Michael needed to stay drug free in order to inherit.

She ate her meal, put away the leftovers, tidied up the kitchen, and looked at the clock above the cupboards.

"Showtime," she announced, ignoring the butterflies suddenly flitting around her stomach.

Monster smiled his doggy smile.

Running upstairs, she changed into her workout gear, found Monster's leash, and selected a baby blue band for him to wear—which he accepted with bemused grace.

"Who's going to be the handsomest dog in class?" she inquired, and Monster tried to lick her chin. She ducked back just in time, laughing.

The parking lot at Sacred Balance was packed with cars. She wedged the Volvo in next to the Stevensons' yellow Hummer, which reminded her that she'd never had a chance to talk to Jennifer about paying for the dry cleaning of her Jil Sander coat. It wasn't the money; it was the principle of the thing. A.J. knew her aunt would not have let such behavior go unchallenged, and if A.J. was going to try to fill Diantha's shoes, she was going to have to be willing to make herself occasionally unpopular. It was kind of a philosophical shift for a former marketing consultant.

She squeezed out past the crookedly parked Hummer, wondering why Jennifer was there since there was no Yoga for Young Adults that night.

Suze was still behind the front desk when she walked in with Monster.

"You're still here?"

Suze smiled self-consciously. "I wanted to see if . . . I was hoping we could talk about something."

Did Suze want a pay raise? How much was A.J. paying her, because Suze's friendly face was beginning to be worth its weight in gold. She smiled. "How about after class?"

"Um, okay." Suze smiled nervously.

Uh-oh. Hopefully Suze wasn't about to give notice. Welcome to the joys of management, A.J. reflected.

On the first floor the Advanced Yoga class was underway. A.J. paused in the doorway to watch the students warm up, making pretzels of their limber bodies. She remembered being that flexible once. And she would be again. It would just take time. And a lot of determination.

Her nerves tightened watching Lily snapping out orders like a field marshal preparing the troops.

It was only too easy to picture Lily as a murderess, but if Lily were going to murder someone, she'd probably do it with her bare hands. She wouldn't have the patience for messing around with hypos and honeybees.

Lily looked up, caught A.J.'s gaze, and glowered.

A.J. smiled at her with bright insincerity and than made her way to the second floor to peek in on Yoga for Cops. There were now six students, all of them female. Simon was virtually beaming as the lady law enforcers went through their moves. A.J. bit back a grin. She tried to picture Jake enrolling in a yoga course and failed.

Glancing at her watch, she realized she was on the verge of being late for teaching her first class. She hurried down the hall. The door to the studio where the Doga class was to be held was closed. Monster began to wag his tail. A.J. pushed open the door and froze.

The brightly lit room was in pandemonium: dogs barking, people yelling—the racket bounced off the hardwood floors. Monster's ears flattened and he tried to back out of the room. A.J. couldn't blame him—escape was her first instinct, too.

"Come on, we're a team," she muttered to Monster, and pulled his leash short. He gave her a doubtful look, but padded obediently beside her as she made her way through the mob to the front of the room.

She could see Chloe and her overweight beagle, as well as several of the other kids from Yoga for Young Adults— including Jennifer Stevenson. Jennifer had brought along a large, bad-tempered-looking purebred German shepherd— so perhaps this would not be the night to bring up the matter of her dry-cleaning bill. The shepherd snapped at Monster as he walked past.

Monster scooted out of the way and gave the other dog a look of almost human outrage.

"Jennifer, control your dog," A.J. ordered sharply.

Jennifer merely gave her a brazen smile before turning to her ever-present posse, who obligingly went off into peels of shrill giggles.

It was going to be a very long class, A.J. thought.

She took her place at the front of the room. "Okay, everyone. Please line up in three straight rows."

The human students obediently began to line up. A.J. took notice of Charlayne Lewis, her old friend Nancy's daughter. Originally Charlayne had seemed to belong to Jennifer's inner circle, but now Charlayne, like Chloe, was on the outside. She stayed at the back of the room with Stu Snyder. *Stu.* A penny dropped for A.J. Stu Snyder must be *the* Stu—the young man Jennifer had been caught with behind the gymnasium by her former boyfriend Steve, who was now Chloe's boyfriend.

Jeez, the place was turning into *Dawson's Creek.*

"Okay." A.J. tried clapping her hands for attention. "We're going to try Down Dog," she announced, which got a few laughs, although she wasn't trying to be funny: Down Dog was, in fact, a yoga pose. "No, seriously," she said. She made a lie-down motion, and Monster slowly settled down on all fours with a groan.

This got more chuckles, and the two-legged students began to try and convince the four-legged students to cooperate.

It occurred to A.J. that a good prerequisite for Doga would be obedience training because half the dogs in the room—and a number of the humans—had apparently never taken direction before.

Jennifer's dog immediately started a snarling match with a silver-haired lady's Akita.

"Fritz!" Jennifer yelled ineffectually before dissolving into giggles. Her friends—neither of them girls A.J. could remember seeing previously—began laughing as well.

"Jennifer!" A.J. called out in annoyance.

Jennifer yanked on Fritz's choke chain and turned an expression of total innocence toward A.J.

A.J. wondered how her aunt had managed to deal with Jennifer. A.J. was already considering banishing her from Sacred Balance. And she could just imagine how that would go over with Lily if she threw the daughter of the town's most influential family out on her ear.

On the far side of the room, a schnauzer got into a slanging match with a shih tzu, and a standard poodle decided to take a bite out of a collie; luckily the collie was mostly hair, and no serious damage was done, but suddenly it was like a barroom brawl for canines. Dogs were growling and snapping, and the human students weren't doing much better.

A.J. stepped in to try to help sort out the dogs and owners.

Over the clamor she heard Jennifer's harsh voice, though she couldn't make out the words. She did hear Chloe's shrill, "You had your chance and you blew it! Steve loves me now!"

A.J. moved toward them in time to hear Jennifer sneer, "Are you sure you're not still on drugs? Because you are *definitely* delusional!"

Chloe drew herself up tall, her face flushed with anger, her eyes bright. "I don't care what you think anymore, Jennifer. Di was right. You're a sad, unhappy, lonely person who only cares about herself."

Jennifer went rigid. "Oh yeah? We'll see who's pathetic when you're in jail for killing Di!"

Taking its cue from Jennifer's agitated voice, Fritz the German shepherd lunged at Chloe. Chloe started back and fell over her beagle, which let out a heart-rending shriek and went scrabbling away, dragging his leash.

"Jeeeezus," A.J. exclaimed. She tried to push through the dogs and people toward the quarreling young women.

Fritz started off in hot pursuit after the beagle, and several of the other dogs decided to join in the fun, dragging their human owners with them. The double doors in the back of the room swung open, and Lily narrowly stepped out of the way as the beagle dived through the doorway followed seconds later by Fritz and a pack of yapping dogs and protesting owners.

Not that A.J. had time to notice, let alone deal with that disaster, as she was occupied with trying to haul Jennifer off of Chloe.

Chloe was squealing and writhing while Jennifer swore an ugly stream of invective, grabbing clumps of the other girl's hair.

"Are you two *crazy?*" A.J. tried to pull Jennifer back, ducking as Jennifer turned and tried to slug her.

"What is going on here?" yelled Lily. One thing for Lily, her voice *definitely* carried. She'd have been very useful in a riot—which A.J.'s class was quickly turning into.

Locking her arms around Jennifer, A.J. tried to throw her off, her own back twinging forbiddingly at the unexpected strain. She was *so* going to regret that move later.

"Get your hands off of me!" Jennifer screamed at A.J. Lily moved in to try to help restrain her. Jennifer clawed at her face. Lily jerked back.

"Why, you little—!"

Sobbing, Chloe scrambled to her feet and ran for the door. Jennifer broke free of Lily's grasp and sprinted after her.

"Don't let her go!" A.J. yelled.

Students gazed at her in bewilderment. No one tried to stop Jennifer as she pelted through the doors after Chloe.

Lily, apparently losing interest in Jennifer, swung her sights back on A.J. "Would you like to explain to me what's going on here?" she demanded.

"I don't need to explain myself or my teaching methods to you!" A.J. shot back. Not that she would exactly describe the last fifteen minutes as her teaching method, but—

"When are you going to face facts? You don't belong here. You have no right to be here. You're turning the studio into a joke!"

"I have every right to be here," A.J. cried, oblivious to the startled and fascinated audience still in the room. "Whether you like it or not, this is my legacy, not yours. This is what Aunt Di intended—well, not *this*—but my being here and being a part of the studio. You can't change that. And if you killed my aunt thinking—"

"*Killed* her?" screamed Lily. "Now you're accusing me of murdering Di? Are you out of your tiny little mind?"

"You don't have an alibi, and it's pretty obvious you're willing to do anything to get the studio."

A.J. knew she needed to stop now. She was one step from getting herself sued for slander. Besides, she had zero proof that Lily had killed Di. In fact, as much as she disliked Lily—which was considerably—Lily was pretty low on her list of suspects.

"To keep the studio out of *your* hands. To keep *you* from destroying everything the rest of us have worked for—everything that Di and I worked for. I *loved* Di. No, we didn't see everything eye to eye, but I respected her and admired her and *loved* her. You know what you're problem is? You want to push in where you don't belong and be part of something you have no part of. You're jealous. You're a jealous, over-aged adolescent, and it's pathetic."

A.J. froze.

Jealous . . . adolescent . . .

And what had Jake said the first night they went for dinner?

Somebody didn't do his homework. . . .

Lily stared at her and then waved a hand in front of her face. "Hello? Did you hear me? Did you hear a word I said?"

"Oh my God," A.J. whispered. "I think I know who killed Aunt Di."

Twenty-five

❧

"**Really?**" sneered Lily. "Who is it now?"

A.J. ignored her, running to the door. "Where are they?" she cried. "Jennifer and Chloe?"

"They ran out," Stu answered. Charlayne, stricken-faced, stood beside him, clutching her miniature schnauzer like a stuffed toy.

A.J. stared at the two of them. "What happened between Jennifer and my aunt?"

"Why ask us?" Stu returned defensively.

Charlayne, a younger, slimmer version of her mother, gazed solemnly back at A.J. "It was good. It was great. The best. At first."

"At first?"

Reluctantly, Charlayne nodded. "Jen was always wild. Even when we were kids. She was always doing stuff to try to get her parent's attention—her mother's attention: drinking, smoking. She got a tattoo when she was thirteen. She was with a guy before we even started high school."

Unexpectedly A.J. felt a twinge for the lost kid Jennifer must have been.

"Then a couple of years ago we all started taking yoga. Di was the only one who could get through to her. Jen loved her. I mean, she laughed at her and pretended she didn't take it seriously, but really she loved the discipline, loved the whole tough-love thing." Charlayne bit her lip.

A.J. thought rapidly. "But then Chloe's dad died and Chloe fell apart . . . and Di started focusing on Chloe."

"I think it was that whole thing with Steve," Charlayne said. She cast her uncomfortable-looking boyfriend an apologetic glance. "She just . . . went off the deep end."

"*How* off the deep end?" demanded A.J.

Stu said gruffly. "Be quiet, Charlie."

"You think she killed Di, don't you?" A.J. charged. She stared from one to the other.

Charlayne's eyes filled with tears. She shook her head. "I can't believe that," she said. "It's too horrible."

It *was* horrible, A.J. thought, but maybe the most horrible part was that it could have been prevented if Jennifer's parents had bothered to involve themselves in her life.

"A.J.!" Lily yelled across the room.

A.J. ignored her, leaving Stu and Charlayne, and running down the hall past milling dogs and their owners. "Has anyone seen Chloe or Jennifer?" she called.

Someone pointed down the staircase. A.J. raced down the stairs, coming to a halt as she spotted Jake and a pair of uniformed officers starting up.

"Jake!" Her relief was cut short when she saw the grimness of his expression as he reached her. "What—?"

"We're looking for Chloe Williams," he said quietly.

A.J. stared, realizing the significance of the uniformed officers. "No. Listen to me. I think I've figured it out."

Exasperation tightened his face. "A.J., I don't have time to argue with you. Is she up there?"

"I'm telling you, you've got it wrong! I'm positive she didn't kill my aunt."

"*A.J.*" His anger was genuine and startling. "This isn't up for debate. Do you want me to slap you with an obstruction charge?"

"She ran downstairs a few minutes ago—with Jennifer Stevenson in pursuit." Now A.J. was equally angry. "And if you'd listen to what I'm trying to say—"

Jake's face had changed before she finished speaking. "Stevenson? The yellow Hummer? She nearly plowed into us as we were pulling into the parking lot."

"Was there another car in front of her? A little Toyota?"

"Yeah," said one of the officers trailing Jake. "There was a Toyota a few yards ahead."

"Jennifer's chasing Chloe. Don't you see what that means?"

"Going which way?" Jake interrupted, turning to the uniformed officer.

"North."

"Away from town—and home?" He seemed puzzled.

A.J.'s eyes went wide with realization. She sucked in a ragged breath. "Oh God! Chloe must be headed for Starlight Farm. She's running to my mother. She's leading Jennifer straight to my mother!"

Jake stared at her. Then he nodded to the uniformed officers. "Okay, let's head out to Starlight Farm." He turned to A.J. "Stay here. I'll call you as soon as we've got them in—"

"You have to be kidding me," A.J. interrupted. She moved past him, starting down the stairs. "I'm not waiting anywhere. You're talking about my *mother*."

"Which is why you're staying right here." He grabbed her arm, his fingers hard in her soft flesh.

A.J. wriggled free. "Look, either I'm going with you or I'm driving on my own, but I'm not staying here when my mother is in danger!"

After a fraught moment Jake seemed to realize they had reached a stand-off. "All right," he growled. "Come on."

The four of them ran downstairs, past the front desk.

"Wow," Suze exclaimed as they rushed past. "Did the class go *that* bad?"

Outside, the uniforms headed for their car, and Jake hustled A.J. into the SUV.

"Buckle up," he ordered, starting the engine. He switched the lights and siren on, and they tore out of the parking lot, the other marked car in pursuit.

"Maybe you better explain to me what you think is going on." Jake had to raise his voice to be heard over the siren. "You think Jennifer Stevenson killed your aunt?"

"Yes, I do. And I realize that she's only nineteen and the daughter of one of the most important families in this county—"

"I don't give a damn about any of that," Jake said shortly. "Why do you think she killed your aunt?"

"I don't know if she really meant to kill her or only frighten her; maybe she doesn't even know for sure. I think she was extremely angry with Aunt Di for what she perceived as a final betrayal. She's horribly jealous of Chloe Williams, both because Chloe ended up with Jennifer's boyfriend Steve Cussler, and because Di was lavishing so much attention on Chloe, trying to help her stay straight after rehab."

"This is very shaky."

"No, it's not. I was just listening to the news this afternoon about a teen shooting in the next county over the same kind of thing. One kid blamed another kid for stealing his girlfriend. It happens. It happens with adults: someone feels jealous or rejected or humiliated and suddenly turns to violence. And, in theory, we're a lot wiser and have a lot more self-control than an adolescent or even someone in her twenties."

"Go on," he said tersely.

"I think the final straw was a dress that Aunt Di borrowed from Nicole Manning. She's the star of—"

"I know who Nicole Manning is."

"Okay. Well, the parcel that was destroyed in the fire at Deer Hollow? That was a designer gown Aunt Di borrowed from Nicole for Chloe to wear to the Midwinter Ball, which Steve—Jennifer's old boyfriend—invited her to attend. I think Jennifer found out about this damn dress and it tipped her over the edge. I think she was hurt and angry and she wanted to pay Aunt Di and Chloe back."

She spared a look out the window as they hurtled down the road. They had to be doing about ninety; it didn't seem nearly fast enough.

To keep herself from thinking about what was happening miles ahead of them, she said, "Do you remember the comment you made when we went out to dinner and you told me about whoever killed Aunt Di not having done his homework?"

"No."

"It was the whole overcomplication of the yoga tie around Aunt Di's neck. She was killed with bee venom, and anyone with half a brain would have to realize that was going to show up in an autopsy, so what was the point of the yoga tie?"

"I know what you think the point was," Jake said. "You think Jennifer used that yoga tie to implicate Chloe."

"Yes, I do. I don't think Jennifer cared whether anyone initially believed Di was strangled or not. I think her intent was to put something implicating Chloe at the scene of the crime, because that's what this was all about. Jealousy of Chloe."

"I'm sorry," Jake said, "but I just don't see a ball gown as a motive for murder."

"I'm not sure it's a motive the way you or I understand motive, but I don't understand why a teen would go into his high school and shoot a bunch of other kids. Jennifer's

hatred of Chloe is pathological. I know she blames Chloe
for stealing her boyfriend; there may be other injuries real
or imagined. She never misses an opportunity to embarrass
or humiliate Chloe. She attacked her in class this evening."

Jake was shaking his head. "A.J., it's not going to hold
up. If Chloe had been killed, then yes, your theory might
make sense, but what was the motive for killing your aunt?"

"Aunt Di was very popular with these kids, and I think
there was a certain amount of rivalry for her attention. If
you knew my aunt . . . She was always on a crusade. Sometimes it was to save a tree or stop kids from drinking milk,
and sometimes it was about rescuing a person. I think for a
time she was involved in rescuing Jennifer, but then she
turned her attention to rescuing Chloe. I don't know how
that changed her relationship with Jennifer. I can't imagine
she stopped caring about her, but maybe Jennifer believed
she did."

Jake seemed to be listening.

"Or it could be that she saw Jennifer for the emotionally
troubled young woman she is. I'm not sure how that would
have played out, but she might have suggested Jennifer
seek counseling. She might have discussed speaking to
Jennifer's parents."

"This is pure speculation." Jake tapped the high beams
as they hit a dark and desolate stretch of road. It seemed to
be taking forever to cross the valley, A.J. thought, gripping
her icy hands together. She had to hang on to something
besides hope. The girls had at least a five-minute head
start. Five minutes was a long time when you were fighting
for your life.

"You must come across stuff like this," she said, staring
at his profile. "You're a cop."

"I'm not a psychologist," Jake said.

She took a deep breath, trying to calm herself, to stay focused. "You said motive isn't as important as means and opportunity. Okay, look at means. Jennifer's mom is crippled

with arthritis. According to Nancy Lewis—Dr. Lewis—
she's tried every cure under the sun. I just read an article
this very afternoon about how Dr. Joseph Broadman tried
to promote the widespread use of apitherapy in the fifties
and sixties."

"Apitherapy being . . . ?"

"Bee products including venom. Bee venom is adminis-
tered via syringe to the arthritic patient intradermally."

Jake threw her a quick look.

"Bee venom? Are you sure Pam Stevenson is using bee
venom?"

"I'd be willing to bet money," A.J. said. "And I have a
lot of money to bet."

Jake's mouth twitched with reluctant humor. He reached
for the radio and made a call requesting backup for a possible hostage situation at Starlight Farm.

He hung up the mic and glanced at her. "Your mother
and her lawyer were at the station this evening. That's how
we discovered the yoga tie belonged to the Williams girl.
Meagher volunteered his services on the kid's behalf."

Chloe's car and the sunshine yellow Hummer were both
parked in front of Elysia's home. The house was ablaze
with light as though Elysia were having a party. The porch
lamp shone welcomingly as Jake pulled up next to the
other cars and turned off the siren. The silence seemed unnatural after the blast of the siren..

A.J. reached for the door handle. He grabbed her.

"No, you don't. This is as far as you go." He glanced in
the rearview mirror as the second cop car pulled up behind
them. "Stay put."

He got out of the SUV and walked back to the other car.

A.J. got out and started for the front porch.

"Whoa!" Jake caught her up as she reached the stairs.
"Where do you think you're going?"

"Inside."

He was shaking his head. "We have no idea what's happening in there. We're going to do this by the book. First we try phoning."

"You don't need to call ahead; she's home," A.J. said. She took advantage of the momentary relaxing of his grip to slip free.

He caught her again as she reached the door. "A.J. . . . Jesus. Listen to me. If we go rushing in there half-cocked somebody could end up injured or dead."

"And somebody could just as easily wind up dead if we sit on our hands out here." She pulled out her set of Elysia's keys and inserted the house key into the front-door lock.

Jake spoke urgently. "Listen to me. A mistake now could be fatal. Do you understand what I'm saying? We don't know if either of those kids is armed or not."

The front door swung silently open. Elysia's voice, oddly untroubled, drifted to them.

"Take it from me, sunshine, you never want to look desperate. Nothing is less attractive to the male of the species. They're like dogs. They can smell your fear."

A second voice, Chloe's, murmured something. She was drowned out by Jennifer's hysterical, "If I can't have Steve, no one can!"

"Well, you certainly can't have him if you do away with yourself," Elysia said easily. "Now sit down and let's think this through."

Jake drew his gun and slipped past A.J. She followed him, staying close to the wall as he drew near the arched entrance to the front room.

Jennifer said with bitter satisfaction, "The yard is full of cops."

"Playing to a full house is always gratifying," Elysia agreed. "Now let's put our heads together and think of the best way to handle this."

"You don't fool me," Jennifer said. "You only care

about *her*. Just like Di. You don't care about the fact that she stole Steve from me. Poor Chloe lost her father. Poor Chloe can't afford a dress. Poor Chloe can't afford college. Maybe if poor Chloe stopped spending her allowance on painkillers—"

"I'm not!" Chloe cried.

A.J. peeked around Jake's shoulder in time to see Jennifer point what looked like a small cannon at Chloe—who happened to be clinging to Elysia. The floor seemed to tilt, and A.J. wondered if she was going to faint. She grabbed Jake's free arm and sunk her nails in. He barely spared her a glance. She wondered if he was really capable of shooting a terrified young woman. She had no doubt Jennifer was.

"Now, shush," Elysia said crisply. "This is silly talk. We need to think how to get you two out of this jam."

"I don't want her out of it," Jennifer said. "I want her *dead*."

Jake stepped out of the safety of the hallway, moving soundlessly toward Jennifer. Elysia's eyes rested on him for a moment and returned to the hysterical girl standing before her.

"I understand, my dear, but the problem is, you can't harm Chloe without destroying yourself. Do *you* understand?"

Chloe's eyes went as wide as saucers as she watched Jake sneaking up behind Jennifer. Noticing the other girl's expression, Jennifer spun around and tried to turn the gun on Jake. He grabbed her arm, yanking it upward, and the pistol fired harmlessly into the ceiling.

Chloe screamed and buried her face in Elysia's shoulder. Elysia made clucking noises.

Jake wrested the gun from Jennifer, who was shrieking like a madwoman, trying to kick and claw him. A herd of cops nearly knocked A.J. to the ground as they rushed in to aid Jake.

Jennifer was thrown to the ground and immobilized in a matter of moments. She sobbed furiously into the carpet.

A.J. gasped, "Mother, are you all right?"

Elysia's face quivered, and for just a moment she looked like she might burst into tears. She put an arm out to A.J., who joined her on the sofa. A.J. locked her arms about her mother's narrow shoulders, breathing in the peculiarly reassuring scents of cigarettes and Opium.

"I've never been so frightened in my life!" A.J. cried. "You were *wonderful*!"

Elysia's cheeks stained a delicate shade of rose. For a moment her eyes fastened doubtfully on her daughter's face "You're joking." She swallowed hard. "Do you really think so?"

"I do," Jake said, looking up from handcuffing the still furiously sobbing and struggling Jennifer. "I think you seriously ought to consider a career in acting."

An hour later Jennifer was in the back of a police car heading for jail, Chloe was in the back of a police car heading for home, and Elysia and A.J. were in the living room bidding good night to Jake.

"And I take back all those dreadful things I said about you," Elysia added, having thanked Jake one final time for saving her life with virtually no structural damage to the house.

"Thank you, ma'am," Jake said gravely.

"I'll walk you out," A.J. offered.

They strolled outside. The night was crisp and clean, the stars twinkling overhead. Their feet crunched on the frosty grass as they walked to the SUV.

"What do you think is going to happen to her?" she asked quietly.

She didn't have to explain to Jake who she meant.

"I don't know. She'll get the best legal advice there is, and given her family's money and influence . . ."

"She needs help. I know it sounds crazy, but I'm sorry for her. I can't help but think how different my life might have been if I hadn't had Aunt Di's stabilizing influence."

Jake said crisply, "Jennifer Stevenson has had every advantage a kid could have growing up, apparently including your own aunt's influence. She's an adult and she's going to have to live by the choices she made."

Nothing warm and fuzzy about a cop's view of the world, thought A.J. Not a lot of patience for mistakes or weakness—which was good to know up front.

She changed the subject, saying, "So Jennifer was watching and waiting for UPS to deliver the dress, and when the dress was finally delivered, she firebombed my house, though not very effectively because it was really only luck that the dress was destroyed."

"She isn't exactly a criminal mastermind," Jake said.

"Do you think she deliberately tried to run me down in the Hummer?"

"I don't know. I believed what she said when I interviewed her, that she took the vehicle on impulse and that she thought it was funny to see you run."

"Playful little tyke," A.J. murmured.

"Yeah. A real charmer." His eyes were grave as he gazed down at her face. "You took a big chance tonight, A.J."

"Sometimes you have to." She realized the truth of that now. "So did you. Thank you. There's no telling what would have happened. . . ."

He tucked an errant wisp of hair behind her ear, and the touch of his fingertips sent shivery sensations across her skin.

"It's finally over," she whispered.

"It doesn't have to be," he said, and kissed her.

Epilogue

❧

The parking lot was packed on a Saturday afternoon in April when Suze MacDougal parked her baby blue Beetle next to A.J.'s Volvo outside Sacred Balance Studio.

Suze got out, wincing as her car door banged into the side of the Volvo. She raked a nervous hand through her hair. But there was nothing to be nervous about. A.J. had been so cool about giving Suze her shot at teaching. She would be making her first official appearance as an instructor at today's open house.

And who cared what Lily thought. Suze was pretty sure Lily wasn't going to be teaching at Sacred Balance for much longer.

Suze walked up the cement path, past the flower beds now in tentative bloom. She pushed through the glass doors and walked into a party. Balloons and streamers filled the crowded lobby. Music floated down from upstairs where free yoga lessons were being offered to anyone interested. Trays of organic goodies and nonalcoholic beverages circulated through the crowd. A sign hanging from the wall announced the reopening of Sacred Balance.

It could happen. . . .

It sure could, thought Suze. And it sure had. The last couple of months had been incredible, starting with Jennifer Stevenson's arrest. Talk about scandal! But the most incredible thing had been the way Mrs. Stevenson had rallied to Jennifer's side—and the way she had changed since Jennifer's trial had started. Instead of continuing to close herself off from the world, she had actually begun volunteer work with disabled teens in the community.

Oh. My. God. Was that Nicole Manning? It *was.*

Suze watched A.J., who was looking incredible in a little black Vera Wang dress, move to greet Nicole. Nicole's breathy voice carried to where Suze stood nibbling on a cracker smeared with crunchy soy nut spread.

"Oh, hey, I got so much free press out of that dress. It was worth every penny. You know the producers are talking about doing a movie of the week? Teen angst is so hot right now."

"You are *so* gracious," A.J. told Nicole.

They air-kissed. A.J. turned to greet Chloe, looking radiant on the arm of her fiancé, Steve Cussler. Suze was really glad *that* had all worked out. Chloe was a sweetie, and she'd sure had more than her share of tough breaks.

A.J. introduced Chloe to Nicole, who proceeded to demonstrate just how gracious she could be.

Spotting Suze, A.J. offered a big grin. "So, how's your first official day as an instructor at Sacred Balance?"

Suze laughed. "Great. How am I doing so far?"

"Great!" A.J.'s eyes moved automatically to the glass doors as new arrivals pushed through.

She didn't exactly look disappointed, but the lanky good-looking guy and his hawkishly handsome companion were clearly not who she was waiting for. Suze had a pretty good idea who A.J. was waiting for.

Maybe a better idea than A.J. did herself.

"Andrew, dear boy!" exclaimed Elysia brushing past them. She was looking, well, extraordinary in a slinky scarlet designer jumpsuit. She embraced A.J.'s ex—and what a shame about *that* guy—and said in a funny tone, "And this must be Nicholas."

Andrew grinned at Nicholas, who grimaced good-naturedly. He was supposed to be FBI or something, and he looked kind of like how FBI guys on TV looked.

Elysia was razzing Andy mercilessly about missing their Broadway outings.

"Mother," A.J. protested. "Give it a rest."

"Hey." Nicholas seemed amused by Elysia. "Better you than me. So long as Andy steers clear of any more murder investigations."

"Nick's gone half the time anyway," Andy admitted, and Nick's eyes rested on his face briefly.

"I might be in the mood for the occasional theater out-ing meself," Mr. Meagher suggested, appearing at Elysia's side with a flute of sparkling cider.

Andy exchanged a smiling look with A.J.

A.J. glanced instinctively at the front entrance. Suze glanced, too. It was Michael Batz and his wife, Lorraine.

Now that was a shocker—when Michael dropped out of the Olympic trials. The word was he had decided he was more suited to coaching than competing. The Batzes were greeted by everyone, and then they moved off into the crowd.

"He'll be here," Suze told A.J.

"Who?"

Suze giggled, and at that moment the front doors opened and Jake walked in. Even if Suze hadn't spotted him, she would have known from the way A.J. got that flushed and sparkly look.

Jake spotted A.J. and moved straight through the crowd; Suze was willing to bet he didn't even know there *was* a crowd.

"Sorry I'm late," he told A.J. He looked her up and down. "You look amazing in that dress."

"Thanks," A.J. said. "Come and get something to eat."

They made a cute couple, no doubt about it. Of course, A.J. was always saying she wasn't ready for a serious relationship yet, and Jake *never* had been ready for a serious relationship as far as anyone in Stillbrook could tell. A lot of people had bets as to how long A.J. would be able to put up with small-town life and small-town attitudes, but Suze had high hopes.

She looked up at the black-and-white art posters with Diantha's slogan beneath, and smiled.

It could happen.

CORPSE POSE

❧

Corpse Pose or *Savasana*, is the final pose of your yoga routine. It's a relaxation pose but it is also useful for meditation.

Step One: Sit on the floor with your legs extended straight in front of you.

Step Two: Lie back on your elbows and slowly lower yourself until you're lying on your back.

Step Three: Spread your legs about hip width; relax your muscles, allowing feet to drop to the side.

Step Four: Gently sweep your arms out along the floor about ten inches from your hips; turn your palms up.

Step Five: Keep your shoulders down and spread wide—don't pinch.

Step Six: Relax your entire body. Empty your mind. Feel the top of your head soften . . . relax the muscles in your face . . . in your throat. Breathe deeply and evenly. Soften your belly . . . soften your groin. Feel the muscles in your thighs release . . . release your calf muscles . . . soften the soles of your feet.

Step Seven: Close your eyes and breathe deeply and evenly through your nose.

Step Eight: Focus on your breathing . . . deep even breaths in . . . and out. Stay in this relaxed and boneless—but focused state—for ten minutes.

Organic Recipes

✥

Cuppa Cocoa

(Serves 2–4)

Ingredients

3½ oz Dark Chocolate (70% Cocoa Solids)
½ cup Organic Double Cream
Organic Greek-style Yogurt
1 shot Espresso Coffee

Directions

1) Chop chocolate into small pieces and place in a thick mixing bowl. Heat cream over a gentle heat in a thick bottomed saucepan until it just reaches boiling. Do not scorch!

2) Add a quarter of the warm cream to the chocolate and stir to melt. Gradually add the remaining cream until the chocolate has completely melted. (NOTE: If the

chocolate does not melt evenly, place the bowl over a saucepan of boiling water like a double-boiler, but make sure the bowl doesn't touch the water.)

3) When chocolate has melted to a smooth and even consistency, place bowl with melted contents in the fridge. Mix the extra thick and creamy Greek-style yogurt with the espresso coffee. Fill two espresso cups—or four regular sized cups—about two-thirds full with the coffee and yogurt mixture.

4) Remove cream and chocolate from the fridge, topping the rest of the cups to the rim. Place espresso cups in the fridge and leave them overnight.

Remove cups from fridge one half hour prior to serving.

Basic Stir Fry
(Serves 6–8)

Ingredients
(All vegetables should be organically grown)

4 oz tempeh (soybean cake, similar to tofu)
8 oz baby portabella mushrooms—organic
2 tbsp minced garlic
1 small chopped onion
Extra virgin olive oil
1 cup frozen peas and carrots
Small bag frozen broccoli

1 cup frozen red, yellow, and green pepper strips
3 tbsp soy sauce
2 cups brown rice

Directions

1) This is almost too simple to require directions! Cube tempeh and chop vegetables.

2) Sauté tempeh, mushrooms, garlic, and onion in olive oil over medium heat.

3) Add peas and carrots, broccoli, pepper strips, soy sauce (or favorite low-sodium marinade) and cook for 10 minutes.

4) Add rice and cook another 5 minutes.

Cozy up with
Berkley Prime Crime

SUSAN WITTIG ALBERT
*Don't miss the nationally bestselling
series featuring herbalist China Bayles.*

LAURA CHILDS
*The Tea Shop Mysteries are the
toast of Charleston, South Carolina.*

KATE KINGSBURY
*The Pennyfoot Hotel Mystery
series is a tea-time delight.*

**For the armchair
detective in you.**

penguin.com